A Time To Kill . . .
A Time To Die

Books by Jack Pearl

A TIME TO KILL . . . A TIME TO DIE
STOCKADE
THE CRUCIFIXION OF PETE MC CABE
BLOOD AND GUTS PATTON
MASQUE OF HONOR (with Ed Linn)

A TIME TO
KILL...
A TIME TO
DIE

A NOVEL BY JACK PEARL

W · W · NORTON & COMPANY · INC · *New York*

FOR

June, Janet, Jill
AND
Mac and Li'l Joe

A Time To Kill . . .

A Time To Die

So on we worked, and waited for the light,
And went without the meat, and cursed the bread;
And Richard Cory, one calm summer night,
Went home and put a bullet through his head.

From "Richard Cory," in *The Children of the Night* by Edwin Arlington Robinson

THE BIG BURN curled over the lodge like a white tidal wave, a sweeping expanse of blowing powder a mile across the top of Mt. Baldy. Looking up at the mountaintop always gave him a queasy feeling in his gut. In the blinding sunlight it seemed as though the towering slope was trembling. On the next beat of his heart, the great wave would break and bury everything in frozen nothingness.

Laced with serpentine ski trails, it held something for all of them amateur and expert alike. Gentle hills. Rills. Dips. Cutting in and out of pines and birches. Broad open slopes. Belly-busting sheer shussing.

With his binoculars he had tracked the couple from the warming hut at the top of the Burn. They had vacillated before finally choosing this run. The man would have preferred an easier trail. She was the better skier. That was evident as soon as they started down.

The man kneeling at the window on the upper floor of the lodge looked at his watch. In approximately three minutes they would hurtle out of the grove of pines off the corner of the lodge and traverse the broad open slope that fell away below the side terrace.

The view from that terrace defied adjectives. The word that best described his own feelings was "grandeur."

Last summer, standing at the low wall with a martini in his hand and smoke from the charring steaks on the grill salivating tongue and palate.

9

He opened the window as far as it would go. The snow mounded on the sill blew in on him, tickling his nostrils like dust. That's how cold it was. The two women huddled together on the bed against the wall and drew the parkas more tightly around their shivering bodies. More than cold, the fear. Cold fear. Their hands were free, but their ankles were shackled together.

The fourth member of the group, male, lay doubled up on a chaise lounge. His hands and feet were bound cruelly tight with baling wire. Wrists bleeding where the wire cut the flesh, his hands purple. Blood on his temple, oozing from a puffy, ugly dark bruise. He was unconscious, unaware of the menace that hung over the mountain.

Just about time. The man at the window picked up the rifle and rested the barrel on the windowsill in front of him. He admired it with his hands and his eyes. A beautiful thing really. It was a .300 H & H Magnum with a Bolvar 8 scope and B & L mounts. Once this same rifle had killed a big-horn ram at 600 yards. He set the scope for 375 yards and bent his head to the eyepiece. He swept the barrel back and forth over the empty slope. Blue white in the shadow of the trees. Dazzling, diamond crystal in the sunlight, so bright it slashed at the tender nerves behind the eyes.

The two women stared at him, mute, terrorized, unwilling to accept the reality of what was happening, not daring to project their thoughts beyond this moment, this incredible point in time. It could not be real. Only a madman . . . And reason balked, here, quivering, teetering on the brink of sanity.

The skiers burst out of the trees around a sharp turn, in an explosion of white powder, as their skis fought for traction on the hard-packed snow. Skidding sideways, the white plumes of soft, icy powder arching high above them. He followed them expertly with the telescopic sight as they traversed the open slope. Weaving like splashes of colored quicksilver across the albino landscape. The girl was definitely the superior skier. She led her partner and was holding back so as not to outdistance him too humiliatingly. Her wedeln form was admirable. Short, tight, quick parallel swings. Her lithe body snaking through the turns. Upper torso erect, steady. Shoulders turned to the fall line of the slope. Good vorlage, he noted, with the ankle and knees, not the waist or hips. Hips in the tight pants undulating as if she were dancing the twist. Buttocks and thighs moving in a grinding up-and-down rhythm that was positively wanton. He experienced a warm tremor in his groin. The wedeln was too fast for him to line her up with any real assurance of success. He moved the scope onto the man.

He was good, classic textbook. Parallel Christie. Perfect crouch, the tips of the skis pressuring the snow. Up-and-down motion, even if a bit too stiff. Stiff in his use of the poles as well, taking the traverse in long, sweeping turns as opposed to the girl's swift, short swings. The marksman did not attempt to follow him with the scope. He gauged the serpentine course of the man and held the rifle steady so the target kept gliding back and forth through the line of sight as it weaved across the snow-blown slope.

The trigger finger tightened until only a hair's breadth of tension would trip the pin. Out. In. Out. Then back through the reticule. One, two seconds at the most, when the intersecting filaments of the sight were following a line segment that extended from the middle of the shoulder blades to the midpoint of the back of the head with the skier's up-and-down motion.

Up—shoulder blades. Down—head. Up. Down. Up. Down.

The sound did not carry far in the cold, dry air. The echo of it off the surrounding peaks fading quickly. The woman was scarcely conscious of the report, dulled as it was by the roaring of the wind in her ears. Certainly it was not a forbidding sound. She felt no great alarm when she looked back over her shoulder and saw her husband tumbling over in the snow, arms, legs, and skis pinwheeling like spokes.

She winced and bit her underlip, praying that he'd come out of it without any broken bones and ploughed to a short, skidding stop some seventy-five yards below where he lay motionless.

She made her way back up the hill breathlessly, tracking a herringbone wake in the white crust. She called his name. And now her heart began to race as she struggled toward the spot where he lay twisted grotesquely in a drift. Unmoving. Silent.

She was frightened, but not panicked. They were old hands at this. She knew she was the better skier, yet she had taken some rough spills herself. More spills than he did, usually, with his more cautious style. He might be stunned, have the wind knocked out of him, she told herself, but it couldn't be serious. Not really serious. Maybe on boiler plate, but not in this soft snow.

Blood on the snow. So red, almost luminous against the blinding white of the snow. Thick, crimson syrup.

"Oh, my God!" she whimpered.

He lay face down, and by some quirk his cap was still in place on his head. The blood was seeping through the wool and running down his neck onto the snow. She kicked off her skis and knelt down beside him to remove the cap. As it came away, the gory sight that was uncovered brutalized her senses. She felt nothing other than total rejection of what her eyes told her. It had to be a fiction. A hallucination composed by the blinding sunlight on the white snow. Snow as well as sand could trick the eye. A man could not possibly have *this* (what she appeared to be seeing) happen to him from taking a fall in the snow.

It surfaced suddenly out of the dark recesses of her subconscious. Two years earlier. They had been vacationing in Vermont. Coming around a bend and seeing the big buck collapsed in the snow, antlers twisted in the underbrush. His blood dripping onto the snow from a massive head wound. Dead eyes glazing as she watched.

She recoiled in horror and clutched her hands to her face. It came back to her. The unfamiliar cracking sound she had heard just before he went down.

She lifted her eyes up the slope they had been traversing, beyond the trees, up the sheer face of snow-dusted rock to the
lodge that sat on top of the bluff. Just the night before, sipping
hot Tom and Jerrys in front of the big warm hearth at the inn,
they had talked about that house. Admiring it with undisguised
envy.

"You'd have to be a millionaire to build a pad like that," her
husband had said.

Sunlight glinted off glass from the upper floor of the lodge.
Light reflected from an open window. A coruscating pinpoint.

The cross-hairs of the reticule were centered between her
stricken eyes. She did not hear the shot. She was dead before the
sound wave passed over the execution site. Lifeless meat in the
snow.

His face revealed nothing of what he was thinking or feeling
when he turned away from the window. He reloaded the rifle
from a box of high-powered ammunition on the dresser.

The dark woman was so incensed by the meaningless act of
violence that her outrage overcame her fear of him.

"Which one has *your* name on it?"

He glanced at her challengingly.

"You won't let them take you alive, will you? I mean, that's
not your style, going out with a whimper. You're a *big* man. You
want to leave with a big bang."

"Shut up!"

"That's what this is all about, isn't it? So you'll get a front-page
obituary?"

He walked over to her, stroking the bolt of the rifle with
his thumb. "I told you to keep quiet."

"For God's sake stop goading him," the blonde woman said
nervously. "He's sick."

"Sick?" The brunete sneered. "He just doesn't have the guts to
face up to life. That's his trouble. Gut-less-ness!"

"You bitch!" He struck her so hard with the back of his hand that she was knocked across the bed. She lay there, stunned, with the blood trickling out of a corner of her mouth.

The blonde shied away from him. "Don't touch me! I told her to stop talking to you like that." She threw up her arms defensively as he raised a hand, but he was only going to massage the tight muscles at the back of his neck. "If you're going to kill us, for God's sake do it quickly."

He laughed softly at her earnestness. "Patience, my dear. Be patient." He walked over to the unconscious man on the lounge and placed the muzzle of the rifle just below the purple bruise on his temple. His finger slid inside the trigger guard.

She averted her eyes.

The dark woman struggled up on one elbow. The sleeve of her coat was stained with blood.

"You know what I think?" she taunted him. "I don't think you can do it. Not here where you can see our faces."

"Will you keep quiet!" The blonde was terror-stricken.

His expression did not change. "You believe that, do you?" he asked in a calm voice. Slowly he swung the rifle away from the man's head and lifted it, fitting the stock into the hollow of his right shoulder. He took careful aim. A fraction to the heart side of the breastbone. Between her small breasts.

"I want you to look your loveliest when you're laid out," he said casually.

"Go ahead," she said. "It takes real courage to shoot a woman." She put a hand to her sore mouth. "Hitting people who can't hit back."

He pointed the rifle down at the floor and stared at her coldly. "You can talk about hurting people. *You* of all people. There are things that hurt a hell of a lot more than a split lip. Or even a bullet . . . But how could an insensitive bitch like you understand?"

"Is that what I am? Insensitive? Listen, the first time I saw you I *knew*. There never was anything in back of that big front you always put on. No guts. Nothing!"

"Oh! Why don't you shut up!" The blonde lurched off the bed to get out of the line of fire. Hobbled by the handcuffs on her ankles, she sprawled face down on the carpet and lay there crying softly.

Pain flared up like a sheet of flame behind his eyes. He closed them and pressed his forehead against the cool metal of the rifle barrel. He had been living with this recurring pain forever it seemed, except for the temporary reprieves provided by drugs and alcohol. In the past few weeks, the pain had achieved new, higher plateaus. He had the notion that if a corkscrew were drilled into his skull the pent-up pressure would erupt like an oil gusher.

It peaked and diminished gradually. He opened his eyes. The way she was looking at him made him want to kill her on the spot.

"*Bitch!*"

"Because your self-pity revolts me?"

He brought up the rifle, aiming at her belly. What she deserved was a gut shot, and the slow agony of dying. Yet his finger would not make the fatal contraction.

"Oh, go to hell!" Perspiration beaded his forehead, cold and slick as congealed oil. He walked away from the bed, back to the window, wiping his face with his sleeve.

He counted six figures milling around the bodies of his first two victims on the slope below. Two more skiing down the trail from the warming hut higher up the mountain. A foursome was traversing up the hill from the bottom of the run. It was clear that, as yet, none of them had any inkling of the peril they were courting. He lifted the sash and poked the rifle barrel out the open window.

The blonde woman lying on the floor moaned. "Oh, no! No more. Why them? They're innocent."

"But are they?" He smiled and pressed the cold eyepiece to his eye socket. Studying the grouping around the still forms in the snow, he picked his next target. A large bearded man wearing a hooded parka. He snapped the shot and let out his breath.

The bearded man went down as if he had been felled by an ax. There was a scream, a woman's scream, that shrilled across the mountain. Someone was pointing in the direction of the lodge. He fired a second shot and another figure collapsed in the snow. They were all screaming now and scattering for cover like ambushed quail. The muzzle flash, a puff of smoke had given him away. He didn't care particularly.

He stared at the four still forms, dark and grotesque against the white snow. They reminded him of Rorschach blots on a sheet of paper.

Then, unexpectedly, a small black dog came trotting out of a clump of foliage and approached the bodies. Ignoring the shouts from the pine grove where the skiers had taken cover, it sniffed and whined around the bearded man, wagging its tail hopefully. A barrage of sticks and pine cones from the grove sent it yelping down the slope with its tail tucked between its legs.

He followed it with the scope as it strove frantically to keep its footing on the hard-packed crust of the steep grade. The frightened animal bellywhopped about fifty feet before its momentum was broken by a shoulder of soft snow against the side of a boulder. It struggled out of the drift onto a patch of clear ground on the lee side of the boulder, where it shook the snow out of its shaggy black coat. Then, unceremoniously, the little mutt lifted its leg.

He lowered the rifle, threw back his head, and began to laugh.

"It's Christmas Eve," he pronounced.

The blonde whimpered. "I don't want to think about it."

The brunette stared at him uncomprehendingly. "You find something amusing about that?"

"A dog out there, he reminds me of the Grand McNish. You remember the McNish?"

"Yes, what about him?"

"You remember that Christmas Eve, don't you? Mac and the punch?" He was overcome by nostalgia. Bittersweet memory.

So real to him that he could close his eyes and he was back there twenty-five years in the past. His eyelids stung, and he swallowed to ease the rawness at the back of his throat.

The woman remembered that Christmas Eve past as well as he did. The fabulous champagne punch and the bandy-legged little Scotch terrier with the pompous title: The Grand McNish! A rare and precious inside joke that would endure until the last one of them was dead.

Yet she hesitated, sensing there was some advantage to be gained from his nostalgia. The madness of the present submerging in the mellowness of the past.

"You mean to say you don't remember the big Christmas Eve party the year the war ended?" He closed the window and turned to face her.

"Oh, vaguely, I guess."

He laughed. "Oh, come on! That was the night . . ."

Marine Corporal Carl Schneider was the last of the old crowd to be discharged from the service on Christmas Eve of 1945. When the train plunged into the tunnel on the final leg into Grand Central Terminal, Carl went into the washroom. He combed his hair, carefully teasing a wavy, blond forelock so that it curled down over his right eyebrow. He washed his hands and straightened his regulation tie. He pulled down the tailored tunic snug over his hips and grinned at himself in the mirror with self-admiration.

"You're a good-looking gyrene, I gotta admit it," he said aloud.

Carl went out into the vestibule, where a Negro porter was stacking luggage. He found his barracks bag and tipped the porter a quarter. The smell of steam seeping up between the cars. Air brakes hissing as they clamped against the wheel drums. The car lurched and he grabbed a sticky hand rail. Suddenly he was frantic with impatience. His heart was racing. For three years he had borne it like a Stoic. Now he couldn't wait. Home. Family. Friends. And Wendy Gates. Not necessarily in that order.

He could close his eyes and see Wendy as clearly as he had seen her that snowy morning back in 1942 on the Long Island Railroad platform waving goodbye to the Camp Lejune Special. Wendy, standing out from the other girls and women who had come to see their men off to war. God, how proud he had been, holding her in his arms, kissing her. He'd known prettier girls than Wendy. She was too thin for one thing. Angular and hollow-cheeked. And her nose was too long and thin. Dirty blond hair that kept falling over one side of her face. Her sex appeal was not blatant. Aristocratic was the way he always thought of her. The way she walked and talked. At nineteen she had been a working model for four years, and was studying drama in the evenings.

"My girl," he said softly. But the words turned sour in his mouth.

The bitter truth was Wendy Gates was in love with Jack Whittaker.

Some of the excitement and elation waned as he shouldered his bag and stepped out onto the platform. But the momentary low dissolved the instant he walked through the upstairs gate into the terminal. There was an enormous revolving Christmas tree in the middle of the waiting room festooned with colored lights and balls and tinsel. Holly wreaths and pine roping. He took a deep breath and could smell the beautiful smells. The crisp, spicy scents of winter. Christmas was just not Christmas without pine and cold and snow. Down on the tropic Caribbean island where he had spent the last two winters, they had decorated holiday wreaths with orchids and other cloying, exotic blooms. The carols blaring out of the loudspeakers in the terminal brought tears to his eyes.

"We Three Kings of Orient Are . . ."

Then they were all over him, mobbing him, pounding his back, digging their fists into his ribs, both of them laughing and talking at once. Forrest Evans and Charlie Roche. Jack Whittaker waited until the others had worked off their animal spirits before he came forward with a big grin on his rugged face. He gripped Carl's hand firmly and squeezed his arm with his other hand with real affection.

"Welcome back, old buddy. Now it really is going to be a merry Christmas."

"Well, let's not stand around jawing," Charlie said. "There's a big party waiting on us men."

That's right." Jack winked at Carl. "And it wouldn't have seemed the same without you there, Carl."

The simple declaration of friendship from Jack moved him far more deeply than the hyperbole of his other friends.

He thought of Jack Whittaker as his best friend, although he knew *he* was not Jack's best friend. Jack gave generously of himself to all of his friends without partiality. He favored no one of them over the others. It seemed to Carl that Jack would not commit that ultimate enclave of self which is essential to genuine intimacy in a relationship between two human beings. Almost without exception his friends vied with each other to win that commitment from Jack. And some of them, particularly Carl, resented him for withholding it.

Carl alternately loved and hated Jack Whittaker. Admiration and envy were inseparable companions in his complex emotions toward Jack. Jack would always be stronger and smarter and richer and more successful than he could ever hope to be. He would not stay abreast of Jack. In the future. The gulf between them would grow wider and wider. He sensed it instinctively. It only made him hang on to Jack more tenaciously in the present.

There was a case of Rheingold in a cooler in Jack Whittaker's car, and the party began as soon as they were on the East Side Drive.

Carl slouched on his spine in the back seat alongside Forrest, a can of beer in one hand.

"Hey, watch it, pal," Forrest complained as Carl's beer slopped over the rim. "These new slacks and jacket set me back sixty bucks."

Carl whistled. "Jesus, you're still a dude, ain't you, Evans? I figured the Army would cure you."

Charlie Roche turned partially around in the front seat and threw one arm over the backrest. He clamped his hand hard over one of Forrest's knees. Charlie was still wearing his combat infantryman's uniform with all his campaign ribbons bedazzled with battle stars, and a purple heart and bronze star.

"What the hell are you talking about, Carl? This dude wasn't in the Army. He spent the war in a country club at MIT."

He laughed, but the vehemence in back of the joke was not lost on anyone. Roche had gone in with the first wave at Red Beach on D-Day, and had battled the Nazi Wehrmacht across France, through the Ardennes, and across Germany to the Elbe River. Forrest Evans had been one of the lucky ten in his engineering company selected to attend the Army Special Service School at the Massachusetts Institute of Technology. When the war in Europe ended, he was lacking only twenty-seven credits for his bachelor of science degree.

"That hurts, you bastard!" Forrest chopped at Charlie's wrist with the edge of his hand, but the other man was too quick for him. He drew back and Forrest hit his own knee.

Charlie sneered at him. "They teach you that at MIT, college boy? Hey, Jack, give me another beer, will you?" He hurled his empty can out the window onto the grassy shoulder of Grand Central Parkway.

"Take it easy, Charlie," Jack cautioned. "We don't want to get stopped by a cop."

"Cops!" Charlie laughed. Shrill and offensive to the ears. "You got to be kidding! You know what I did to a squad of MP's in Paris one night? A squad, there must have been fifty of them." His excitement was real. "Just me and my bud in this alley, back to back. Yah! Yah YAH!" His hands slashed the empty air with vicious karate chops. "This way and that, they kept coming at us from all directions. We had to cut our way through a wall of human flesh."

"Cut it out, Charlie!" Jack shouted in rare anger. "You want to drive us off the road? Jerk!"

Carl was tense. Charlie Roche had had that effect on him as far back as he could remember. With his bushy red hair and wild eyes, Roche looked like a mad prophet. There was a madness that came over him at times, usually when he was drinking heavily. But he settled down obediently now, cackling at his recollection of the memorable evening in Paris.

"Hey, Charlie, where did you get that ring?" Carl asked to get his mind onto another subject. Is that rock for real?"

Charlie clenched his fist and displayed the large gold ring on the second finger of his left hand. The stone seemed to give off sparks as spokes of light from the overhead parkway lamps cut through it.

"You better believe it's real," he said. "This here sparkler is the 'spoils of war,' I guess you might say."

"You took it off a dead kraut?" Carl asked. The idea of it made him self-conscious. He felt inferior to men such as Jack and Charlie who had been in the midst of the real war. Carl had served his tour of overseas duty on a tropical island standing in front of the gate of a two-star general's villa. The South-Atlantic Naval Defense Force was what they had called it. What it really was, was four hours of monotonous guard duty daily, followed up by twenty hours of sleeping, drinking, and whoring. And by the end of his assignment that got almost as monotonous as the duty.

"What did you do in the war, daddy?"

"I wuz in the Younited-States-Mar-ines, son."

And hope the kid would let it go at that.

Charlie was staring strangely at the ring, wearing an expression of private amusement. He stroked the stone with a finger of his other hand.

"Yeah, I took it off a dead kraut." He looked up at Carl and grinned. "He didn't want to let go of it, the s.o.b. I had to cut off his finger to lift it."

Forrest's and Carl's laughter was subdued; it seemed chicken not to laugh at all. Only Jack Whittaker's face remained impassive. He took a can from the carton sitting on the seat between them and tossed it into Roche's lap.

"Here, drink your beer," he said.

Charlie winked at him. "Thanks. That's my old bud." He took a long swallow and wiped foam off his upper lip with his sleeve. "Say, Carl, wait until you see Jack's new broad. I should say broads. There are two of them got the hots for old Jackson here."

"Three," Forrest corrected him. "You're leaving out Wendy."

Charlie looked directly at Carl. "So I did. Old, reliable Wendy. She's been carrying the torch for Jack so long she hardly counts any more. It's like she's joined a nunnery."

Carl was glad it was dark in the car. His face was burning. "Tell me about your new girls, Jack." He wanted to steer the conversation away from Wendy.

"The first thing I'll tell you is that they're not *my* girls. I invited them to even up the boys and girls tonight. There are a couple of guys you haven't met who are going to be at the party, Carl."

"New guys?" Carl experienced the stab of resentment he always got when Jack Whittaker spread his friendship outside their own circle of friends.

"One's an old Army buddy, Wally Kaiser. The other guy I met at work."

"You mean you've got a job already, Jack?" Carl was vexed. "I thought we were going to bum around a few months and raise hell. That's what we always said we'd do in our letters."

Jack laughed. "Don't worry, buddy, we are going to raise hell. Holy hell. Ordinarily I wouldn't have gone out looking for a job so soon, but this one came looking for me." He hesitated. "I got it through a friend of Wendy's. Someone she'd worked for at the National Broadcasting Company. It's in their TV department."

"TV? What's that?"

"Television. You know, radio with moving pictures."

Carl laughed. "Oh, sure. Like in Tom Swift and Buck Rogers."

Jack was serious. "It's not sci-fi any longer, Carl. It won't be long before TV will be the greatest craze in this country. And I'm in on the ground floor. Right now, my biggest responsibility is to see that the coffee cups stay full. I guess you'd say I'm an apprentice. But it's not going to stay that way long."

Carl shook his head. "I don't know, Jack. It doesn't sound like much of a future to me. I thought you were going to school on the GI Bill?"

"Oh, I'll get around to that. Maybe next September. Right now I want to make some money, so you and I can raise that hell you were talking about."

Carl loved him once more. He leaned forward and gripped Jack's shoulder. "Now you're talking, buddy. So let's get back to these new broads. You got one helluva nerve fixing up two strangers with tail when you knew old horny Carl was on his way."

"These kids aren't tail, Carl. They're nice girls."

Charlie Roche hooted. "Sure they are. This little one, she has it so bad for Jack you can almost smell it. God, she's stacked too. I swear, Jack, why don't you do the humane thing and screw that poor little gal?"

"Jack's buddy from NBC will cool her off, you can rely on it," Forrest declared. "They were hitting it off fine when we left to pick up Carl. I think the other girl is more Jack's type. Tall brunette with striking gams. Cool and sophisticated, but very, very sexy. I could go for her myself except that I am already spoken for."

Charlie Roche turned on him loudly. "Evans, you have got to be kidding. I mean, you aren't seriously thinking of marrying that flat-chested, bony-assed broad?"

Forrest Evans was unflappable. "Beauty is only skin deep. But
I don't expect that a crude bastard like you would understand
that, Roche. Pat DiSalle happens to be an educated, intelligent,
extremely stimulating young lady and—"

Roche cut him off with a wild whoop. "And her old man is
loaded, buddy. Plus which he is on a first-name basis with Joe
Kennedy and all the bigwigs at Hyannisport. And that broad is
going to be Mr. Forrest Evans' passport to fame and fortune.
Ain't that the truth?"

For the first time since they had left the terminal there was
absolute silence in the car.

Finally Forrest said defensively "Oh, come off it, you bums.
It's a good match all around. I am marrying what I want. And
Pat is marrying what she wants."

"That's okay, Forrest," Jack told him. "You don't owe anybody any explanations about your personal life."

"Thanks, Jack. I know I don't. But I don't want you to
think—"

"It's enough, Forrest. Let's change the subject."

Up front Charlie Roche let out a curdling howl. "Damn you
guys and your broads! All they do, I say, is take up valuable time
when you could be boozing it up and playing shuffleboard and
darts at the local pub. Man, do I ever have a thirst. Pass me
another Rheingold, Jackson."

"I'm cutting you off, Charlie," Jack refused. "You keep this up
and you won't even be around to taste that seventy-five-dollar
punch we made to toast the return of the prodigal."

"Shit! The way you talk, you act like I was the only one who'd
been away," Carl said. But he was grateful nevertheless.

"You're right, Carl," Jack said soberly. "After three years in
the Army, it began to seem as if I'd been a soldier all my life. As
if home was someplace I'd read about in a book or seen in a
movie. Now that I've been back for two months, it's the other
way around. It's as if there never had been any Army. As if I had
never left home at all. Funny."

"Funny! You must be some kind of a nut, Whittaker, I mean

it." Charlie's voice was strident again. "You may not know you ever left home. But God damn it, *I* sure know it!" He punched the dashboard hard with his fist. The big ring cut into his finger just below the knuckle, drawing blood.

"God damn, Charlie!" Jack complained. "Stop busting up old Bessie!"

"Drop dead, Whittaker!" Charlie growled, sucking his injured finger. "Can't this tin lizzie go any faster? I'm thirsty for that million-dollar punch."

The Christmas punch had been Jack Whittaker's idea. It was concocted of six bottles of New York State champagne, one bottle each of Hennessy's brandy, Gordon's gin, and Cointreau, one quart of fresh strawberries, and two ounces of crème de cacao. All of the ingredients were mixed together in an oversized punch bowl rented from a local caterer. There was a twenty-pound block of ice floating in the punch to cool it. Nevertheless, before they left to meet Carl Schneider at Grand Central Station, Jack and Forrest Evans had carried the huge bowl out onto the open back porch of Jack's house, where the temperature was twenty-nine degrees. As a precautionary measure, Jack tied his pugnacious Scotch terrier to the porch railing. Just a week earlier a case of beer had been stolen off the same porch. They would all rest easier with the Grand McNish guarding the treasure.

When they arrived back at the house with Carl at nine-thirty, Kate Adams and Tess Blue pulled Jack off into the kitchen for a private talk. Kate and Tess, who had gone to grammar school and high school with Jack and the other boys, functioned as unofficial hostesses at most of the house parties, buying and preparing the food, emptying ashtrays, filling peanut and pretzel dishes and policing up the disorder after a party was over.

Kate, the more serious of the two, looked as if she were going to cry. "Jack . . . the punch . . ." The words gagged her.

He was stricken. "My God! Don't tell me somebody got by the Grand McNish?"

She shook her head.

"Then what is it? Speak up, girl!"

"You tell him," she appealed to Tess.

Tess, a big bawdy blonde, began to giggle. Once started, she couldn't stop. Gasping, she finally got it out. "It's the McNish himself."

"He drank the punch? I don't believe it."

Tess was too broken up to say any more. But Kate found her voice. "The dog lifted his leg on it."

"Oh, no!" Jack staggered over to a kitchen chair and sat down heavily. "*In* the punch itself, or just on the outside of the bowl?"

"There's no way of telling for sure."

"Oh, my God!" He buried his face in his hands.

"What are we going to do?" Kate asked helplessly.

Tess managed to control her hysterics long enough to offer a suggestion. "I know what you can't do, Jack. You can't go out and tell those guys who kicked in to buy this golden elixir that your pooch sent all that beautiful booze down the drain."

"What can I tell them?"

"Nothing."

"Nothing. You mean—?"

"Exactly."

"You're terrible," Kate shrieked.

"It's the only logical thing to do. Look, all the three of us know for sure is that the McNish lifted his leg *on* the bowl. Chances are, he didn't get any over the rim. He's a short dog, and that's a tall bowl."

Kate grimaced. "I still couldn't drink it, knowing."

"So don't." The dilemma appealed immensely to Tess's broad sense of humor. "We know, we don't drink the punch. Frankly, I like Scotch better anyway. What they don't know won't hurt them."

"Well . . . that doesn't follow," Jack said. The beer he had swilled in the car was giving him a sour stomach.

"Don't be a jerk. I read in some societies they drink urine."

"Please." Kate shut her eyes and shuddered.

Jack got up, walked out onto the back porch. The girls had retied the Grand McNish out of reach of the big cut-glass bowl. The bandylegged little Scotty tucked his tail between his legs and looked away from him.

"It's all right, Mac," Jack consoled him. "It's my fault, not yours. I don't blame you for mistaking it for a rich man's fire hydrant."

He bent over and made a rough estimate of the height of the Scotty's hindquarters. Then he went over to the punch bowl and computed the distance from floor to rim with his eye. It was a stand-off, he decided. The odds of McNish's clearing the rim were no better than the odds that he didn't. On that note of cautious optimism, Jack went back inside and announced: "We don't tell 'em anything."

It proved to be the correct decision. The champagne punch was the high spot of the party. "Magnificent" and "stupendous" were some of the less hyperbolic adjectives used to describe it. But it was Forrest Evans' solemn declaration that caused Tess to collapse in a puddle of mirth on the carpet, and supplied the punch line for the comic episode when it was narrated, over and over, in the years that followed.

"I've never tasted anything like this, Jack. You're to be congratulated. It's got—I can't quite place it—that something extra in it!"

He was insensitive to the fine snow blowing into his face and up his sleeve and to the icy metal freezing to his sweaty palm where the rifle barrel rested on it, and to the harsh glare of the sun on the slope falling off sharply on this side of the lodge. That time twenty-five years in the past was more real to him than the time he was living.

Memory complemented life the way the aging process improved fine wine. An event remembered acquired body and bouquet and dimension, distilled from one's own hindsight and the insight of others who were a part of the event as well. One

*man's participation in the past was but a single thread woven
through the fabric of people and places and happenings that made
up the whole tapestry of life. The present was inscrutable. His
vision was too narrow and restricted to perceive any meaning to
it. It was only from the distant vantage point that he could look
back in time and recognize the design that his solitary thread
traces through the tapestry.*

*The Grand McNish and the champagne punch. One fragment
of an evening, a week, a month, an era. Any one man's part of
it only a solitary thread.*

He stood at a window in another room, looking out on the
west side of the mountain. A gap in the treetops framed the
Toonerville Trolley passage of the chairs on a distant ski lift.
Swaying in their jerky ascension up the ratchet cable in endless
succession like shooting-gallery ducks . . .

The youth was in high spirits as he rode the lift up to the top
of Big Burn. He cut his eyes to the side, covertly studying the
profile of his companion on the double chair, and discreetly increasing the pressure of his thigh and hip against her. Even
through the layers of their clothing, her warmth and softness
excited him. What was even more stimulating than the physical
contact itself, she did not withdraw from him.

The girl was quite aware of his leg against hers, and that he
was observing her reaction, and she was delighted on both counts.
Last night, after they had sung until they were both hoarse with
the group around the fire in the lounge, he had escorted her to
her room. At the door he had kissed her passionately. And she
had responded to his ardor. Up to a point. Shyly, but firmly, she
had declined the invitation to have a nightcap in his room. Earlier
he had dropped the casual gambit that his roommate was spending
the night with friends in Aspen.

But tonight, well, if he repeated the invitation and if his roomie
was still away, she *might* change her mind. *Kismet*, she told herself airily. Let fate decide. If it was meant to happen, then let it

happen. He would not have to resort to force. He was good looking. Cool. She really dug him the most.

Impulsively, she reached over and put her mittened hand on
top of his. Surprised and pleased, he turned his head and smiled.

"Really living, aren't we, doll?"

He put an arm around her shoulders and pulled her toward
him, trying to kiss her.

"Hey, slow down," she protested feebly, "we're in public."

"In case you haven't noticed." He laughed and jerked his
thumb back in the direction of the couple in the chair behind
them.

She looked and giggled. "Wow!"

"Those two are *really* making out." He drew her close again,
and this time she let him kiss her. Closing her eyes, deliciously
aware of the tingling nerve endings.

Without warning, he pulled away from her violently, gasping.
"Jesus!"

The coy vanity crossed her mind that he had been overcome
by lust for her irresistible white body. Then she saw his face.
Stunned, stricken, and, as she watched, the color drained swiftly
out of his rosy cheeks. His flesh took on the lifeless tone of wax
fruit.

She was startled, but not frightened. "What on earth is it?
Don't you feel well?"

"My back," he said in a fading voice. "It feels like I've been
. . ." She couldn't make out the last word. It sounded as if he
had said "shot." But that was crazy.

Then his eyes rolled back up into his head and he sagged
limply in the chair and started to slip underneath the safety bar.

She screamed and lunged for him. The cumbersome skis
strapped to her feet handicapped her efforts to grab hold of him.
When she twisted around, they got tangled with his skis, and
shoved him even further out of the chair. She held on to his
jacket desperately, shouting in futile hysteria.

"Help! Won't someone please help me?"

Her mittens were dragged off, and he was gone, tumbling toward the snow-covered boulders some thirty feet below.

The sight of fresh blood on the back and seat of the chair where he had been filled her with horrified disbelief. His last words rang in her mind:

". . . *like I've been* . . ." He had said it! ". . . *shot* . . ."

At the same instant the wooden hand bar in front of her seemed to explode. Splinters stabbed into her face and neck and hands.

Someone was shooting at her too!

Seized by unreasoning panic, she pushed up the damaged bar, and leaped out of the chair. Her screams, as she fell, were joined by those of the passengers in the other chairs up and down the mountain.

The ski run where the first shootings had occurred was shut down promptly. At the upper and lower stations of the chair lift there was bedlam. The operator at the bottom had stopped the lift when the first inaccurate but logical report had come down to him, mouth to mouth, from the lift's passengers, that somebody had fallen out of one of the double chairs "by accident."

Five minutes passed—after three more passengers had been shot—before his frantic manager got him on the phone and shouted: "Get that Goddamned thing moving! There's a sniper firing at the lift! All those poor slobs are trapped up there dangling like sitting ducks."

And, before all of the chairs had deposited their riders at the top station, three more passengers had been shot, and seven hysterical people had jumped to the ground, some of them suffering serious injuries.

Snowmass-at-Aspen, the largest and most lavish winter resort in the Western United States, was under siege.

The state police sedan skidded to a halt in front of the West Village police station. Captain Lester Dorn and Lieutenant Dave Potts were out of the car and taking the courthouse steps three at a stride by the time the fading siren ceased its wailing. The red turret lamp on top of the roof continued to flash its alarm.

Police Chief Phil Wexler of Aspen was conferring with Police Chief Max Lanier of West Village—the smaller town servicing Snowmass—in front of a large map of the resort area hanging on a wall of the small office. Paul Malone, the county sheriff, was there too. As well as some faces Dorn didn't recognize.

Greetings were terse.

"What's the story, Phil?" Dorn asked Wexler.

"Better get it from Chief Lanier. He's been on top of it all the way."

"There's this sniper, maybe more than one, holed up in a lodge right here." Lanier put a finger on the site between the ski trail where the first shootings had happened and the lift which had been the follow-up target.

"First he picked off a man and wife as they were skiing down this trail here. The others walked into the ambush without suspecting a thing. He killed one of them and wounded another feller, not too bad."

He moved his finger across the map to the lift, identified by a broken black line. "Then he turns his gun on the lift. Jesus! That must have been awful for those poor people, trapped in those chairs like that. He killed one young fellow to start with. And his girl panicked and jumped. She's all right, broken leg and a bad case of shock. Before they got all the passengers off safely, he'd killed one more woman and wounded five others. Seven more took their chances, I don't blame them, and jumped for it. Couple broken legs and arms. One's got internal injuries, but nothing fatal."

Dorn sagged back against the desk and tipped up the brim of his trooper's Stetson. "Jesus Christ! Five dead and six wounded. Not counting the ones who jumped."

"All of it in a little under a half hour," Chief Wexler put in. "He's a killer, no doubt about it. Like that boy down in Texas that shot all those people from the tower."

Dorn lit a cigarette and burned down a third of it with one

enormous inhalation. "Max, you said something about there might be more than one feller up in that lodge?"

"That's right, a cab brought two men and two women up to the lodge from the airport late yesterday afternoon. It was a chartered flight. Bad luck, the driver was new on the job. Otherwise he might have recognized who they were. The owners are pretty well known around here. It's one of the biggest private lodges at Snowmass."

"What about the airline that flew them up here? They must have a record of the passengers' names."

"Dead end there too. The flight was from Denver Airport. They do so much business this season, one face is the same as another. They're pretty sure it was a man chartered the flight. He paid in cash. And the passengers were logged as 'Mr. and Mrs. J. Smith' and 'Mr. and Mrs. R. Jones.' "

Dorn looked pained. "Now, that's original. Who are the owners?"

Lanier nodded to a slim, dark man, wearing a red tie on a red shirt underneath his open mackinaw. "This here is Sid Feldman. He does accounting and some public relations for the corporation runs Snowmass."

Feldman cleared his throat self-importantly. "Actually, it's owned jointly by three men. They're all very well off." He handed Dorn a list he had prepared.

The state police captain and Sheriff Malone studied it together.

John W. Whittaker—novelist, playwright, producer
Wallace Kaiser—President, Reynolds, Kaiser and Price
(ad firm in New York City)
Forrest Evans—Board Chairman, Evans Heavy Equipment
Corporation (heavy construction machinery)

"I've heard of Whittaker," Dorn said. "He's on a lot of those late-night television talk shows."

The sheriff nodded. "Big people, all right. It don't make sense their kind being mixed up in something like this."

"Maybe they're high on whiskey or drugs," Lanier offered. "There's been lots of talk about some of the wild parties going on up there."

"No drunk or junkie could do that kind of shooting," Phil Wexler denied it. "This guy—I think we can rule out the women —is an expert marksman. Those weren't just lucky shots, the ones he hit on the lift. Range must be a thousand yards or more."

Dorn looked to Dave Potts, who had been a sniper with a special services outfit in Vietnam. "What do you think, Dave?"

Potts was not overly impressed with the killer's marksmanship. "A thousand yards was a routine shot. We used a bolt-action Remington 700 with a variable power scope. I've bagged VCs at twelve, thirteen hundred yards. One of our dingers blew off a Cong officer's head at sixteen hundred yards. Almost a mile. What I mean is, given a finely balanced target rifle and a powerful scope sight, almost any experienced hunter could score at a thousand yards. Especially if he's got the rifle firmly propped, like on a windowsill."

Sheriff Malone concurred. "He's got a point, Les. That's why the conservation people are trying to push through legislation prohibiting hunters from shooting with scopes. Game don't have a sporting chance."

"Hmmm . . ." Dorn rubbed the side of a thumb against his jawbone. "Mr. Feldman, do the fellers who own the lodge do any hunting?"

"Oh, sure. They have some kind of a gun club, I think. I'll see what I can find out about it. A few of the local men are professional guides."

"Thanks," Dorn said coolly. "But the police can handle whatever interrogation has to be done."

"Of course." Feldman was deflated.

"I still bet there's booze or drugs involved," Chief Lanier maintained.

Sid Feldman cleared his throat and favored Lanier with an apologetic grin. "One thing . . . these rumors about wild parties up at that lodge tend to be exaggerated. They're spread around, usually, by the people here who aren't invited to them."

Dorn suppressed an appreciative smile. "That figures."

"The owners are very responsible and respectable people," Feldman continued. "So are their guests, the ones I've met."

"They have a lot of guests up there? Out of towners?"

"A fair amount. Some are regulars. Some I don't know."

Dorn frowned. "Then, for all we know neither of the two men up there now are necessarily any of the owners. They could be friends who came here with or without the knowledge of Whittaker, Kaiser, or—" he looked down at the list Feldman had given him "—or Evans?"

Feldman nodded. "That's right."

"Well . . ." Dorn said, with some indecision, to the sheriff. "I imagine the owners should be notified what's happening up there. Just in case. That's valuable real estate. Find out whether those four are up there with the owners' consent, and, if so, who they are."

"Good point, Les," Chief Lanier concurred. "The lodge stands to be shot up pretty bad before this is over. The right and legal thing to do is to let the owners know." He paused before amending. "If it isn't them up there."

"It's more important than that, Max," Dorn told him. "I want to find out who's behind that rifle. Run a check on him. Friends, relatives. Maybe he's even been under a doctor's care recently. If we can get some clue as to what set him off like this, we might be able to talk him down without any more shooting." He looked at Sheriff Malone. "Paul, can your office handle that angle? The local police where they live will check them out for you."

Sheriff Malone was pleased to oblige. "You bet, Les. We'll get right on it."

"Good." Dorn turned to Chief Lanier. "Okay, Max, so what action have you taken so far about this sniper?"

Looking very uncomfortable, Lanier shifted his eyes away from Dorn. "Well . . . so far I just ordered everybody to stay clear of the area. I mean, anyone who can shoot like that could pick you off better than a half mile away. They brought out the dead and wounded from Big Burn while he was shooting at the lift. The warming hut was evacuated by way of Sam's Knob, station on top. I thought . . ." He let it trail off, but all the men present knew what Max Lanier thought.

Law enforcement in affluent resorts like Snowmass and Aspen almost exclusively was dealing with nonviolent crimes. Routine misdemeanors, nasty drunks, or an occasional light-fingered ski bum. Assault and battery was a rarity. Murder was unheard of. Mass slaughter such as had taken place on Mt. Baldy that morning was unthinkable. Lanier was eager to let somebody else think about it for him. None of them blamed him. Including Sheriff Malone, who technically was the ranking law officer among them.

"You got your men coming in, right, Les?" he inquired affably.

"Two squads of state riot police. With all the equipment. Gas, bullet-proof vests, and shields. Two of the best snipers in the troop. A police helicopter is on its way too. . . ."

"Could I offer a suggestion, Captain?" Sid Feldman asked. He touched the knot of his tie self-consciously. They were all looking at him with the special sufferance that policemen reserve for civilians. Particularly small bookish civilians like Feldman.

Dorn let him hang a while before drawling. "Well . . . sure, now, Mr. Feldman. What's on your mind?"

Feldman's eyes were owlish behind his thick lenses. "Maybe there's a quick way to find out who the people up at the lodge are."

"How's that?"

"Ask them?"

"Oh, hell!" A deputy snickered.

Even Dorn wore a thin smile. "And just how would we go about doing that, Mr. Feldman? You volunteering to walk up to the front door waving a white flag?"

Feldman's smile was superior. "That won't be necessary, captain. All you have to do is phone the lodge. That line is operative all year." He took a small spiral notebook out of his shirt pocket, opened the cover and tore off a page." He handed it to Dorn. "Here's the number."

Dorn felt like a damned fool and showed it. "It's worth trying, anyway," he said trying to minimize Feldman's idea. It was a small thing to do, he knew, and added immediately, "I should have thought of it myself." He sat down behind Chief Lanier's desk and picked up the phone.

The phone at the lodge rang monotonously over and over. Dorn stopped counting after ten.

"I guess they're not about to answer," he said finally, and he was about to hang up when a man's voice came on.

"What is it?" The voice was calm.

"This is Captain Dorn of the Colorado State Police. Who are you, and who do you have up there with you?"

"It doesn't matter." Calm and flat.

"Are the others alive?"

A hesitation. "They're alive. But that may change at any time now."

Dorn spoke with as much authority as he could to a phone. "Okay, mister. Now, you listen to me, and listen carefully. You leave those people be and you put down your rifle and come out with your hands high. You're in bad trouble. But no trouble is as bad as being dead."

The voice was amused and contemptuous. "The four of us up here are going to be dead, one way or another, no matter what happens. And, if you try to break in here and take me, I'll sure as hell kill as many of you as I can too. Don't be a fool, captain. Don't try it. It just means it'll be sooner than I had planned."

He betrayed no signs of tension or hysteria. Relaxed and curiously "rational." To Dorn that was the giveaway. Any man who could be so detached after gunning down innocent people at random had to be a dangerous mental case. He had to be treated very gingerly.

"That a fact?" Dorn replied casually. "Well . . . just when are you planning to do it? Kill them and yourself?" Needling him a little. "There are a couple of squads of riot police on their way here. You know, you could save the taxpayers a lot of money if you'd let us know what your timetable is."

The sniper laughed. "I like your sense of humor, captain. I don't want to kill you. So do us both a favor and stay where you are. Send your riot police on their way to more important business. And keep away from this part of the mountain.

"Do your thing, and let me do mine. Don't worry about us. Goodbye, captain." The line clicked and went dead.

Dorn tried unsuccessfully to call back, but there was a busy signal. "He's taken it off the hook," he said, hanging up. He briefed the others on the phone conversation.

"You think he means what he said, Les?" Sheriff Malone asked.

"I'm convinced of it, Paul." Dorn was grim.

"And there ain't nothing *any* of us can do except to sit tight," Lanier said, eager to emphasize that Dorn, Malone, all of them, were as helpless and impotent as he had been while the massacre was going on.

Dorn got up and placed a comradely hand on Chief Lanier's shoulder. "Now, I'd like to go up and look over that lodge." His mouth curled wryly. "From a safe distance . . . You did the right thing, Max. Clear out the area and wait for the shock troops. They're trained to do this kind of a job."

Wexler frowned. "You're not going to go in after him, are you? You just told us he was serious about killing the hostages."

"I don't know, Phil." Dorn sighed. "I'm not sure what to do right now. Maybe there's nothing to do. We'll just have to take it slow. Play it by ear. He nodded to Lieutenant Dave Potts. "Come on, Dave. And get the rifle and binoculars from the car. We might get a shot at him.

Accompanied by Sid Feldman, Chief Lanier, Chief Wexler, and Sheriff Malone, the troopers rode the lift up to Sam's Knob. From the restaurant, they went south across Mt. Baldy on snowshoes. Led by Lanier, they went downhill so that they would approach the lodge from due north. Lanier explained this maneuver.

"All the windows on both floors are shuttered except for that one bedroom. He did all his shooting from those windows. He can cover the road from there too."

Dorn nodded. "But he can't draw a bead on us coming up from this side?"

"I guess he doesn't figure on anyone moving in on him from this direction," the sheriff reasoned. "That high ground around him is plenty steep on three sides. I wouldn't want to climb up there with all this snow and ice."

"But he must be keeping a lookout, just in case," Feldman cautioned. "Those shutters all have air vents he can see out."

Dorn scowled. He still harbored a faint resentment toward the slight bookkeeper—that's how he thought of Feldman, as a slight bookkeeper with weak eyes hunched on a high stool over a ledger, and wearing a green eyeshade. But he was not about to discount any advice he offered. Aside from having a deductive mind, Feldman probably knew the topography of Mt. Baldy and the layout of the lodge better than any of the police officers did.

He studied the lodge, less than five-hundred yards away, through field glasses. It was a handsome reproduction of a Swiss chalet. Standing on a high promontory, stark against the blue sky, it looked as indomitable as a fortress, with its shuttered windows and wide eaves.

"We could take him when it's dark. If he waits that long," Dorn said. "Hell, he's got to sleep sometime."

Feldman shook his head, his face solemn. "It wouldn't work. I know every piece of material that went into that lodge. Those shutters, solid oak. By the time you could break one of them down and get inside, he'd have plenty of warning, even if he was asleep."

Dorn was in the act of lighting a cigarette when Sheriff Lanier shouted. "Hey! Something's moving up there!"

The captain brought up the binoculars quickly and scanned the lodge. The shutters were open on one second-story window on this north side. The sash lifted, and he glimpsed an arm (checkered shirt, he filed it away in his memory file). Then a shoulder, the arm extending as the rifle barrel slid menacingly out the window.

"Get down!" Dorn cried. "He's spotted us." Feldman had been right. The sniper was maintaining an alert surveillance of the ground around his fortress. They were safely in cover behind a small rise before the first bullet *zinged* overhead, the report chasing after it an instant later.

Lieutenant Potts started for the top of the rise on his belly, cradling his rifle in the hollows of his elbows.

"Where the hell do you think you're going?" Dorn called after him.

"I want to see if I can get a shot at him."

Dorn weighed the idea. It was a .264 Winchester, firing a 140-grain slug, plenty of gun to do the job. And it had a Lyman sight. Dave Potts was the best sharpshooter in the troop. He was still deliberating when Potts got to the top and began lining up his target. Dave Potts never had a chance to get off the shot.

Stunned, Dorn saw Potts jerk and rear up. Without a word, he shuddered and sank down motionless in the snow, his finger caught in the trigger guard of the Winchester. The sound of the shot from the lodge cracked with authority, and even before he crawled up to where Potts lay, Dorn knew he was dead.

His instinct was confirmed by the massive hole in the back of Potts' skull where the heavy slug had exited.

In the bedroom on the far side of the house, the women huddled together shivering on the floor in front of an electric heater he had brought up from the cellar at the request of the blonde woman. It wasn't really cold in the room any more. They were bundled up in coats and blankets, and the sun was beating down on the roof over their heads. The chill that blew over their bodies, the ice that layered over the flesh and jellied the marrow deep inside the bones came from within. The closeness of death.

They sat in tense silence for some minutes after the last shot sounded. At last the dark woman spoke.

"It's stopped, I think."

The other woman said nothing. Her eyes were glassy. Her hands and feet were numb. So numb she couldn't feel them at all. So were her nose and lips and cheeks. Merciful shock.

"If only I could get downstairs while he's gone," the brunette said. "If I could get to the den, where the rifles are—"

"You're as crazy as he is," the blonde told her. "The way our feet are shackled. Anyway, he always locks the door."

"He might forget."

The dazed eyes. The vacant eyes looked right through her. "You don't really believe that. You're only talking to keep up your courage. All that nonsense before, running off at the mouth about some stupid party twenty-five years ago.

The dark woman gripped her shoulders and shook her roughly. "You listen to me! 'All that nonsense' just may have saved our lives. He was thinking about killing us then. I could read it in his face. Talking about the party distracted him. He was interested, couldn't you tell? You don't have to be a psychologist to know where all this started. I mean, he just didn't wake up yesterday morning and decide to shoot up the world. In the old days they said insane people were 'possessed'? It's true. He's possessed. Possessed by the past."

"Talking isn't going to stop him from killing us." The blonde woman had begun to accept the fact that her death sentence was irreversible. Now and then she would experience a morbid anxiety to have it over and done with.

"And you're going to sit there like a dumb cow while he shoots you between the eyes?" The woman's total submissiveness angered the dark woman. "Can't you get it through your brain that every minute we can get his mind off the present—*this, here, now*—is time gained? The more time we can gain, the better our chances. There are police out there, cracking their brains to try and come up with a plan to save us. We've got to buy time, do you understand?"

The blonde nodded her head. "I—I—guess so."

"All right, now when he comes back here, you and I are going to talk. Talk and more talk. I'll cue you, don't worry. And just say anything at all that comes into your mind. It doesn't matter what. As long as we can make him listen to us."

He was only too eager to listen. Finding out things about that Christmas Eve that he had not known before. He wanted to hear more. All the missing threads of so many days and nights. Then, perhaps, he could better understand. Why he was here now with a rifle in his hands. He took a long swallow of bourbon from the bottle on the floor beside him. It deadened the aching in his throat. The pain in his head receded into a bearable knot of tightness at the base of his skull.

It was the third time Mae Edsel had gone upstairs to repair her lipstick. The boys had booby-trapped the rooms on the ground floor with mistletoe and were taking frequent advantage of it.

"My mouth is actually sore," she said, touching it tenderly with the colored tube.

"Don't knock it!" Wendy Gates smiled. "The only real pest is that Wally Kaiser. He's so passionate when he kisses you, you get the feeling he's going to rape you."

Mae laughed. "Oh, he's only putting on an act. Wally's all right."

"Oh?" Wendy was laconic. "Well, I suppose you know him better than I do."

"Not really. He comes into the office occasionally with layouts from the ad agency where he works. He's Jack's friend."

"You see much of Jack?"

"Not during working hours. I'm a secretary in the front office. Jack's at the studio."

"And after hours?"

It was not a casual question. Mae knew it. She was seated at the vanity in Jack's mother's room with her back to the blonde girl.

She shrugged. "Drinks. Dinner twice. We're friends." She watched Wendy in the mirror. She was sitting on the bed, legs crossed, swinging her foot to the beat of the music blaring in the room below. Mae was uncomfortably aware that she was being appraised. "Sized up" was more accurate. She suspected why too.

"Have you known Jack long, Wendy?" Her question was not as casual as it sounded either.

"About five years. As long as I've known the rest of the crowd." Her gaze moved up the backs of the dark girl's legs. They were long and shapely. Mae had the best figure of any of the girls there. *Damn it!* But her face was not outstanding, she consoled herself. Pretty but ordinary. Her wide brown eyes were her best feature. Wendy looked at her own reflection in the vanity mirror, pleased by what she saw. Fine bone structure, large almond-shaped eyes, green as emeralds.

Mae put away the lipstick and teased her bangs with a comb. "This is the first time I've met any of the kids. They all seem so nice. . . ." She winced inwardly at how banal it sounded. "I mean, Jean and I are outsiders, but you're all so friendly. So often, when people have been close friends for a long time, they resent new people being brought in."

Wendy smiled as she lit a cigarette. "You mean the gals don't like the competition? Haven't you noticed that the boys and girls in this crowd aren't paired off? Everybody plays the field. We're a communal group, I suppose you'd say."

Mae laughed. "You make it sound like one of those religious sects where they practice free love."

Wendy's green eyes were amused. "Help yourself."

"Now you're pulling my leg. It is unusual though. Such an attractive group of young people and there aren't any romances."

"I didn't say that," Wendy said, no longer smiling. "There are attractions. It wouldn't be natural if there weren't. As they say, boys and girls are different, and *vive la différence:* But there haven't been any hot love affairs. Not so far, anyway."

Mae turned around on the vanity bench. "I heard that Carl and Tess were almost engaged once."

"Oh, that. Before the war. But it was kid stuff. Tess actually did get engaged to a sailor after Carl went into the Marines, and she sent Carl a 'Dear John' letter." Her expression was faintly contemptuous. "The poor girl didn't know that Carl had gotten over her long before she got over him."

Mae was going to ask how Wendy knew about that, but caught herself. It was obvious how Wendy knew. Mae had seen the hunger in Carl's eyes when he danced with Wendy. Just the way he looked at her across a room.

"How do you like your date?" Wendy asked her unexpectedly.

"My date?" Mae's eyebrows arched in surprise. "I didn't know I had a date."

"Wally Kaiser and Jack's friend from work were invited to balance up the boys and girls. You and Jean."

"But you said before that everybody plays the field in this crowd?"

Wendy's smile was as sweet as sugar laced with arsenic. "That's true, but you and Jean and Wally and Dean aren't really in the crowd."

Mae knew how to use her claws too. She grinned and replied: "My date certainly can't be Wally. Not the way he and Carl have been tom-catting after you all evening, Wendy."

The observation stripped away Wendy's pretense of friendliness. "That's an uncouth way of putting it," she said coldly.

"But so apt, dear."

Wendy stood up. "We'd better get back to the party before they think we fell in.

Walking down the stairs, Wendy was sullen, thinking over what Mae had said about Wally and Carl. Her tom-cat metaphor was not all that apt. What they were really like was two dogs, bickering and snarling over a bone. They had taken an instant dis-

like to each other, and she was caught in the middle. The two of
them had been crowding her all night until she thought she'd
smother if she didn't get away from them. Her mouth twisted
wryly. Most girls she knew would be floating on Cloud Nine if
two handsome males were competing for their affection. Wendy
was flattered. But neither Wally nor Carl was the one man she
desired.

Jack Whittaker greeted them at the foot of the stairs. When
he smiled at her, Wendy's knees jellied, and her stomach felt like
it did when she rode down in a fast elevator. She couldn't control it. She had fallen in love with Jack the first time she saw him.

Wendy was still a virgin at twenty-one, although innumerable
men had done their best to alter her status. The one man she
wanted to sleep with had never asked her.

She held out her hand to him as she neared the bottom of the
stairs. "Dance with me, Jack." Before he could protest—she
knew he didn't care for dancing—she said, "You promised before."

He laughed. "I did, didn't I?" He took her hand and led her
into the big sunporch. The rug had been rolled up for dancing.
One dim lamp sat on a table in a corner of the room. There were
three couples gliding and swaying dreamily to the music of Harry
James. Their faces were shadowed.

Her green eyes, faintly luminous in the dimness, were unblinking and brazen. "There now, dancing isn't all that bad, it is?"

He grinned. "A girl could get in a lot of trouble dancing the
way you do."

"A girl only dances the way I do with someone very special."

He laughed and whacked her bottom playfully. "Stop trying
to act like a hussy. It's not your role, Wendy."

She pouted. "Damn it, Jack, it's not an act. Is your mother
coming home tonight?"

"How did my mother get into this conversation?" he asked.
"No, she's staying over at Marcia's. She likes to be there when
the kids open their gifts in the morning."

When he had been inducted into the service, Jack had tried to persuade his widowed mother either to rent or sell the big house and move in with his married sister Marcia. Now he was glad that she had rejected his advice. It was good to come home to a "home."

"Then you'll be here all alone. That's not right on your first Christmas home."

He realized what she was up to now. Firmly he pushed her away, opening a gap between their bodies.

"Damn you, Jack Whittaker!" Tears sparkled in her eyes. "Stop treating me as if I were your little sister."

"Hey, keep it down." He looked around uneasily, but the other couples were wrapped in the trance of Harry's high, bitter-sweet trumpet.

". . . a kiss . . . the beginning of a love affair . . . A tender kiss . . ."

"Kiss me, Jack," she said softly.

"Wendy," he pleaded.

"For old time's sake."

He turned his head away from her, not answering. It was a worse rebuff than saying "No."

Her voice was very small, and for a bad moment he was afraid she was going to cry. "Don't do that to me, Jack. Please don't act as if I don't exist. I love you, Jack."

"Don't, Wendy."

"But it's true. And I think you could love me, if only you'd let yourself." She paused and looked up at him with a wistful smile. "I read once that love can be contagious. And I've got such a bad case that—"

"You're a wonderful girl, and I adore you," he overrode her with jovial brusqueness that did not quite come off. "You're beautiful and desirable and there are times—like right now—when I find you almost irresistible."

She went slack in his arms, a giving up. "Almost . . . but not quite." Then tonelessly, "Merry Christmas."

Gratefully he saw Carl come through the door and head toward them. *God bless the United States Marines.*

Carl wore a sullen expression and his voice was surly.

"Am I interrupting anything important?"

"Of course not, buddy. Want to cut in? Be my guest." He smiled at Wendy. "Thanks, doll. I hope I didn't crush too many of your toes."

She jerked out of his grasp without answering him. He had inflicted the final indignity on her, dumping her unceremoniously —even eagerly—into the arms of another man.

Carl was a much better dancer than Jack. He led with authority, and she had to concentrate to follow the intricate patterns of his steps. The slow tempo of Harry James made him impatient. "Somebody reject that platter, huh? Put on a lindy."

"Drop dead," Forrest Evans said as he and Mae Edsel glided past. "It's only got a little more to play. Miller's 'American Patrol' is coming up next."

"You know what they call this grunt and rub music at Parris Island?" Carl's laugh was nasty. "Speaking of which, you and old Jackson were putting on quite a show yourselves."

She drew away from him contemptuously. "Carl, you don't own me. How many times do I have to tell you that? Here you're only home one night and you're starting the same thing all over again."

His voice was flat. "And you haven't changed either. Still carrying the torch for Jack. You know something, Wendy? We have more in common than you think. We both want something we can't have. I want you, and you want Jack. People have been drawn close to one another on less than that."

She turned her head and looked at him for the first time. There was a quizzical expression in her eyes.

"I never thought of you as a philosopher, Carl."

"There's a lot of things you don't know about me." As casually as he could, he asked her, "Did you tell Kaiser you'd go out on a date with him?"

"If I did, it's none of your business," she told him.

Captain Dorn set up temporary headquarters in Sheriff Lanier's office in West Village. From there he directed by radio the operations of the dual state police command posts at the warming shack on top of the Big Burn and at the halfway point at Sam's Knob.

Sergeant "Casey" Jones, in charge of Sam's Knob, reported that the police 'copter was making its approach to the lodge.

"Thanks, Case," Dorn said. "Now get off the line. I want to talk to the bird now."

The 'copter's pilot came in weakly through static and engine noise. "I made one pass over the house at about five hundred feet. Everything looks quiet enough. I'll be making my next approach at about a hundred."

"You watch yourself," Dorn warned him. "This guy can knock the eye out of a crow at a hundred feet."

"I got Dick Eastman here with me. He wants to know if he should try to pick off the sniper if he shows himself?"

Dorn frowned into the mike. "Potts tried that. And he's dead. I don't know, Bill. We better play it cool for a while, until we come up with some definite plan of action. Let me know if you spot anything interesting, will you, Bill?"

Dorn snorted and put down the mike. He was halfway through his third pack of Camels, and it was only past noon. Sheriff Malone came into the office in a big hurry. "Les, I was just on the phone with the governor. He says the FBI is standing by."

"Oh, great!" Dorn spit out a shard of tobacco. "Let's call out the National Guard. Then we can have a real winter carnival."

Malone lumbered around the room like a great bear in his thick coat and fur hat. "They can invite themselves if it turns out that those three hostages he's holding were brought across the state line against their will."

"Jesus!" Dorn was irate. "What do they think the FBI's going to do that we can't do? Send in Efrem Zimbalist, Junior, with his tommygun and bullet-proof vest? Listen, we can have that killer laid cold in fifteen minutes if we're willing to sacrifice a half-dozen more lives."

"Sure, Les, I know that. Look, I know you're doing the best you can."

Chief Lanier covered a small smile with his coffee cup, thinking how fortunate he had been to hand off the buck to the state police.

"One other thing." Malone looked embarrassed. "The governor wants us to set up press headquarters here in West Village. The story has already hit the headlines on some special editions back east. It won't be long before the place is swarming with newsmen. TV people too."

Dorn swore under his breath. "Max, will you talk to Sid Feldman about that?"

"Sure thing, Les," Lanier said, glad of this small responsibility. With a trace of self-importance, he added, "I'll be glad to handle liaison between your office and the press."

Dorn grinned in spite of everything. "That's what I've always needed—a press secretary."

Malone took a notebook out of his coat pocket. "On the big wheels who own the lodge, nothing yet. I never would have believed how hard it is to get in touch with people like that. Especially on Christmas Eve. In New York Whittaker's office is already closed. Half day. The police there went to his apartment, but there's nobody home."

"Christmas Eve." Dorn pounded one huge fist onto the desk in frustration. "Rich ones like that, they just might take off for a week or two around the holidays."

"That's a fact. Kaiser's secretary said he and his wife flew down to Haiti a couple of days ago. She doesn't know where to reach him. He phoned her day before yesterday to say he didn't like the hotel they were staying at and was checking out. He was going to call her again when they were settled in a new place. She's still waiting to hear."

"What about Evans?"

Malone flipped the page. "Forrest Evans . . . The Cleveland police spoke to his oldest daughter. She told them her parents left early this morning on a short vacation."

"Damn!" Dorn punched his thigh.

"One thing, though, Les." Malone had kept the one positive item for last. "The girl said they were on their way up here."

"Snowmass?" he asked incredulously.

"Yup. The lodge. Supposed to be a big Christmas party."

Captain Dorn let out a long, low whistle and sat up alertly. "Now, what about that! Well, that could be our first break. At least we know it isn't the Evanses up at the lodge."

Malone nodded. "I've got a man standing by at the airport to corral them when they arrive."

"Good." The captain stood up and walked to a window, looking up the mountain. "A big Christmas party up there. I'll be damned! Well, when Evans gets here, we'll find out who was on the guest list."

"I think we can eliminate the Kaisers as well as the Evanses," Malone said.

"Hell, no!" Dorn swung away from the window to face him. "The Kaisers might have checked out of that hotel in Haiti and come straight back here. So far, the only ones we can definitely eliminate are Evans and his wife."

The phone on the desk rang and Dorn picked it up quickly. "Dorn here . . . Yeah, Clem . . . Is that a fact?" A look of satisfaction came over his lean face. "Every little bit helps. You bet. Thanks." He put down the phone.

"One more present and accounted for," he said. "Whittaker's kid cousin. Name of Louis Santini."

"Feldman mentioned him. He flew a jet fighter in Korea. Came home on a Section Eight discharge after a hundred missions. I figured he might be a candidate for our mystery sniper."

"No chance. He just got in at the airport on a charter flight. Seems he was invited to the party too."

"You know, Les," Malone reflected, "it doesn't make a hell of a lot of difference which one of 'em is up in the lodge behind that rifle. Our problem's the same. How do we get him before he gets any more of us?"

Dorn was mildly annoyed by the sheriff's subtle implication that his preoccupation with the identity of the sniper was a diversion to avoid confronting the main issue.

Bluntly, he reproached Malone. "Look, Paul, if you have any bright ideas how to take that fellow up there, let me in on them."

Malone shifted uncomfortably. "Ah, hell, Les! I only meant . . ." He stalled there. Just as the thousand-and-one solutions that Dorn's mind had been playing with since this monster had been dumped in his lap had all come to rest in limbo.

The sheriff scratched his head, looking foolish.

"Paul, we got to get a handle on this situation," Dorn said less sharply. "Until we find something to grip on to, we just don't have any control over what's going on inside that lodge. Right now it's a Mexican standoff. He's got us by the short hairs. Like I told Max before, maybe one of the other people due up here can help us find the answer to your question: how to get him out of there without any more bloodshed."

The chopper's rotor blades beat the air like the wings of a great bird. It flew an elliptical pattern around the lodge, swooping lower and lower with each complete turn.

Dick Eastman shouted to the pilot over the loudness of the engine and rotors. "Bring her in real slow like from the south next time. Maybe I can see something through the windows with the shutters open."

"You heard the captain, Dick," Sergeant Carter objected. "He said to play it cool."

"I ain't going to pick a fight. I just want to have a look with the glasses." He picked up a pair of high-powered field glasses and focused them on the snowy ridge below. When the lodge was due north of them Carter cut the throttle and eased the stick forward. Hands and feet working the controls with the skilled coordination of an organist, he maneuvered the ship in to within 150 feet of the corner of the lodge, providing Eastman with a slanted view of the two unshuttered windows on adjacent walls of the upstairs bedroom.

"If he opens one of those windows, we get out of here fast!" he said.

The two men were watching those two windows with such concentration that they did not see the shutter inch open slowly on a window further along the side of the house. A rifle barrel poked out of the crack.

The shot smashed through the right side of the curved plexiglass windshield, barely missing Eastman's head and exiting through the door on the pilot's side behind Carter's shoulders.

"What the hell!" Carter's arms and legs overreacted, sending the tumbling 'copter out of control.

"We're going to crack up!" Eastman yelled.

There was no further conversation, as Carter had to rally all of his physical and mental resources in the contest against machine and nature. Battling the balky controls, he was struck by the strong conviction—original for him after all his years of flying—that it was, indeed, contrary to the natural order of things for man to fly.

There was a heart-stopping instant of panic as the ground rose up to meet them, spinning like an enormous turntable. Then, indebted more to luck than to his skill, the helicopter shied away from its disaster and lunged straight up into the air. Mind and muscle obeyed the programming of training and experience. He righted the chopper, trimmed the stabilizing rotors, and hit the throttle. They ran like hell!

Crouching at the window where he had set up the ambush, the sniper flung open the shutters wide and tracked the chopper's wild gyrations through the scope sight. Lines of displeasure tightened his face when she did not crash. As the chopper fled, he aimed at the small rotors on the tail section, firing, one, two, three shots, with the cool, unhurried poise of a professional hunter.

"Gotcha!" he exclaimed with satisfaction as the tail began to swing from one side to the other. The ship flew on a way, doing its crazy little dance. It canted to one side, fluttering. Abruptly it seemed to stall and fall away sharply to that side. It was losing altitude very fast. The last he saw, it plunged down out of sight beyond a grove of tall pine trees.

The flock winging off into the sky, a graceful feathered arrow-head. The stragglers, strung out in its wake, born losers, and knowing they were, from their terrified squawking. The big mallard with the green head and white throat band. The gun led it perfectly, but the shot was low. Still, the bird was winged, and it went down spiraling around the dangling wing into the water.

From the blind on the other side of the cove, Charlie Roche's voice called out: "You're a lousy shot!" He then went on to demonstrate his own proficiency by sending the two tail-end stragglers plunging like stones into the marsh grass with two quick blasts of shot.

That was the summer of 1946, near the DiSalle hunting lodge in Maine. Forrest Evans' future father-in-law—the couple had become officially engaged in April—had given Forrest a key to the lodge along with permission to visit there whenever he liked. It was a large, luxurious dwelling with eight bedrooms upstairs and a spacious den with a well-stocked bar. The picture window in the den looked out on a lake. The swimming, fishing, and boating were excellent. And in winter it was the heartland of the skiing region.

The weekend was to have been the first of many happy times at the DiSalle lodge. The way things worked out, it was the one and only time the crowd vacationed there together. Afterward, it was generally accepted that what happened there that summer was directly responsible for their breaking up.

Looking back now, though, he realized that what had appeared to be a cause *at the time was, in reality, a first clear* symptom *of a long-standing ailment which was already in the terminal stage when it manifested itself.*

The friction which had existed between Carl Schneider and Wally Kaiser since their first meeting had grown worse in the months since Christmas. Carl made no secret of his dislike for Wally. Wally treated Schneider with courteous contempt. In fact, he affected an air of condescension toward all of them with the exception of Jack Whittaker. Even Wendy Gates, whom he dated frequently, was put off by him.

"He's so damned superior," she confided to Jack. "Out in public he's just about perfect. Holding doors for you, lighting your cigarette, all those little things that women should find endearing in a man. He even sent my mother flowers on her birthday. Oh, he's a gentleman with a capital 'G.' But you always come home after being out with Wally feeling deflated somehow. As if he expects a girl to curtsy and say: 'I'm so grateful because big, wonderful *you* wasted your valuable time on little, nothing old me.'"

Jack laughed. "That's ridiculous. It's all in your mind. Wally is crazy about you. I know he is."

"He may say it, but he doesn't show it. Not in the ways that really matter. If it's all in my own mind, it's only because Wally put it there. I can't help it, Jack. It's not just me. I can't think of one of us who truly thinks of Wally as a friend."

"I do, or I wouldn't have him around as much as I do."

"I'm sorry you do, Jack. He doesn't fit. He thinks he's better than the rest of us."

"That's not true. Wally's a good egg. Let me tell you something. I lived with this man in the Army for three years. When our outfit moved up from Naples to Rome, I had my leg in a cast, and it looked as if they'd have to leave me behind. Wally wouldn't hear of it. Why, he must have carried me on his back half of the way. A man without feeling? No. More than muscle, that took heart. There's a lot of feeling dammed up inside Wally

Kaiser. He's not cold and aloof, or superior. He's as frightened and insecure as all the rest of us."

She was surprised and curious. Not at what Jack had said about Wally. Maybe Wally was hiding behind a façade of aloofness. The surprising thing was what he was saying about himself. In all the years she had known Jack Whittaker it had never occurred to her that he could be frightened or insecure. He was the great, infallible father figure to all of them.

A group of human beings who share an intimate association over a long period of time function together like the parts of a machine, turning one on the other in complementary harmony, each one contributing in its own fashion to a common purpose. Inevitably, an erosion takes place, a loss of lubricity; friction shows up the inherent weakness of the parts. The harmonious function is impaired; ultimately it breaks down. Which is exactly what was happening to Jack's old friends.

Jack Whittaker was playing chess in a corner of the den with Wally Kaiser. Forrest Evans and his fiancée were out walking in the moonlight. "Looking for someplace to make out," as Carl delicately put it. It was a warm night with a full moon.

Carl was sitting at the bar listening to the broadcast of a Yankee night game. The girls were occupied with chores in the kitchen and other parts of the lodge.

Charlie Roche, self-appointed bartender, stood alone at the el of the bar, playing with an ancient flintlock pistol, one of a pair that Clinton DiSalle had mounted on his backbar. Roche's khaki army shirt was rolled up to his elbows.

It was a standing joke, which Charlie sternly ignored, that he never really felt well dressed without some article of his retired service wardrobe. A pair of sox, a field jacket, or a shirt.

Charlie had been drinking heavily all afternoon and evening to ease the discomfort of a bad sunburn, and he was in a belligerent mood. His eyes were wilder than usual.

Jack's and Wally's glasses had been empty for perhaps ten minutes when Wally called to Charlie.

"Get on the ball, bartender, or we may just forget to tip you."

Charlie glared at him sullenly but said nothing. Absently he shoved the pistol underneath his belt and began to mix the drinks. He brought them over, taking his time, and, after serving them, he stood there watching Jack ponder his next move. Wally leaned back in his chair and glanced up at Charlie. He saw the gun and grinned.

"Oh, why don't you come off it, Roche? The war's over."

"Huh?" Charlie missed the point.

"That cap pistol. You going to play cops and robbers?"

Charlie's sunburned face got even redder. If Jack had said the same things to him, he would have laughed and played along with the joke. But Wally Kaiser had a way of making the most innocent statement sound smug and insulting.

Charlie bridled. A man of action rather than words, he jerked the pistol out of his belt and pointed it at Wally's head.

"Yeah, want to play? Bang! Bang! You're dead. And don't I wish the damned thing was loaded."

Distracted from the game, Jack looked up. He rose halfway out of the chair at the sight of the pistol pointing at Wally.

Wally, who had been brought up in a Quaker home, detested weapons and the violence they stood for. When he was inducted into the Army he had at first refused to carry a rifle. The threat of a court-martial and some strong persuasion by Jack Whittaker had succeeded in making him accept a compromise. But privately he had vowed to Jack that he would never fire the rifle at another human being, German or Jap. In Company B's brief service on the Fifth Army front in Italy, it had been engaged in several fire fights, but Jack was certain that Wally always aimed over the heads of the enemy troops on the other side of the Arno River.

"Don't point that thing at me, Roche," Wally said. His voice was too quiet, and he was very pale.

"Up yours, Kaiser!" Charlie sneered and jammed the muzzle of the pistol against Wally's head.

Wally's hand came up fast and grabbed the gun, wrenching it

out of Charlie's hand. Calmly he put the pistol into his own pocket.

"Children shouldn't be allowed to play with firearms," he said in the snide way that everyone found so objectionable.

Charlie's fury was a palpable force in the room that commanded all attention. His eyes bulged. His throat swelled.

"You—you—" The words would not come out until his tension found release in some violent action. He slapped Wally with his right hand. As hard as Jack had ever seen a man slapped. The blow flung Wally's head to the side and almost knocked him out of the chair. Before he could recover, Charlie backhanded the other side of his face.

Then the words came in a rush. *"You lousy, stinking bastard! I'm going to beat that pretty smirking face of yours to a pulp. Get up!"*

To the amazement of the other men, Wally ignored him. Acted as if he weren't there. Ugly red welts were puffing up his right cheek and his neck and jawbone on the left side. He touched them with his fingertips, nodding to Jack. Pale and expressionless.

"Your move, Whittaker," he said as if nothing out of the ordinary had happened.

Charlie stared at him in disbelief. "Didn't you hear what I said to you?"

"I said it's your move, Jack," Wally repeated.

Charlie pounded both fists down in the middle of the chess board, scattering the pieces. "You yellow bastard! Get up and fight!" He lost all control now. Picking up one of the full glasses, he hurled it across the room. It smashed into the wall, spraying Scotch, water, and glass splinters over the pine paneling and the floor.

Calmly, Wally took his pipe out of his pocket and proceeded to fill it from a tobacco pouch at one side of the chess board.

The brutal savagery of Roche's challenge and Kaiser's refusal to respond to it or, worse, even acknowledge that he had been challenged, had a strange, unpredictable effect on Jack Whittaker. Roche was a bully. He accepted that. What really confounded him was Wally's infuriating passivity. As if Roche's presence had such small relevance for him that Roche ceased to exist in his mind.

Unexpectedly—it was as unexpected for him as it was for the others—Jack stood up, knocking his chair over. He picked up a drink and threw it in Wally's face. Then he went after Charlie Roche.

Charlie was too startled to defend himself. Jack hit him hard on the chin, and he went down. He sat on the floor, dazed, looking up at Jack in bewilderment. Cool-headed, even-tempered Jack. Arbiter of conflicts among his friends as far back as Charlie could remember. He couldn't believe what was happening.

Jack reached down, grabbed his shirt front and pulled Charlie to his feet. His legs were shaky, and he swayed from side to side in Jack's grasp, arms hanging slack at his sides.

"Hey, buddy . . ." he said thickly, trying to grin through his split lips.

Jack drew back his fist to hit him again as Wally and Carl pounced on him from behind. He let go of the shirt and Charlie staggered back and leaned heavily against the bar. Jack did not struggle against the men who were restraining him.

"Okay . . . It's all right." Docilely, he allowed Wally to lead him out onto the porch, while Carl attended to Charlie.

Wally sighed in exasperation. "Honestly, Whittaker, that's the last thing I would have expected from you."

Jack stared straight ahead out across the dark lake. "I don't know. . . . I just don't know."

Wally took out a handkerchief and mopped his wet face and the front of his shirt. "The trouble is, Jack," he said with the disapproving air of a headmaster, "you've been associating with barbarians like Roche so long that it's beginning to rub off on you."

"Don't talk down to me, Wally." Jack was pale and tense.

"But it's true, old boy. Whatever were you thinking of?"

Jack glared at him. "How could you sit there and let him knock you around and pretend that nothing had happened?"

Wally shrugged and gingerly fingered the rising mouse under his right eye. "I could have pinned his ears back, but what would it have proved? Just another example of violence breeding violence."

It was not a coward's rationalization. Jack had put on the gloves many times with Wally in the Army gym during basic training and the brawny dark man was a skillful boxer.

Jack shook his head. "Somebody had to stop him."

"No dice, Whittaker," Wally snapped. "Don't blame me because *you* lost your head."

"Damn you, Wally!" Jack said in annoyance. "It was your fault, the whole thing. You're always baiting Charlie, and tonight you went too far. He's got a low boiling point when he drinks too much. You know that. Yet you deliberately—"

Wally wouldn't let him finish. "*I* went too far?" His black eyes glowed. "That son of a bitch aimed that gun at my head!"

"Oh, hell! That pistol hasn't been fired in over a hundred years. It's an ornament."

"No matter! He's lucky I didn't ram it down his throat."

The discussion ended as Charlie Roche came ambling out onto the terrace, holding an ice cube wrapped in a handkerchief to his split lip. He held up one hand with the palm facing them and grinned sheepishly.

"Peace . . . Say, that's a wicked right cross you've got, old buddy. We're going to match you with Louis."

"I'm sorry, Charlie." He offered his jaw. "Look, you want a free shot at me, go ahead."

Charlie laughed. "That's mighty tempting, kid. But no thanks. I had one coming, I guess."

"At least you admit it, that's something," Wally said testily.

"Wally!" Jack rebuked him.

"It's okay." Charlie could handle it now. He put out his hand to Wally. "My apologies to you, Kaiser."

"Accepted." Wally disregarded the outstretched hand and lit his pipe. "Well, now that we've got everything settled, let's go in and finish our chess game. I have the board memorized so there won't be any problem—"

"Not tonight," Jack cut him off. "I'm going for a walk along the beach."

"I'll join you," Wally said.

"No! I want to be alone." Jack turned abruptly and vaulted over the low brick wall that bounded the terrace and strode off with his hands jammed deep into his pockets.

Jack Whittaker couldn't sleep. The luminous hands of his wristwatch read three-thirty. He got out of bed and put on his swim trunks. He left the room on bare feet so he wouldn't wake Wally, snoring in the other twin bed, and went downstairs and out the terrace door. The moon was down, and the air moving in off the black lake was cool. In the distance he could hear dull rumbling of thunder, and sheet lightning flashed against the sky on the eastern horizon.

In contrast to the night air, the water felt warm on his legs as he waded into the lake. He swam leisurely toward the square silhouette of the float anchored about a hundred yards off the beach. When he reached the float, he turned on his back and floated with one hand resting lightly on the boarding ladder.

It was a pleasant, sensual sensation, suspended weightless in the tepid water. His body rising and falling rhythmically with the gentle pulsations of the lake. He felt immersed in the teeming force of the universe, an infinitesimal but unique particle of life sweeping to some unknown destiny on the tide of creation.

The stars were hidden by the thick, swirling overcast blowing in from the nearby ocean. He lay there an eternity, ears submerged, listening to the crooning voice of the lake. He was part of the tide, as the tide was part of him, coursing through his body, fiercely alive in his loins. He ached with sexual desire.

Something wet and alive touched his shoulder. Gasping, he thrashed upright in the water. Only the sound of the woman's voice stopped him from striking out at the dim shape beside him.

"I'm sorry, Jack. I didn't mean to startle you."

The sheet lightning flared again, closer this time, illuminating Wendy Gates, with her fair hair plastered wetly to her skull. The quick, stark flash accentuated the classic angularity of her face and bare shoulders. She laughed at him.

"Don't mind me. I couldn't sleep either."

"You look like a sea siren," he said. Lightning lit up the sky again. "Your hair reminds me of seaweed."

"Well, *thanks* a heap. You sure know how to flatter a gal! Don't mind if I hitch on, do you? You get pooped fast treading lake water." He was between her and the ladder, so she held on to his shoulder. He was chary of the pressure of her long fingers.

"What are we doing out here at this time of night?"

The tempo of the lightning was quickening, and the thunder was louder.

She stroked the side of his neck. "I thought a dip in the lake would cool me off." He was intensely aware of her breathing. "You know what they say: '. . . a walk and a cold shower.' Is that what you're doing here, Jack?"

Her knee brushed his thigh, and he shivered. He had never been so keenly aware of Wendy's femaleness as he was at this moment. She moved so that his leg slipped between her thighs. He tried to back away from her, but his buttocks hit the ladder.

"Wendy . . . we should go back . . ." He faltered. "There's a storm coming."

The last part of it was drowned out by a clap of thunder that shook the earth. No heat lightning this time, a bright jagged dagger tearing apart the sky and stabbing down into the forest on the far side of the lake.

She threw her arms around his neck and thrust herself against him. "Oh, Jack!"

The feel of her took his breath away. She was naked! Her

bare breasts flattened against his chest. Her thighs clamped his thigh in a tight, hot vise.

"My God!" he exclaimed. "Wendy!"

"Please, Jack, let it happen. Just this one time." She kissed him with her mouth open. Her tongue was slippery, squirming in his mouth. She put one hand down inside the waistband of his trunks, stroking his taut belly. He moaned as her fingers closed over him, caressing, coaxing.

"There!" She was triumphant. "You want me. You can't deny it, darling!"

He was holding on to the ladder with one hand, and trying to shove her away with the other. He was no match for her. No matter how many times he went over it in his mind later, the doubt always remained. Had he really wanted to stop it from happening? Or was the truth on her side.

There was nothing he could say. His body was speaking for him with greater eloquence than any words. He pulled down his trunks to his ankles. They came gliding together in the warm water, her legs spreading wide to envelop him. Thighs shimmering palely like water lilies. He penetrated her with a smoothness and ease that surprised Wendy. The loss of her virginity was not painful at all, as she had expected it would be. The lubricity of the lake water may have helped. Far more likely, she decided when it was done, the excruciating delight of the experience had surpassed whatever small discomfort attended the event.

The first drops of rain began to fall on the lake, as a thunderbolt of fire rammed into the earth with the force of a gigantic pile driver. It seemed to Jack Whittaker that the entire world was shaken by it.

Carter and Eastman on stretchers were transported by motor sleigh to Sam's Knob. Carter's right leg was broken. Eastman had a mild concussion as a result of his helmet's being knocked off when the helicopter crashed. Both were suffering from multiple bruises and shock. Nothing more serious than that.

Dorn was at the restaurant with the sheriff and Chief Lanier when they were brought in. The pilot described what had happened, before he and Eastman were taken down to East Village in the lift.

"He outsmarted us, that's all there was to it," he concluded gloomily. "No excuses, captain. You warned us he was dangerous." He shook his head, lamenting, "I feel awful cracking up that chopper."

Dorn patted his shoulder. "Don't worry about it, Bill. Nobody's blaming you. Anyway, the chopper isn't in too bad shape. It came down in a lot of soft snow in these trees. I'm just happy you're alive."

Sid Feldman came into the restaurant while the two injured men were being carried out to the lift.

"I just heard about it, captain. Are they going to be all right?"

"Yeah, they won't be flying for a while, but they're in fair shape." He grimaced. "I wish I could say as much for myself." His bloodshot eyes swept the restaurant, empty except for the police. All of the skiers had been cleared off Mt. Baldy. "Say, could anyone use a burger and a mug of coffee? I haven't had anything to eat since supper last night."

Dorn, Lanier, and Feldman sat down at a table. Sheriff Malone went off to phone his office. The manager of the restaurant took their orders. He and a short-order cook were the only ones on duty. The police had ordered the rest of the staff down to West Village.

"What a time that lunatic picked to blow his top," he complained as he scribbled on a pad. "Christmas Eve. We figured to do our biggest trade of the season today. All the extra help we put on, they'll have to be paid, you know."

"That's a shame," Dorn drawled. He and Feldman exchanged sidelong looks.

When the manager left for the kitchen, Feldman took a newspaper clipping out of his pocket and placed it on the table in front of Dorn. "I dug this out of our Chamber of Commerce files. I don't know if it means anything, but I thought you'd be interested."

The item featured a small photo of a stocky man with wavy red hair and a pumpkin grin. About forty-five, Dorn judged. He was kneeling beside a dead big-horn ram in the snow, cradling a rifle in his arms. Dorn read the story beneath the picture.

. . . shot by Mr. Charles Roche currently vacationing at Snowmass.

Mr. Roche who served with the U.S. Army Infantry during World War Two as a sniper won first place in the National High-Power Rifle Championships in . . .

Dorn looked up at Feldman. "Now, what about that!"
"Read it all."

. . . scored his kill with a single bullet at a distance of 700 yards. This remarkable shot was made with a .300 H & H Magnum rifle mounted with a Balvar S scope. . . .

Dorn flipped the clipping to Lanier.
"What do you think?" Feldman asked.
"It could be him," Dorn admitted. "But not necessarily. You know what Potts told us. Given the right gun with a high-powered telescopic sight, any good marksman could have winged off those shots."

He doused his butt in a cup of cold coffee that had been left on the table.

Sergeant Casey Jones joined them at the table. "Captain, I pulled back our picket lines around the lodge like you ordered. About fifteen hundred yards. Except for the six men with high-powered target rifles. They're posted so they can cover any side of the building if he shows himself."

Dorn shook his head negatively. "No, Case, I changed my mind. I want them pulled back too."

Sheriff Malone frowned and tugged nervously at one ear.

"You think that's a good idea, Les? I mean, if one of those police snipers can get a shot at him—?"

"Like Carter and Eastman did, and Dave Potts?" Dorn cut him off sharply. "No, I'm not risking any more troopers if I can help it."

"That's our job, taking risks," Malone said quietly.

Dorn looked straight into the sheriff's eyes, not saying anything until Malone averted his gaze. Then he spoke, even more quietly than Malone had.

"I'm in charge here, Paul. It's my responsibility. You know, even if one of our snipers did pick him off, there'd be no guarantee it would be a bull's-eye. If they didn't hit him in a vital area, the first thing he'd do would be to finish off those hostages quick. At least that's what I'd do if I was him."

Sheriff Malone hunched his thick shoulders inside his great fur coat and remained silent.

One of the troopers who were standing around restlessly awaiting orders put a coin in the juke box. The music blasted through the restaurant.

"... so all your cares and troubles fade from sight
when old St. Nick comes down your chimney
Late tonight ... So count your lucky stars ..."

Dorn turned in his chair and thrust out an arm pointing at the juke box. In a quiet, ominous voice he said, "Somebody kill that thing. Right now!"

The women were watching at the window when the helicopter crashed. "My God!" the blonde screamed. "He's killed them too!"

The other woman shuddered and pulled her coat close around her. She went back to the bed and sat down. Staring vacantly at the handcuffs that shackled her slim ankles.

He came into the room wearing a childlike smile. A child reporting a proud accomplishment to adults. "Did you see that?

Did you? They thought they were going to pull a fast one. Man, was that pilot ever surprised when I sandbagged them from the other room! I could see his face through the scope."

"Oh, you're a real killer! No doubt about it," the brunette said.

The smile wiped off his face. "What kind of a crack was that?"

The funny thing was she hadn't meant it the way he thought. But the slip had been a dangerous one. She could see that. His rigid gaze. The way his fingers fondled the rifle bolt.

"What I meant to say—" her mouth was dry, "—was that you are phenomenal with that rifle. I knew all of you boys could shoot. But you're something else again. The way you shot down that plane was simply amazing."

He relaxed, the smiling, prideful child once more. "You know, with a more powerful scope I could pick off a target at better than a mile, I'll bet?"

"I'll bet you could, easily." She wanted to keep him like this. "You always did everything well that you set your mind to."

The flattery was transparent to him, and the smile was shaded with irony now. "That isn't true, and you know it. What ever happened to 'gutless'?"

"I didn't mean that. I'm sorry, now, I said it. We all say things we don't mean when we're angry or frightened."

"Do we? What is it the Romans used to say about drunkenness and truth? *In vino veritas.* We speak the truth when our inhibitions are broken down. Anger and fright can produce the same results. By the way, which are you? Angry or frightened?"

"Some of both. Aren't they the same thing? That's why frightened people are always getting bitten by dogs. They smell the same, fear and hostility."

He glanced toward the huddled figure of the blonde woman. "She's just frightened. Afraid for her own neck. She doesn't care what happens to you or to me. Or if I shot another dozen people out there, she really wouldn't give a damn."

"That's not true!" the blonde woman whimpered. "How can you be so heartless?" She shook her head, groping for the courage to say what was on her mind. "You're a *brute!* A sadistic brute." Her voice gave out in a tremulous whine on the final words.

He laughed at her. "Well spoken, my dear. Bravo! Now let's examine this objectively. You girls should get together. One thinks I'm gutless. The other thinks I'm a sadistic brute. Now, which is it?"

The dark woman opened her mouth, changed her mind. But he guessed what she had been about to say.

"Or maybe they go together, is that it?"

She didn't answer him.

He walked over to the half-full bottle of bourbon on the dresser and took a long swallow. He wiped the mouth of the bottle and offered it to her.

"Here, have some of this *vino* and give us some more *veritas.*"

She didn't want a drink, but she accepted the bottle. She had a wild, dangerous impulse to throw whiskey into his eyes. If she could blind him, there might be a chance she could get the rifle away from him. She held the bottle with both hands, breathless, heart racing. He was standing close to her, with the rifle cradled loosely in the crook of one arm. His queer little smile seemed to be challenging her.

She lifted the bottle to her lips. Would it be better to take a mouthful of whiskey and spit it in his face? No, that would dilute it. The thing to do was to hurl it right from the bottle. But the neck was so narrow. Could she get enough of it into his eyes?

"Well, what are you going to do with it?"

The adrenalin, which had been pumping furiously into her bloodstream, priming her for the rash act, spent itself so abruptly she almost collapsed. She backed up until her trembling legs struck the bed, and sat down. She barely had strength to tilt the bottle up. The raw bourbon backed up in her dry throat and spilled out the sides of her mouth.

"Aren't you the messy one?" he taunted. He took the bottle away from her and gazed at her in silence until she looked up at him.

"That wouldn't have been very smart of you, dear. Your time on this earth is short enough as it is."

The other woman began to snivel again. "Why are you doing this to us? Why are you doing this to yourself?"

"Because I'm a gutless, sadistic brute, remember?" He had another drink, wiping a hand across his lips. "But you're really not the one to be casting stones. Not after some of the things that *you*'ve done."

"Me?" the blonde woman said huffily.

"*You!*"

"It's true," the dark woman agreed with him. "You're no saint. Neither am I. We've both done our share of hurting in this life. All of us have. You know, I used to think the crowd broke up because we all grew up. Like the stalks of a plant all branching out in their own directions. Now, I'm beginning to wonder whether the crowd ever did break up at all. *Really*, that is."

"What are you talking about?" He pulled a chair over near the bed and sat down.

"Well, it's been twenty years for most of us. You know, since we began to live our own lives without stopping to consider whether or not our friends would approve."

He chuckled. ". . . *Those wedding bells are breaking up that old gang of mine. . . .*"

"That was part of it, of course. Families. Careers too . . ." The line of her mouth was hard. "You boys, for example. An ad man, a television producer, a shoe salesman, pot-luck stew, isn't it? Some of you have nothing in common at all. But the old tie has always been there. You've always kept in touch, even if it was only once or twice a year. Why?"

He was perplexed. "Old friends, isn't that reason enough?"

"No, and you know it isn't friendship. Human beings aren't drawn together out of love. Oh, that can be there too. But it isn't the dominant attraction. The primitive, animal need. We must satisfy our need to flagellate and to be flagellated. Pain and pleasure. The recognition that 'here is a person I can hurt' or 'here is a person who can hurt me.' It's the basis of most enduring human relationships. What draws people together even after the joys of love and companionship have withered away."

"I didn't ask for a lecture in freshman psychology," he told her with faint mockery.

"You're right, it's that basic," she countered. Knowing damned well she was mouthing a lot of glib generalities, but knowing too that he had an obsessive preoccupation with his own human relationships, past and present. She could tell that, in spite of his flippancy, he was eager to talk about the subject, and quite deliberately she fed his interest.

"Isn't that the reason most marriages break up? The partners have lost the ability to hurt each other." Nodding at the other woman. "We were talking about marriages before, the people we know. Not one of them is what you could call a really successful marriage. Most of them were failures even before the minister finished the ceremony." She smiled. " ' 'Till death do us part . . .' "

"I suppose you include my marriage in the last group?" Idly he stroked the top of the scope with his thumb. His eyes were watchful.

"That's always been your trouble, thinking your own problems were unique. That yours is a very special tragedy. Look around you, for God's sake! Your friends."

"I never concerned myself with the private lives of my friends," he said stiffly.

"But you did. Constantly. Otherwise what are the four of us doing here? Our lives are hopelessly mixed up together. Private lives!" she scoffed. "That's funny! You attend enough cocktail parties, bridges, sit at the club bar, you come to realize there's no such thing as privacy. We might just as well have our bedrooms bugged and post transcriptions on a public bulletin board. At least that way the facts would be straight. Pick any

marriage. Yours, mine, anybody we know. And I'll give you
the history of its decline and fall."

When Dorn got back to headquarters in West Village, the
corporal at the desk in the reception room informed him that
Louis Santini was waiting to see him.

"I told him to wait in the interrogation room."

Dorn grinned. "Chief Lanier do much interrogating in there?"

Swensen's ears reddened. "Naw! We use it as a storeroom
mostly."

"Why didn't you have him wait in the chief's office?"

"There's somebody else waiting there. Two fellers from the
Federal Bureau of Investigation."

Dorn rolled his eyes heavenward and went into the office expecting the worst. Happily he was wrong.

The FBI men, Paul Hardy and Steve Anker, were in their
mid-thirties. They were natty dressers, Dorn observed, and did
not wear black topcoats and black fedoras as propaganda would
have it. They reminded him of a couple of traveling salesmen,
self-conscious and apologetic about ringing the doorbell.

"We're not up here in an official capacity, captain," Hardy
explained. "I'm not even sure the case is within our jurisdiction.
At least, not until there's definite proof that the killer has kid-
naped the hostages and transported them across a state line."

"I don't think he did kidnap them," Dorn said. "They came
up here together on a charter plane, and if all four weren't doing
it of their own free will somebody would have been bound to
notice. The way it was, they were just four anonymous faces in
a crowd of holiday travelers."

The agent nodded. "That makes sense. Anyway, as I said,
the FBI is here on standby at the invitation of the governor of
Colorado."

"And you're welcome," Dorn said, relieved and grateful that
an army of cloak-and-dagger boys hadn't descended on Snowmass primed to blast their way into the besieged hunting lodge.

Dorn recapitulated the tragic events that had transpired since
the first fatal shots exploded over the slopes in early morning.
When he was finished, the FBI men were in solemn agreement
with his handling of the situation.

"There doesn't seem a damn thing anyone can do under the
circumstances without getting those three hostages killed except
to sit tight and wait him out," Anker said. He was a slim man
with dark hair and heavy-rimmed glasses.

"Until he makes up his mind to finish the job," his partner
added grimly.

"The longer he puts it off, the better the chances are that he
won't do it."

Dorn's gray eyes narrowed. "How so?"

"Just an educated guess." Anker shrugged. "Some of them
I've come up against, they seem to be acting out their hostility,
and when the scene is played through, they come out meek as
lambs." His mouth curled down at the edges. "There are others
who have to finish it the way they planned. Kill and kill, until
they're killed or blow out their own brains. If only we knew
who he is, what he's like, it would provide some indication of
which way he'll go."

"No luck so far on that score," Dorn informed them. "I'm
hoping Whittaker's cousin can provide us with some clues. He's
here now. I'll bring him in." He picked up the phone and asked
Corporal Swensen to send in Louis Santini.

Santini was a fair, sandy-haired man of gangling proportions.
He stumbled as he crossed the threshold into the police chief's
office, and his large feet became awkwardly tangled when he
turned to sit down in a chair alongside the desk. His legs were
too long for his body in a way that reminded Dorn of Li'l Abner
in the funny papers. When he was folded up in a chair, he
appeared smaller. He smiled self-consciously at the captain and
the FBI agents. Dorn tried to put him at ease.

"I was wondering how they stuffed you into the cockpit of
a jet fighter," he joked.

"It was a tight squeeze," Santini admitted. He had a pleasant, boyish face. Dorn found it difficult to believe that he was old enough to have been a fighter pilot in the Korean War. He lit a cigarette with trembling fingers which the other men pretended not to notice.

"Jack Whittaker is your cousin, Mr. Santini?" Dorn asked him.

"More like a brother really." A muscle fluttered in his right eyelid. "Hell! I'd walk the plank for Jack."

"Oh?" Dorn exchanged curious looks with the agents.

"You see, I was in a real bad way after I got out of the air force. Drugs. I was shot down over the Sea of Japan on my hundred-and-fifth mission. Badly burned. I got hooked in the hospital. It happens more than most people realize. I couldn't kick it, so they finally discharged me." He smiled bitterly. "Section Eight. I guess they thought they were doing me a favor. The folks back home would take more kindly to a nut than to a junkie. I was in a bad way." The smile faded. "I was on all kinds of drugs, you name it. I was scraping bottom and trying to burrow my way down even deeper, when Jack took charge of me." He made an expansive gesture with his huge hands. "Well, I've been straight now since sixty-two. . . . But enough of my life and bad times. What's going on up at the lodge?"

"Just what the sheriff's men told you at the airport. I don't know if you heard about the helicopter yet. The sniper shot down a bird and banged up two of my men."

Santini nodded. "The corporal told me when I got here." His hands tightened on the arms of the chair as he asked tersely, "Do you know who it is up there? Doing the shooting?"

"No. We thought you'd be able to give us some idea. How many people were invited to spend Christmas at the lodge?"

"I honestly don't know. The last time I saw Jack was on the Coast, right after Thanksgiving. It wasn't an invitation, really. He wasn't even sure he was going to make it himself with his tight schedule. He said there was going to be a gang at the lodge over the holidays, and that I should go too if I didn't have anything better to do." He shrugged. "I didn't—I'm single. So here I am."

Dorn frowned. The FBI remained a silent, discreet but very alert presence in the background.

"You say you don't know if your cousin intended to spend Christmas at Snowmass?"

"He wanted to make it, but he said he wouldn't know for sure until the last week. Like I said, I haven't spoken to him in almost a month. The first I heard about the killings up here was over the radio in a coffeeshop at the Denver Airport. Right off, I phoned Jack's sister, Marcia. She'd heard, too, over the radio. She didn't know where Jack was either. She saw him in New York about a week ago, but he still hadn't decided about coming up here for Christmas. She hasn't been able to contact Jack's wife. They split up last month, and, while Jack was on the coast, she moved out of the New York apartment without telling anyone where she was going."

Dorn's eyebrows bunched with interest. "So Whittaker and his wife split up, did they?" He scraped back his chair and stood up. He came around the desk and planted one lean buttock on a corner of the desk top.

The FBI agents drew in closer, the three of them making a tighter circle around Santini. The restive stirrings of hounds onto a scent. Dorn approached it cautiously.

"That might be significant. Then again it could be nothing at all. . . . Mr. Santini, you've got an idea that Jack Whittaker might be behind that rifle up there?"

"I told you I don't know," Santini's voice was noticeably distressed. He clamped his hands together over one knobby knee.

"But you're worried about it?"

"You're damned right I'm worried." He looked up and Dorn read the fear and the apprehension in his eyes. "One thing I do know. *If* it is Jack, I'm going to find out."

"How would you manage that?"

"I can go up there. If it is Jack, he won't shoot me."

"I don't see how we can risk that, Mr. Santini," Dorn said gently, understanding the deep affection and loyalty this man felt for his cousin, and admiring his courage. "The trouble is, if it is Whittaker, it's not the same man you know. This man is a deranged killer."

One of the FBI men offered an opinion unobtrusively. "Yes, Mr. Santini, and your close relationship with him could even be a drawback in this instance. In his unstable condition, he might harbor intense hostility and suspicion toward the people who are closest to him."

Santini kept shaking his head. "No, you're wrong. Jack wouldn't harm me."

"Maybe, maybe not. But if it isn't him you damned well will get shot! I'm sorry, but we can't let you do it," Dorn said with regret. "But look, Mr. Santini, you can still give us some valuable help. Aside from your cousin, you knew the people who used to come up to Snowmass pretty well, didn't you?"

Santini didn't answer right away. A smile that conveyed nostalgia.

"I guess I did. Most of them. The regulars."

"Well, let's start with the owners. Were they on good terms with each other?"

The question amused Santini. "Oh, they got along well enough. But if you mean, Were they good friends? The answer is 'no'!"

Dorn frowned. "That doesn't make much sense. When three men invest money in a piece of expensive real estate like that lodge, they'd have to be pretty close friends, wouldn't you say? Or they *were* good friends when they decided to do it."

"No, you're wrong, captain. If *you* want to call what those three had 'friendship,' okay. I'd say they were held together by a common social and financial status, for one thing. That's an obvious reason for people to clique up. With the three of them force of habit was an even more important reason. Jack and Forrest had practically grown up together. They'd known Wally Kaiser since World War Two. Almost like members of a family, they knew each other's weaknesses and how to exploit them. Do you know what I mean?"

"I'm not sure," Dorn said. He glanced at Agent Hardy, who looked baffled by what Santini was trying to express.

"It's not easy to explain; you have to live with it." The young man held up his hands, gesticulating as if endeavoring to snatch a meaning out of thin air. "You see, they could afford each other emotionally and temperamentally as well as financially. That was far more important than having money in the bank. There were other old friends like Charlie Roche and Carl Schneider too who didn't fit in financially, but they were on an equal footing with Jack and the others—at least when they got together at Snowmass." He grinned. "Me too, Jack's poor relation. Being younger, I wasn't a real insider of course. To tell the truth, I don't think they cared about each other at all as they got older. Hell, if it wasn't Roche telling Kaiser off, then it was Kaiser telling Evans off. They were always battling about something. What I'm getting at is, they seemed to practice a kind of amnesty among themselves that would not have been workable with other people they knew and cared for a damned sight more than they cared for each other. Does that make any sense at all?"

"Vaguely," Dorn admitted. "But I think I'm beginning to get the picture. A sort of familiarity that made things easier. They can let down their hair with each other."

"That's how it was."

Dorn cast his weary eyes in the direction of the office's single window. Outside the frosted panes, the snow was falling harder, and he could hear, faintly, the sound of a juke-box rock group belting out an all but unrecognizable rendition of *Silent Night*.

"Another thing they had in common was the gun club."

"Just who was in the gun club?" Dorn asked him.

"Club is the wrong word for it, really. I mean, it was strictly informal. Forrest kept talking about drafting a charter and affiliating with some big national society, but that's all that ever came of it. Talk."

"You belong?"

Santini laughed softly. "Oh, I tagged along once in a while. The truth is I hate the 'great outdoors.' And guns."

"Then you'd say that everyone who visited the lodge did some shooting?"

"I suppose so. With the exception of the women."

"How was their marksmanship?"

Santini lit another cigarette as he gave that some consideration. His hands were steadier now.

"Well . . . Charlie Roche is a crack shot. He's won medals and cups."

"I know. What about your cousin?"

"Jack? . . . He's above average. I'd say Jack, and Carl Schneider are the best of the group. Wally Kaiser and Forrest Evans are average."

Captain Dorn picked up a notebook from the desk and copied down the unfamiliar names. Out of the corners of his eyes he saw that one of the FBI men was making notes too.

"Schneider and Roche . . . You mentioned before that they weren't in it financially with Whittaker and the other men who owned the lodge."

"That's right. Charlie and Carl and Forrest and Jack were kids together. Like family." He grinned. "Poor relations like me. No, that's not fair classing Carl with a bum like me. I don't have any responsibilities, so I drift with the tide. Odd jobs, you know. Carl is a good family man. It's just that he never made it big like Jack and the others."

"What about Roche?"

Santini wore a sour look. "Charlie Roche? Well . . . he's

something else again. He's a wheel in the Legion or one of
the veterans' organizations. Charlie can't wait until World War
Three starts."

Dorn made a notation and underlined it. The agent looked up
from his notes and their eyes met meaningfully.

"That one could stand some checking," the FBI man commented. "The bureau can probably handle it faster than you
can, captain."

Dorn nodded. "Be my guest. . . . Mr. Santini, any group of
men is bound to produce a fair amount of personality clashes.
Was there *real* bad blood between any of them?"

Santini thought about it, screwing up his face. "Well . . .
sometimes things heated up when they were drinking. They all
were—" He caught himself with a hollow laugh. "*Were.* Now
why did I say that. They *are* heavy drinkers."

"There were fights when they were drinking?"

"Sometimes. A few bad ones I can remember the times I was
with them at the lodge. Schneider has always been jealous of
his wife."

"With reason?"

Santini shifted uncomfortably in the chair. "I guess so.
Wendy's a bit of a flirt. I think she does it to bug him. He and
Wally Kaiser slugged it out on the outdoor terrace a couple
of years ago when Carl caught him and Wendy out there after
midnight. I don't know exactly what he caught them at, but
it was a bad scene. They almost went over the wall, and that's
a helluva fall, before the rest of the guys pulled them apart."

Dorn fingered his heavy jaw. The stubble itched like steel
wool, even though he had shaved that morning.

"A couple of years ago, you say. How was their relationship
after that? Bad?"

"Not really. That is, they didn't show it if it was. The next
morning everybody behaved normally, as if the whole thing had
never happened. I mean, hell, it could have been any one of

the men Carl went after. He was that way. Jealous particularly of—" He stopped short, his expression disturbed.

"Particularly jealous of who?" Dorn pressed him, sensing the reason he had clammed up.

"Nothing really."

"Jack Whittaker, that's what you were about to say, wasn't it? She and your cousin were fooling around?"

Santini was unhappy. "No, Jack wouldn't lay a hand on her. He used to say Wendy was bad news. You see, when they were much younger, Wendy carried a torch for Jack. He never encouraged her. But her husband knew about it, so he was always watching her extra close when she and Jack were together."

"Did they always bring the women with them when they came to Snowmass?"

"No, as a matter of fact, the wives—or girl friends, Charlie Roche and I would bring a girl once in a while—only came along on special occasions. Holidays."

"Christmas?"

"Yes, there were some Christmas parties at the lodge, but it didn't work out too well for the couples with kids."

"When was the last time they were up here?"

"The last time the whole gang met up here was on Labor Day. I was here too. They were talking about having a blast over the Christmas–New Year's week."

Dorn tapped a butt on the back of one brown hand and slipped it into his mouth. "How were things between them Labor Day? Was there any hard feeling that you were aware of?"

Santini was too elaborate about clearing his throat. "Excuse me, captain. Could I have a drink of water, please."

"Sure thing." Dorn grinned. "Would you like something stronger? If memory serves me, Max always has a bottle stashed in one of these drawers."

"Thanks. I could use a drink."

Dorn went behind the desk and began searching through drawers. He came up with a nearly full bottle of Old Crow. He looked around the room.

"As a matter of fact, I think we could all use a drink, what do you say?"

"Amen," said Hardy, and the other agent smiled approvingly.

"Now, you were saying that your cousin had some trouble over the Labor Day weekend," Dorn said casually.

"Yes, Jack and Roche—" It was out before he realized he had been decoyed.

Lou Santini slouched in his chair with one knee propped up against the edge of the table, morosely contemplating the litter of what had been an indifferent poker game strewn across the green-felt playing surface. Stale drinks, scattered chips, a disorder of cards, mounded ashtrays, and hanging over it all a pall of cigarette and cigar smoke so thick it would take a shovel to clear it out. The hour was after three and the women had long since retired. But none of the men were inclined to break up the party and go to bed.

Santini was disgusted with himself. His head ached from too much booze. His throat was raw from too much smoking. He had dropped one hundred dollars—one hundred more than he could afford to lose. And that meant the humiliation of accepting another handout from Jack. What really bugged him was that he could have been in the sack all these unfruitful hours with the cute little United hostess he had brought along to Snowmass from L.A. By now she'd have locked her door on him, lying there in the dark doing a slow burn.

The story of my life! Making all the wrong turns.

Inevitably the conversation had found its way into Vietnam, leading to a heated discussion dominated by Charlie Roche, arguing the cause of the hawks, and Wally Kaiser, arguing the case of the doves.

The years had not mellowed Roche. He was the same wild-eyed, flaming Barbarossa who had loved every moment of *his* war and who wore, with the mystique of a wedding band, the ring he had hacked off a dead German's finger. Roche had never married and had no intention of doing so. He was married to an ideal: the power and the glory of the American fighting machine. Deputy commander of a militant veterans' organization, he traveled all over the United States, and the world, carrying the word to U.S. troops in foreign lands. He pounded the table with both fists, roaring:

"They got to know that the President is behind them! The people are behind them! The whole Goddamned country is behind them—"

"Five thousand miles behind them," Evans' sotto voce earned him a scowl.

"And these yellow-belly peaceniks back here ain't fit to clean out the latrines they shit in."

"You know what you're like, Charlie?" Wally said. "You're that old ram at the stockyards that leads the sheep up the ramp into the slaughterhouse!"

Roche was livid. "And you're a crummy traitor who'd see his country pulled down by the Commies!"

"To the guillotine with the traitors!" Wally threw a handful of cards into the air so they cascaded down all over Roche. "There, you've got your own victory parade, patriot—confetti and all!"

"Damned right, to the guillotine!" Roche picked up a fistful of chips and hurled them into Kaiser's face.

"At ease!" Jack Whittaker shouted as Roche and Wally came half out of their chairs. "Keep it cool, men. Go soak your heads under a shower and get to bed."

The belligerents sat down again, but Roche was not finished. He shook a fist in the air. "Do you know the only thing that's going to straighten out this country? Laying real muscle on the traitors. The black militants. The campus bums! They preach violence, okay. Let 'em have violence. I say let's have more of

Kent State and Jackson State! All right! What the hell do they count, a handful of worthless traitors, weighed against the lives of our boys dying to preserve freedom and democracy?"

"Jesus Christ!" Forrest Evans' mouth and nostrils were white and pinched with restrained anger. "Are you for real?" He looked around the table. "Jack . . . Wally . . . Lou . . . What is it with this—this—so-called man."

"What was that?" Roche started to get up again.

"No, I don't mean to suggest you're queer, Charlie," Forrest waved him down. "You don't have to prove your masculinity by swinging at me. You could beat me into a pulp, *man!* It's semantics I'm talking about! 'Man' as opposed to 'beast.' Humanity versus inhumanity. The truth is, Charlie, you don't have a spark of humanity in you. You don't give a damn who gets murdered. U.S. soldiers, Vietnamese women and kids, or college kids. Just so long as the killing goes merrily on."

"You son of a bitch!" Roche spat on the table top. "I ought to—"

"To kill me, right?"

Roche's face was purple. He took three deep breaths before he answered Evans. His voice was calm. Dangerously calm. Tension, an invisible magnet, pulled the men into a tighter grouping around the poker table.

"I know you think I'm a slob, Evans. You too, Kaiser. You sit in your penthouses with a glass of twenty-dollar Scotch in one hand and a black-market Cuban cigar in the other watching the news clips from Vietnam on the TV. And the ones showing the punk college kids spitting on the cops and tossing bricks at the National Guard. And it offends your sensitive stomachs when you see a few dead bodies. I got news for you, friends. When the final body count is in at the end of this century, the ones killed by bullets will add up to peanuts compared to the ones run down by your souped-up cars and overcome by the shit pouring out of your factory's smoke stacks, Evans!"

Wally snorted derisively. "This is too much. Roche is worried about our ecology. Don't tell me, Roche. Let me guess. You've got the simple and efficient answer to all of the world's problems. Pollution, the population explosion, everything. One full-scale atomic war and we vaporize all the garbage and all the excess kids. Instant ecology!"

"It could come down to that." Roche was perfectly serious. He took a long swallow of his beer and wiped his hand across his mouth. "But first things first. We've got to get behind our boys one hundred percent. Get this damned war over with instead of sabotaging what they're doing."

"And what are the boys doing?" Carl asked unexpectedly. Up until now he had treated the discussion with sleepy detachment. "Fighting a war they don't understand. A war that's eating their guts out because the South Vietnamese hate them as much as they hate the Cong. So they hate back and strike back. Killing innocent women and kids. *Kill! Kill! Kill!*"

Lou Santini tensed as Carl got slowly to his feet. In all the years he had known Carl Schneider, he had never seen him so angry. It went deeper than anger.

The years had taken a greater toll on Carl than they had on the other members of the group. His round shoulders and prematurely graying hair made him appear older than he was. His tall, lanky body swayed noticeably. He was drunker than Santini had imagined.

His voice shook with emotion. "You called Wally Kaiser a 'crummy traitor.' By your definition a traitor is anyone who's sick to death of seeing the youth of America bled white. For a lost cause in Indochina!"

He wagged a bony finger at Roche. "Let me tell you something, Roche. I lost a kid brother in Vietnam back in sixty-seven. God! It was a heartbreaker, having him die *there*. For what? I sent back his Silver Star to the Defense Department. It was an insult!"

His sobbing intake of breath was a harsh sound in the still room. "I only wish to hell he had died in a campus protest. You

know what, Roche, if there's a traitor in this room—it's *you!*
You're a bloodthirsty bastard who's a traitor to the whole human
race!"

Roche went for him straight across the table. Ferociously. Jack
Whittaker and Forrest Evans were shoved out of their chairs
and the table toppled over backwards. Glassware, chips, cards,
and ashtrays flew in all directions.

It was a brief but bloody and brutal contest. Before they were
separated, Carl was spouting blood from a broken nose, and
Roche had a split cheek, and two of his teeth lay on the floor.

Santini wrapped his arms around Carl and pulled him away.
He didn't resist. But Forrest Evans and Wally Kaiser could not
hold Roche. He was an enraged animal. It took a slap in the
face by Jack Whittaker to subdue him. Not a cruel blow. The
way he would have hit a hysterical woman.

Charlie Roche resented Jack's slap more than the insults and
the blows which Carl had inflicted on him. Santini was appalled
by the cold hatred he saw on Roche's face.

"You hit me once before, Jack," Roche said quietly. "I let
you get away with it. This time—you went too far."

"Cool off, Charlie. Get a good night's sleep and we'll talk
about it in the morning." Jack placed a conciliatory hand on his
shoulder, but he shook it off.

"No, we won't talk about it in the morning. Because I won't
be here in the morning. I'm leaving right now." The vehemence
of his parting remark shocked all of them. "If I hang around this
dump even one hour longer, I just might put a slug into some-
bodys' brain!"

"And he did leave," Santini concluded his account of the Labor Day weekend for Dorn and the other officers. "In the middle
of the night. I drove him to the airport. He didn't consider me
a part of the clique, so he was civil to me, at least. On the
way down he said something strange—about how he never really
felt comfortable at Snowmass. It was too much of an ivory
tower, not part of the real world. A 'utopia for the idle and

indolent' was how he described it. He was all acid. Said that he wished to hell if the Reds ever hit us with a sneak attack that the first ICBM's would land on Mt. Baldy!"

Slouched on one corner of the desk, Dorn was beating a light tattoo against a desk leg with his heel. From the expressions on the faces of the FBI agents he sensed that their reactions to Santini's story were running close to his own.

"It just could be him," he said aloud.

"Roche?" Santini sounded skeptical. "No, he wouldn't come back to Snowmass after that Labor Day blowup. Besides, he wasn't invited."

"Maybe he didn't wait to be invited," Dorn speculated.

They all were silent for a while, digesting that theory.

Finally Dorn went back and sat down behind the desk. "We'll sit on it until the FBI checks up on Mr. Roche. Right now, I better check in with Casey up at Sam's Knob." With a hand on the phone, he asked Santini. "Where are you staying?"

The big man shook his head. "I came straight here from the airport."

"You won't stand a chance of getting a room, the way things are. We can put you up at the state police barracks, if you don't mind the accommodations." His gaze traveled to the FBI agents. "You fellows are welcome too."

They all thanked him, but Santini expressed the common feeling: "I don't think any of us are going to get much sack time until this is over."

"Yeah." The captain grimaced and massaged a crick in the back of his neck with callused fingers. Before he could pick up the phone, Swensen buzzed him.

"Captain . . . Sheriff Malone just came in with a Mr. and Mrs. Evans. . . ."

Santini made a move to get up and leave, but Dorn waved him back down. "You can stay. In fact I'd like you to hear what the Evanses have to say. You're a friend. I don't think they'll mind."

Forrest Evans shook hands solemnly with Santini, and his

wife offered her cheek. Santini bent down self-conscious and awkward and bussed her high on the temple.

Evans spoke rapidly and nervously. "Lou, what a nightmare to walk into. It can't actually be happening, I kept telling myself all the way in from the airport."

"And on Christmas Eve," Pat Evans chimed in. "Oh, Lou, you don't think it's Jack—"

"Nonsense!" Evans snapped. "I don't believe it's any of our crowd. I was telling Sheriff Malone. With all due respect to Jack Whittaker, that boy has some real kooky friends. Arty, if you know what I mean. Greenwich Village. Haight-Ashbury. Jack's brought some of them up here before. How do we know a tribe of them didn't come back on their own and bust into the lodge to raise hell? Hell, yes! They're probably flying on LSD or something like that!"

"That's been suggested, but I think we've got to rule it out," Dorn advised him. "From what little we have been able to learn about the two couples who moved in up there yesterday, they seemed like respectable, conventional people. They had luggage and keys to the lodge."

Evans shook his head in bewilderment. "It's mad! It doesn't make any sense. No one we know would do a thing like this. Mass murder!"

Pat Evans shivered and hugged her mink coat more tightly around her scrawny body. Dorn could not help but observe, unchivalrously, that she was a singularly unattractive woman. In marked contrast to her husband, who, with his silvering temples and fine profile, reminded Dorn of the male models who posed for the liquor ads in *Playboy* magazine.

"I understand you are in charge of things at Snowmass?" Evans asked him.

"For the duration of this emergency," Dorn replied. He introduced himself and the FBI agents.

Evans was flabbergasted. "My God! The FBI! I had no idea this was having national repercussions!"

Hardy grinned and explained. "We're standing in the wings, you could say, sir. Just in case we're needed."

"Please sit down, Mr. and Mrs. Evans." Dorn went to the door and asked Corporal Swensen to bring in more chairs. When they were settled, he questioned Evans.

"Do you know how many people were planning to join this party and who they are?"

Evans licked his lips. "Aside from Pat and me . . . well, now, let's see. The Kaisers are coming, but they won't be here until late tonight. Wally has business in Haiti . . . someplace in the West Indies. They're planning to fly back directly to Denver."

"That ties in with what we have so far on the Kaisers," Dorn told Hardy and Ankers. "Apparently they are in Haiti." With a policeman's predilection for exactness, he refused to write off the Kaisers until they were positively placed in Haiti by the responsible authorities. But there had to be more plausible subjects.

"Who else? To your knowledge were any of them scheduled to arrive yesterday?"

Evans looked questioningly at his wife. "I don't know, do you, dear? Most of our gatherings at Snowmass are outrageously informal. Off the cuff. Come-as-you-are-and-when-you-can-get-here."

Pat Evans pursed her thin lips. "Nooooo . . . not unless it was Jack. His plans were indefinite. The last word we had from him was, let's see, last Thursday, wasn't it, Forrest?"

"Yes. He said he was battling a deadline on some show he's writing for television. But that he was sure he'd be able to make it up to Snowmass by Christmas Day."

Dorn picked up a paperweight from Lanier's desk. A miniature Santa in a globe filled with water and swirling particles that gave the illusion of snow.

"That doesn't tell us much about Whittaker," he observed. "Where was he when he phoned you, Mr. Evans?"

"In New York. His office."

Santini questioned Forrest Evans. "Forrest, what about Carl and Wendy? Were they coming up here?"

"Yes, they were. Wally Kaiser talked with Wendy on Monday. He said the Schneiders were due in Aspen late this afternoon or this evening."

"Well, four of 'em showed up early," Dorn said. "Now, is that all of them? You and your wife, the Schneiders, the Kaisers, Mr. Santini? And Jack Whittaker as a probable?"

"Yes, that's the whole list." Evans hesitated. "Unless Jack or Wally invited someone else without telling me."

"That's always possible," Dorn said, tapping his pencil on the arm of his chair. "I was asking Mr. Santini before. What about Charles Roche? You think there's any chance that he was invited?"

Evans snorted derisively. "Not on your life! Jack and I discussed Roche last time we talked. And I told him flatly that Roche was out."

Dorn sat up and leaned forward. "Then Whittaker did have some idea of asking him?"

"Oh, not really. He asked me whether I had heard from Charlie since Labor Day. There was a fracas—"

"I know. Mr. Santini told us about it."

Evans shook his head. "Then you know that he wouldn't have come even if we had invited him."

"Hmmm . . ." Dorn was sorting it out in his head. Still unaccounted for were Whittaker, Roche, the Kaisers, and the Schneiders. The way it looked, though, it was fairly certain that the Kaisers were out of the picture. That left Whittaker, Roche, and the Schneiders and—it lit up his mind like a flashbulb: *Whittaker's estranged wife!*

"Mr. Evans, is there any quick way we can check to find out if the Schneiders caught a flight out of New York this morning?"

"Oh, they're on their way, all right," Evans said positively. "Or Carl would have let us know."

"But my point is, could they have changed their plans and

come out here a day early?" Dorn spelled it out. "The fact is, four people arrived in Snowmass yesterday afternoon, and they're up in that lodge now." He jerked his thumb back over his shoulder in the direction of the mountain."

Evans' face was a complete blank. He shook his head. "I just can't understand it. It doesn't make any sense."

"We could phone Wendy's parents," Pat Evans suggested. "The Schneider children are spending Christmas with them."

"Hell!" And scare the kids and the old folks!" her husband disapproved.

"No need to," Dorn said. "Mrs. Evans could do it and ask kind of casually what flight the Schneiders took."

"I don't have their number with me," she remembered.

"That's all right. We'll have the operator check it out for us," Dorn told her. "What's the name?"

"Gates. Mr. and Mrs. Wendell Gates, of Greenwich, Connecticut."

Dorn relayed the information to Corporal Swensen and put down the phone. "He'll let us know when they reach the party."

Dorn was thinking of what Santini had told them earlier. That Wendy Schneider was a flirt. That her husband had been jealous of both Whittaker and Kaiser. It led him onto a track that posed a sensitive question for Forrest Evans.

"Mr. Evans . . . any problems that you or your wife are aware of that might have been troubling any of your friends? The Schneiders, the Kaisers, Mr. Whittaker? You know, business worries, illness—" he purposely skipped a beat for emphasis "—marital discord?"

Evans smiled, expressing his amusement at the absurdity of such a question. "Captain Dorn. You are talking, generally, about ninety percent of the people in the Unted States. Not only my friends. Illness. Business and money problems. Bad marriages!"

Dorn did not miss the reproachful look from the wife. Neither did Evans. He said with a trace of self-consciousness, "I can say, and I think Lou Santini would agree with me, that, of all the old crowd, Pat and I are the only ones who have a really solid marriage."

Pat Evans smiled and lowered her eyes.

"Then the others do have marital problems?"

Evans laughed harshly. "Big problems. You know Jack and his wife are separated?"

"Yes, but what about the Kaisers and the Schneiders?"

Evans sighed and crossed his legs. He unwrapped an expensive cigar and studied it reflectively. "Well . . . it's not something you can describe in a few words. . . ."

He waited as the phone rang and Dorn picked it up. "Out of service . . . All right, Swensen, thanks." He looked up at Evans. "The Gateses' phone is temporarily out of service. An ice storm. We'll keep trying. . . . Now, you were saying, Mr. Evans?"

As everyone expected, Forrest Evans was the first of them to marry after the war. One year from the day he was discharged, Patricia Ann DiSalle became Mrs. Forrest Evans in St. Bartholomew's Episcopal Church on Park Avenue in New York City. Pat's brother was the best man and Carl Schneider, Jack Whittaker, and Charlie Roche were ushers.

With his B.S. in engineering framed on the wall of their new Cape Cod cottage in Greenwich, Connecticut, Forrest began a year's apprenticeship with a firm whose board chairman happened to be his wife's uncle.

As it worked out the family's nepotism was more than justified by his performance. Ambitious, hard-working, and versatile, Forrest displayed a talent for salesmanship and public relations to match his grasp of the technical side of the business. He knew the value of a corporate image. Two years later he resigned and bought a junior partnership in a small Cleveland, Ohio, firm that manufactured heavy engineering equipment, with the help of a generous loan from his father-in-law.

In 1955, he bought out the other two partners and expanded the operation. Within two years after that, the Evans Heavy

Equipment Company went public, and he paid back the loan in full to Fulton DiSalle in the form of stock. Before he was thirty-five, Forrest had banked his first million, and was well on his way to the second.

The Evanses saw very little of Jack Whittaker during the next few years. His work was demanding more and more of his time. He had been appointed assistant to the producer of a new television dramatic program that the studio was preparing. There were his night courses at the Columbia University Extension. In addition, he was writing free-lance radio soap operas on his own time and putting together the outline for a projected play.

Two or three times a year Jack, Carl, Wally, and Charlie got together for an evening of drinking and poker. And, occasionally, spin-offs of the old crowd would meet at a party. They tended to stick together at these affairs, and usually they would go bar hopping afterward. In parting they always promised half-heartedly: "We have just got to get together more often."

They saw less and less of each other.

As his business prospered and expanded, Forrest Evans had to travel back and forth between Cleveland and New York, and he and Wally and Jack began to meet regularly at Toots Shor's and 21. Sometimes there were girls, young aspiring models and actresses eager to make an impresson on Jack and Wally.

Jack's name was appearing with notable mention in the television trade papers. He was co-producer of a dramatic series and director of a weekly situation comedy.

Wally Kaiser was vice-president of visual media in one of the highest-billing ad agencies in the world. A small but fast-moving agency on Madison Avenue was trying to lure him away with an offer of a full partnership.

Carl Schneider was a casualty when the monthly poker games gave way to supper and serious drinking at expensive New York night spots. Carl was an ambitious, hard-working shoe salesman for Florsheim. He was well liked by his employers and in line for a district managership. But he was not in the high income bracket enjoyed by his more creative friends. He was not bitter over it; he had always known that someday Jack Whittaker would be out of reach. Jack and the others, on the other hand, had too much respect for Carl's pride to have him tag along as a free-loader.

Time and rhyme are irrelevant in things remembered. The order of events is unimportant. True chronology is measured in the heart, not by calendar or watch. What happened one, ten, twenty years in the past can be more real than the present. The parts and pieces of a life are scattered over time's landscape like fragments of a jigsaw puzzle. The keen mind's eye sorts them out. Match the right ones. Discard the ones that fool the eye. Parts missing. Blanks in the picture but the salient features are true.

Wally Kaiser, Jack Whittaker, Carl Schneider, all married within a single year. The circumstances, implausible, capricious, laced with delicious irony. Something out of a novel by Fielding or Hardy. . . . He tightened the grip of his hands on the rifle. Cold steel. Smooth polished wood. The rifle was reality.

Jack Whittaker and Mae Edsel started sleeping together in 1948. They had come back to Mae's apartment after watching the rehearsal of a half-hour television variety show. Jack was associate producer, his first major credit. Mae fixed an after-midnight lunch of sandwiches and bourbon on the rocks. He ate half a sandwich and drank three double whiskeys. Mae disapproved.

"You've been hitting the sauce pretty hard lately, haven't you?"

"Everybody needs a hobby," he said lightly.

"Just don't let it turn into a vocation. You drink too much, all of you. Wally's the worst. What is it, Jack, the war?"

"Oh, hell! I suppose that's as good an excuse as any." He lit a cigarette and stared at the half sandwich on his plate. "We drink to escape. Not from the war, that's death, war is. It's life we drink to escape from."

She frowned. "I don't understand. Your life is just beginning now. You have a good job, and it's work you care about. What are you escaping from?"

He grinned and winked. "I can tell you what Wally and Forrest and the rest of them are trying to escape from. But me— that's top secret."

"You don't know what it is, that's the trouble, isn't it?"

He shrugged. "Maybe you're right. But I didn't come up here to discuss human psychology, young lady. I came up here to neck."

She smiled and studied his face, in three-quarter profile, as he refilled his bourbon glass. Wendy Gates, most women she knew thought he was handsome, charming, witty, good natured. Mae had known far more handsome men. His dark good looks —he was good looking, not handsome—were sharp, angular. The side he presented to his friends, she suspected, was but one facet of an extremely complicated personality. In repose, when his guard was down, his expression was naturally brooding. His mouth and eyes became sullen. When he drank too much he brooded. And his temper was quick. The friends he had known for so many years had been surprised by his savage attack on Charlie Roche at the DiSalle's hunting lodge. It hadn't surprised Mae. There was a dark, unpredictable side to Jack Whittaker. When they were alone, he sometimes would expose this side of himself to her, warily, watchfully, testing her it seemed. Mae was flattered that he favored her, showing this bitter, cynical part of his nature to her rather than to his older friends. Rather than to Wendy Gates.

All of these elements contributed, in some way that she could not explain, to the powerful sexual attraction that Mae felt for Jack.

"So let's neck," she said. She got up from the table and walked to the couch that opened up into a bed. Casually, she unzipped

her skirt and stepped out of it. She removed her blouse and hung
blouse and skirt neatly over a chair back.

Jack remained at the table, smoking and swirling his bourbon
in the water tumbler. He looked amused, but the fingers of one
hand drummed nervously on the table top.

"What are you doing?"

"Do you have any idea how much it costs to get a blouse and
skirt cleaned and pressed these days? I get rumpled when I neck.
Last time you were here, I ran a brand-new pair of nylons too."

She sat down on the couch, drew up the hem of her slip and
unfastened her garters. Humming, she bent and rolled one stocking down her thigh, over her knee and calf, all the way down
to her ankle. She slipped it daintily off her foot. The simplicity
of this small act, so feminine, so natural, performed without any
coyness or wile, moved him deeply. He felt as though a precious
privilege had been granted him, letting him observe this small,
innocent boudoir intimacy. He had seen Mae's fine legs and figure on exhibition in a two-piece bathing suit, but there was a
subtle and meaningful difference between public and private
exposure.

He put out his cigarette and walked to the couch as she finished removing the other stocking. She was blushing, and her
eyes shyly lifted to meet his eyes. They were dark and luminous.

"I'll bet you think I'm a hussy," she said.

"I think you're beautiful and desirable." He sat down on the
couch and put his arms around her, slipping his hands under
the back of her slip. She shivered as his hands touched her bare
flesh, his fingers fumbling at her bra hook.

In the past they had always terminated their lovemaking short
of intercourse. The limit had been set by Jack, not Mae.

"I want to take off everything tonight," she whispered in his
ear, and took his ear lobe gently between her teeth. "Please,
Jack, I want us to be naked together. That's all. We won't do
it if you don't want to, but I don't want all these silly clothes
separating us."

He was still warm and vulnerable from the elation he had experienced watching her remove her stockings. She had never removed all of her clothing for him. The idea of it pleased him. The two of them undressing, going to bed together. Touching in the dark. Not just in lust, but in peace and contentment. The comfort of not being alone. Having someone to share the terror as well as the joy. Someone to care. Someone to care for. The frightening revelation came to him.

His agitated face loomed above her.

"What is it?" she asked.

"Mae!" Her name came out as an exclamation. "I think I love you!"

She smiled and moved against him. "Then show me. Love me. Love me, Jack." She moaned as he came into her. She knew then too. "Oh, Jack! Darling! I love you, oh so much."

The older he became, the more Jack Whittaker was struck by the parallel between love and the theater. A marriage or an affair, like a play, might run for years to rave reviews, and by every critical standard qualify as an eminent success. Yet, as the players could tell if they dared, the thrill and excitement of the first night could never be recaptured in the succeeding performances. Spontaneity submerged in repetition. The spark of life glowing dimmer and dimmer in the performances. Until life was extinguished. Actors in false roles, saying words the spectators expect to hear.

In the spring of 1950, Mae announced that she was pregnant. She was unemotional about it, so courageous that Jack almost believed he loved her as he had believed he loved her on that first night of consummation.

"I'll go away and have the baby," she said. "I have an aunt in Sioux Falls. I can stay there. I'll buy a wedding band and say my husband was run over by a bus."

He had to laugh. "You couldn't sell a gold brick like that even in Sioux Falls. Why don't we get you an abortion?"

"Not that." She was so defiant, so full of uncompromising de-

termination, that he didn't bother to argue the point. "Are you
certain about it?" he asked.

"I'm not, but the rabbit is. He died out of conviction."

Jack nodded and lit a cigarette. He took her arm and steered
her into a bar. "I think we better talk about this over a drink."

"A drink!" she said, in the somewhat stern and reprimanding
tone that he always associated with his mother and with other
men's wives. "That's your solution to every problem, isn't it,
Jack? A drink!"

"It's safer than sex," he muttered.

She pulled away from him, angry. "You should have thought
of that before—"

"I know. I'm sorry. I don't mean to be sarcastic." He smiled
at her and helped her into a booth in a corner. "Look, let's not
cut each other to pieces. It happened. It is a fact. It is not the
end of the world." He took her hand. "Mae, honestly, I want
you to marry me. I want you to have the baby. Our baby."

Her eyes filled up. Her throat was so thick she could not
speak until she swallowed once, twice, three times. "Jack—are
you sure? You're not just saying it to make things easier for me,
are you?"

He clasped her hand, white, frail, and cold, between his big
warm hands. She looked so damned small, frightened, and helpless. He could have cried for her his chest ached so badly. His
pity was so enormous.

"I'm saying it because I want things to work out this way
for the two of us." He grinned. "The three of us, should I
say?"

"Oh, Jack, darling." She came into his arms and buried her
face against his chest. He stroked her hair while she cried, mut-
ing the sobs in the collar of his topcoat.

"It will be a ball." He heard himself talking as if listening to
a stranger in the next booth. "I make more than enough right
now to support a family. And I'm red hot at the network now.
You know that. In the fall I'm due to get my own show. That's

what Harry Fuller told me, and Harry tells it like it is. He says
the old man thinks I've got a born genius for this medium. . . ."
    *If any of his writers had given him lines like this he would
have poleaxed the script with a blue pencil.*
    After that they went home to Mae's place. While she was
fixing supper, Jack went out to buy a jar of Russian caviar and
a magnum of Moët champagne.
    "A night to remember," he told Mae.
    While he was out he phoned Carla March, a girl he had met
a month earlier at a literary cocktail party. Ten minutes after
they had been introduced, they left the dull affair together. Jack
bought two six-packs of beer and they spent the evening at
Carla's apartment, drinking bourbon boilermakers and discussing
the modern novel, theater, television as an art form, philosophy,
and sex, in that order. And they summed up the last issue with
a definitive conclusion. They went to bed.
    Afterward they agreed soberly, not without reverence, that it
had been good for both of them. The best for both of them.
    Carla had short auburn hair that she wore close to her head
like a coppery skullcap and lavender eyes. She was shorter than
Mae, but her figure was every bit as good. Her breasts were
perfect. She was a reader in the theatrical offices of Stacey
Keene, the theatrical producer and impresario, who had four
shows running simultaneously on Broadway.
    Jack had managed to see Carla one night a week since that
first meeting by lying to Mae that he was playing cards with
the boys. The last time they had been together he had given
Carla a first draft of his play to read. When he called, she was
bursting with excitement.
    "It's wonderful, Jack. Honestly, I've already warned Stacey
that it's going to be his next hit."
    "I'm glad you like it, Carla." His mouth was dry and the
words sounded so stinking and formal.
    "It needs work, darling. I'd like to help you with the rewrite
before The Man reads it. I've had experience doing that. Did

you know I practically outlined the new third act for Walter Manten's last play?"

"I couldn't let you do that, Carla. It's enough that you took the time to read it."

"I was crazy to read it . . . you know that." His flat, impersonal reaction to her news disturbed her. "Jack, I want to help you. You'd be doing me the favor. It's a great play, and it would be a privilege for me to be associated with it." She laughed self-consciously. "And it would be a labor of love besides."

"I appreciate it, Carla."

There was a long, appraising silence at her end. When she spoke again, her voice was tight. "Jack . . . is anything the matter? You sound so strange. As if we were talking about nothing more important than your laundry list."

He took a deep breath, let it out slowly. "Carla . . . it isn't important. Not any longer."

She *knew* then and she was too gracious a lady to pretend she didn't know in order to put him through the wringer—even though he owed that much suffering to her—of making torturous, heartbreaking explanations.

Her voice was controlled, but she could not hide her pain from him any more than he could hide his pain from her.

"You didn't tell her, did you?"

"No, not about us. I wanted to, but it was too late."

"Too late? Why, Jack? What happened?"

"I'm going to be married, Carla."

"Married? Oh, my darling. Jack, I—"

"Let's not play word games with it, Carla. I've said it. There's really nothing else to say. Is there?"

"I suppose not."

It was easier now for both of them. The crisis was past. They could speak now with the polite voices of strangers.

"Jack, this doesn't make a bit of difference about the play. It's still good. I want Mr. Keene to see it. About the rewrite . . ."

"Never mind, Carla. I appreciate it, but, to tell you the truth, I think I'm going to have to shelve the script for a while. The next few months are going to be very busy. You understand, I've got this new show at the network to think about and—" He blocked on the rest of it.

"Sure, Jack . . . I understand . . . Well . . . all the luck in the world to . . . to you and your wife." She rushed the last words together in a breathless garbling and hung up before he could hear the involuntary wail of despair torn from deep inside of her.

"Goodbye, love," he whispered into the dead phone.

A few days after that, Wendy Gates visited him at his Rockefeller Plaza office. She was lithe and tanned, her hair streaked with pale, sun-bleached strands. The tawny effect was heightened by a tight, short yellow shift printed with gold and yellow flowers. She dazzled.

He kissed her cheek when she entered and took her by the hand, leading her to the couch along one wall.

"You look great, Wendy. Gorgeous. Been a long time."

"Thanks, Jack. It has been a long time."

"I heard you were traveling in stock?"

"Yes, we played a month in Florida. I quit when the company moved on to Texas."

He lit her cigarette and sat down beside her. "The old Florida sun. It agrees with you."

She studied him in silence through the drifting smoke of the cigarette with her large unblinking green eyes. Years had gone by since he had made love to Wendy that stormy night at the lake. It was childish, irrational for him to feel so defensive when ever he was in her presence. Yet time kept on adding to his legacy of guilt and regret.

"What's on your mind, doll? Say, do you have a lunch date?"

"Thanks, but I do. And a supper date too."

"You don't waste any time, do you? Who's the lucky guy? Anyone I know?"

"Yes, you know both of them."

"Both?"

"Yes, I'm having lunch with Carl and supper with Wally."

He was surprised. "Carl Schneider? I haven't seen Carl in months. How is he?"

"All right, I guess. At least he sounds fine. You're the only one I've seen since I got back. I spoke to Carl and Wally on the phone." Her eyes narrowed like a cat's. "Carl didn't have too much to say. But Wally was full of news."

The muscles behind his jawbones tightened. "Oh? Such as?"

"Congratulations!" she said with undisguised bitterness.

He understood why she was here now. "Thanks, Wendy. I guess it's about time I settled down." Her arched eyebrow told him how lame it sounded.

"Whatever happened to all that crap about steering clear of involvements? All that monastic dedication to your career? The man who didn't want to love or be loved?"

He tried to dismiss it lightly.

"That was a long time ago, Wendy. Life looks awfully over-whelming to an ex-GI with a discharge in one hand and his severance pay in the other. Three hundred lousy bucks, total assets. No job. No education. No—"

"No shit!" she interjected. "But not so overwhelming as to stop you from shacking up with Mae Edsel for the past four years!"

"Jesus! Wendy!" Her outburst shook him. He automatically glanced toward the office door, thankful that his secretary had closed it on her way out.

Wendy laughed. "What's the matter? Don't they know about you and Mae around here? After all, she works in the front office. Or has she handed in her resignation to devote her full time to setting up your little love nest?"

Jack saw himself in the mirror on the wall behind the couch. His ashen face frightened him. Numbness was spreading through his body. Like death. His heart galloped wildly. He was choking. Reality was slipping away from him. Somehow he reached the desk and sat back in his chair with his eyes closed. All the while aware of her strident, accusing voice.

"The worst part of it is, you don't even love Mae. That's the rottenest part of all. *You don't love her!*"

"Wendy—I'd appreciate it if you'd leave now."

"With pleasure." She stood up and buttoned her coat.

"I'm sorry about this, Wendy," he told her.

"I believe you are, Jack," she said calmly.

"I *am* sorry!" He lit a cigarette and crushed the empty matchbox savagely in his fist. "Hell! Homer knew what he was talking about. The gods sit up there on top of the mountain and play games with our petty lives. They have a macabre sense of humor, don't they?"

"Do they?" Wendy smiled. Not at him, but inward at some personal satisfaction denied to him. "Jack . . . what would you say if I told you I might be getting married very soon myself?"

"I'd wish you both long life and happiness." He wondered if she was serious. "Who's the lucky man?"

The green eyes, flecked with gold specks, regarded him with uncompromising vengeance. A lioness closing on her prey to apply the crunch.

"Ask me tomorrow," she said. She ran a pink tongue across her top lip. "Goodbye, Jack. And tell Mae I hope she has a miscarriage."

After she was gone, he poured himself a drink. It had been a rough session, but in a way he was glad it had happened. For complex reasons that he could not define, and which he felt reflected poorly both on his character and his manhood, he had dreaded this confrontation with Wendy Gates. The moment when he would face her and tell her that he was marrying Mae Edsel. Now it was over. Good riddance.

Four months after Jack Whittaker and Mae Edsel were married before a justice of the peace, Wendy Gates was wed to Carl Schneider in a large, formal church wedding.

The wedding reception was a reunion of sorts. They were all there with the exception of the Whittakers. Jack's absence disappointed everyone. Carl, who had counted on Jack to be his best man, would never forgive him for what he believed was an intentional cut.

Wendy smiled smugly at his childish disappointment. "I'm sure Jack has his reasons for not coming."

"Jack Whittaker can go to hell for all I care!"

But he did care, and Wendy knew it.

Mae was bothered by Jack's refusal to attend the wedding almost as much as Carl was. His excuse that he had to be in California that weekend was a lie.

"I know why you don't want to go. You're ashamed of being seen with me." She said it lightly, but privately she was not so sure.

Jack looked at her over the theater section of the *Times* and smiled. "Now that's a classic pregnant female for you."

She spanned her swelling belly with both hands and grimaced in distaste. "I *am* pregnant. Seven months."

"And you look every bit of it," he said wisely. "And I like the look." He stared her straight in the eye.

That night, as they were getting ready for bed, Wally Kaiser pounded on their door. He had come from the reception and was so drunk that he kept listing to one side when he walked. Jack helped him to a chair, while Mae went into the kitchen to make coffee. Wally's slurring monologue carried to her from the living room.

"Beu'ful weddin' . . . Beu'ful bride . . . All brides are beu'ful, they say. . . . Not like her . . . Wendy . . . Wendy . . . Oh, my God!"

All of a sudden he began to weep. It distressed her out of all proportion. She recalled the old saying: "Nobody likes to see a grown man cry." It was true. You stereotyped your friends, and then when they drifted away from the roles you assigned to them, you were dismayed. She had always seen Wally as a suave, handsome playboy, poised and in command. Romance was a game to Wally. He played the field. He dated so many different girls that Mae was continually embarrassing herself, and Jack, by confusing their names when they went out in foursomes.

She had always known Wally was attracted to Wendy, but she had never suspected his feeling for her was so deep. She leaned back against the sink while the coffee perked, with the knuckles of one hand pressed against her mouth, listening to his outpouring of unsuspected emotion with mixed feelings of pity and disappointment and fascination. And resenting Wendy, curiously, for having the power to inflict this pain on her husband's friend.

His anguish seemed to sober Wally. "I know she's a bitch, Jack. So do you. But she's in my blood. I wanted her. I still want her. She doesn't love Schneider. She doesn't love either of us. But, hell, I still would have married her on any terms. I told her that. She just laughed at me. So help me God, Jack, the day she accepted Carl's proposal, I took her to dinner that same night. Would you believe this? I asked her to marry me that night. Do you know what her answer was? She laughed and said: 'You're too late, dear. I told Carl I'd marry him at lunch this afternoon!' Now is that a bitch for you? She only married Carl to spite you, Jack!"

Nausea engulfed Mae. The room seemed to tilt as she turned and groped frantically for the edge of the sink. Her hands touched the slippery counter, lost their hold, and she fell. Her distended abdomen crashed against the stainless-steel ledge.

Six hours later, Jack Whittaker stood in the dim, bleak corridor of a hospital hearing the white-jacketed, beetle-browed resident: "There was no chance at all for the baby. Your wife is mighty lucky to be alive." The blue eyes, remote behind the thick lenses, sliding away from him. In guilt? Embarrassment? Pity? The awkwardness one human feels in the presence of another's tragedy. What does one say to the surviving kin?

"We had to do a partial hysterectomy, Mr. Whittaker, but she's going to be all right."

Alone again. All numbness. Wendy's face leering at him: *"And tell Mae I hope she has a miscarriage!"*

The day he brought Mae home from the hospital was like coming back to his mother's house the day they had buried her, two years before. A sense of permanent loss, a crippling, the sense an amputee has that a vital hand or foot is gone forever.

He wanted to avoid the subject that was uppermost in both their minds, but Mae would not shirk the reality.

"We won't be able to have any more babies, you know that?" she said as they had martinis later that afternoon.

He shrugged. "If we decide we really want one, we can always adopt."

"You didn't want this baby, did you, Jack?"

"For Christ's sake, Mae, neither one of us did. We weren't married. Once we were, we got used to the idea."

She replied with an odd, small laugh. "Used to the idea. Yes, I suppose so. The same way I'll get used to the idea that—"

"Will you stop it, Mae. It's academic, all of it. I think I'll mix another batch." He went into the kitchen.

Two months later Jack and Wally were drinking at the bar in P.J.'s on Third Avenue when Wally nudged him.

"Look who just walked in."

It was Carl Schneider. He was heavier than Jack remembered him, ruddier, puffier in the jowls. As he came up to them, Jack could see that he was getting prematurely gray.

He greeted them with a surly smile. "Well, if it isn't the pin-stripe twins. Say, aren't you off course? Twenty-one is over thataway."

"We're slumming," Wally said coolly. "What are you doing out alone, lover boy? Don't tell me the honeymoon fever has faded so soon?"

"Up yours!" Carl scowled and signaled the bartender.

"Not mine, lover," Wally taunted him. "Is that your problem? Poor Wendy."

Jack moved to avert the threatening hostilities.

"Congratulations, Carl—belatedly." He offered his hand.

Carl ignored the hand and said to the bartender, "Double Scotch on the rocks. Best in the house. And put it on a separate check."

It went on like that for almost fifteen minutes. Carl and Wally exchanging insults thinly veiled as jokes. Jack insinuating himself between them as a buffer, taking his punishment passively.

"We missed you at the wedding, Jack," Carl said. "Especially Wendy, she missed you."

Jack sensed imminent peril.

"Mae and I were sorry too. It was just one of those things that couldn't be avoided."

"Just one of those things," Carl said archly. "From the song of the same name. How does that song go, Jackson? Something about 'crazy flings' and 'gossamer wings.' "

His mouth was smiling, but his eyes were as hard as stones.

"Crazy flings, that's what that wife of mine thrives on. Talk about crazy. You know we spent our honeymoon up at the DiSalle lodge, compliments of Forrest and Pat. Damned nice of them. You remember the lodge, don't you, Jack?"

Jack nodded, staring into his glass.

"You remember that float in the lake? Sure you do. Anyway, this crazy bride of mine, you know what she wants to do? She wants to go skinny dipping in the middle of the night and make love in the water. Have you ever heard of anything so crazy, Jack?"

Wally laughed. "And you're complaining? All women should be that kind of crazy, Schneider. How was it?"

"I don't know," Carl answered. "It rained and we never got to try it. But I'll accept Wendy's word for it. It must be a ball."

Jack looked at his watch. "I hate to break it up, gentlemen, but

I'm meeting Mae at Sardi's. Good to see you, Carl. And give
my best to Wendy. Mae's too."

"I'll do that, Jack." He was resting one elbow on the bar with
his big hand wrapped around his drink. Without warning, the
sturdy old-fashioned glass shattered in his fingers, spraying the
counter with Scotch and pieces of broken glass. Blood welled
up brightly from a wicked gash on the inside of his thumb.

They looked on, stunned Jack, Wally, the bartender, and the
strangers around him.

Then Carl laughed, took out his handkerchief, and wrapped it
around his hand. "You tell J.P. I'm going to sue him, Larry," he
said to the bartender. "Cheap glassware!"

On their way across town in a cab, Wally said to Jack. "Carl
has a king-sized chip on his shoulder. He was bad enough in the
old days, but now he's obnoxious. Sore as a boil. It's funny when
you think about it. Carl is one of the rare guys in this world who
get to marry the girl of his dreams. And what has it done for
him? Nothing. Makes you wonder, doesn't it?"

"About what?" Jack replied, not really listening. Unable to rid
his mind of Carl's face when he said, *"But I'll accept Wendy's
word for it!"*

"The trouble with marriage—any marriage, not just Carl's—is
that the partners cannot love equally. One of them is always
loved less, and that one has to feel cheated. The secret of a good
marriage—not perfect, there's no such animal—is to marry a girl
who puts *you* on a pedestal, instead of the way it is with Carl
and Wendy." He took a little address book out of his jacket
pocket. "Yes, my friend, before I relegate this sex directory to
the ash bin, I am going to make sure I have the right mate.
Beauty, brains, and worships Wallace Kaiser."

Six months after that conversation, Wally Kaiser married Diana
Carlson, a fashion editor for *Vogue* magazine. Jack knew very
little about the girl, because that same year he and Mae moved
to Los Angeles. The network transferred him to Hollywood to

head the production and writing staff of a new television series which would be filmed at Warner Brothers' motion-picture studios.

Wally and Diana were married in a civil ceremony and flew to Hawaii for their honeymoon. They stopped over in L.A. on the way to spend a few days with the Whittakers, and from what Jack could see, Diana conformed perfectly to all of the attributes that Wally required in an "ideal" wife.

She was lovely, in face and form. She was intelligent and a talented editor. She called Wally "dear one," and that he was dear to her, infinitely precious in fact, there could be no doubt. She idolized him with her every word and gesture and expression.

"He's the most beautiful and brilliant man I've ever met," she confided to Mae, gushing happiness and brightness all over the place.

"She's too much," Mae told Jack. "Maybe she'd come over better in New York in February, but there's too much sunshine and sugar water in California as it is. Coals to Newcastle, you know what I mean? That poor man! You'd think he'd die of diabetic shock on that steady diet of pure molasses she feeds him."

"Meow-w-w-w," Jack chided her. "Just because she's an old-fashioned girl who treats her husband with the proper respect and adoration he deserves as lord and master of the household, you've got a burr under your tail. You're scared a few more gals like Diana may bring on a reactionary trend in the battle of the sexes. Keep 'em barefoot and pregnant, that's what my Scotch grandfather used to say." He caught himself too late, flinching from her bruised expression.

He went to her and embraced her, brushing back soft tendrils of hair from her temple with his lips. "Seriously, I don't like the girl either." He thought about Diana soberly. "I can't help feeling that all that saccharine must be covering a very bitter pill."

When Dorn finished questioning the Evanses, he had a police car drive them over to Aspen. Forrest was confident that among

his numerous acquaintances in the resort town he would find
someone to put them up for the night.

His wife wanted to fly back home immediately, but Forrest
was adamant.

"No, we're going to stay here and see this thing through, Pat.
After all, these are our friends."

She fixed him with a disdainful look and said just loud enough
for him to hear: "*Our* friends?"

They were gone only a few minutes when Max Lanier phoned
Dorn from Sam's Knob. "I think we got trouble, Les. One of
the boys just reported in that somebody slipped through our
picket line and he thinks the feller's headed for the lodge."

"God damn!" Dorn swore softly, his face grave. "One of those
reporters, sure as hell. You got a bullhorn up there, Max?"

"Yup."

"Okay. I'll be up there as soon as I can." He slammed down
the phone. "Hardy and Anker, you want to come along?"

Santini stood up, towering over the six-foot police captain by
at least four inches. "Can I come too?" He saw Dorn's hesitation
and added quickly. "There's a chance my cousin is in that lodge."

"All right. If Whittaker is the one, maybe you can do something. Don't ask me what. Let's go."

Light snow was falling as they drove to the lift station, and by
the time they were halfway up the fall was heavy. In the premature dusk visibility worsened rapidly. Darkness closed in over
the mountain like a shroud.

With the coming of darkness, he closed and latched the shutters. The two women were napping restlessly on the bed under
a blanket. He turned the electric heater to low and left the room
quietly, locking the door after him. He loosened the rifle's leather
sling and shouldered it, military fashion, as he began a leisurely
patrol of the upper floor. Room by room.

Carefully opening a shutter in each room, he scanned the terrain both with his naked eye and his field glasses. Visibility was

poor on the darkening, snow-whorled slopes falling away from the lodge. He took care not to expose himself unduly, mindful of the threat that could be lurking in every shadowed patch of trees and every defile. An enemy sharpshooter waiting for just such an opportunity.

As far as he could make out, the mountain was deserted on all sides of the lodge. To the south he studied the pinpoint of light at Sam's Knob. Far below twinkled West Village, a fairy-tale vision, miniatures underneath a Christmas tree.

His eyes misted, remembering other Christmases. His mother's smiling face—she had been more of a child than he was at the holiday season, bubbling with good will and excitement as they decorated the tree. And love. He retched the raw canker loose from the back of his throat and slammed the shutter closed.

Downstairs he inspected with meticulous care the heavy oaken shutters and the locks that fastened them. He was not concerned with the possibility of a frontal assault on his—he smiled—his citadel. He shut his eyes and visualized them storming up the snow-blown incline the way the Nazis had charged up a hill in an old war movie he had watched on TV, the heavy fifty-calibers blowing them over like rows of dominoes. His spine was alive, tingling, his blood pulsing in his arms and legs with the anticipation of imminent action. How they would pay when the time came! In blood! For every foot they advanced on the mountainside. For every step they advanced up the staircase. And, finally, barricaded within the last bastion.

He went into the kitchen and turned on the lights. It was safe. The shutters blacked out the windows effectively. He had checked that the night before. He propped the rifle up in a corner and began to prepare supper for the four of them. A cozy, intimate supper, like so many other suppers they had enjoyed together at Snowmass. He laughed softly at his little joke.

While the coffee was perking, he opened a canned ham and cut thick slices of it for sandwiches, spreading the jelly from the ham on the bread in place of butter. Butter and eggs were among the few foodstuffs not stocked in abundance in the lodge's cupboards and freezer. Last night he had taken an inventory, estimating that four people could eat well for more than a month before their rations were exhausted.

A month. His sense of humor surfaced briefly, a rare occurrence during these last weeks. There was no doubt in his mind he could hold out for a month. It was a tempting challenge. Holding at bay half the police force of Colorado. Possibly the National Guard as well. What sport!

His smile was wiped away as a squirming worm of pain bored into the thin, sensitive flesh between skin and bone at the base of the skull, and resumed its gnawing, a cannibal termite ravenous for his brain. No, a month would be a luxury he could not afford in his condition. In the beginning the blackouts were infrequent, no more than once every few months, and over in a matter of seconds. Now they were happening every four or five days. The last one had come two nights ago while he was untying his shoes, and he had been unconscious for at least five minutes. A wave of panic constricted his throat. Suppose . . . this very instant, it should happen. Who could tell? This time he might even black out for ten, twenty minutes. More! Time enough for his hostages . . . or the police . . .

Trembling so badly that he could not have used the rifle to save his life, he staggered out of the kitchen, down the hall to the den. The bar! Oasis for the lost, doomed, and dispossessed! He didn't like vodka, but it was the only bottle that was open. Half full. He pulled the cork, tossed it away and lifted the bottle to his lips with both shaking hands.

It tasted like wet ashes, making him want to retch, but he took a deep breath and held it down. The vileness of it comforted him. A throwback from childhood, his mother forcing ipecac down his gullet when he had croup.

"Of course it tastes awful. Good medicine always tastes bad. It's the medicine working, honey, killing the germs."

He shuddered and sank down on a bar stool, still holding the bottle. The good medicine was doing its work. He was limp now, covered with cold sweat underneath his heavy woolen clothing. The warmth of the alcohol radiating out of his belly, relaxing his tense muscles, ridiculed his fear. He wasn't going to black out. Not for another two or three days at least. There were always advance signs, he realized after the attacks were over. A numbness of fingertips and toes, a blurring of vision, imperceptible warnings that he usually chose to ignore when he was up to his ears in work. He flexed his fingers and toes. Focused on the nipple of a nude statuette on the back bar. Nothing wrong with him! He was just fine.

Nevertheless, it might be wiser to attend to the business upstairs before too much more time elapsed. He thought about it while he finished preparing the supper back in the kitchen.

Upstairs the dark woman sat up on the bed and swung her stockinged feet to the floor. She groaned. Her joints were stiff. Her muscles ached. She bent over and worked the steel cuffs as high as she could on her calves to relieve the irritation. Her thin, bony ankles were raw and welted under the torn nylons.

A dim lamp on the dresser was the only illumination in the room. It was quiet except for the humming of the electric heater and an occasional guttural snore from the sleeping woman beside her.

She stood up and hobbled slowly over to the chaise longue where the unconscious man lay motionless, looking as if he were already dead. Maybe he was, she thought without emotion. Lucky stiff!

"Hey, I made a funny," she said aloud, and she felt like giggling. *I must be going mad!*

She bent over the man and picked up a limp hand. Cold as death. Marble. The faint thready pulsations in his wrist on her fingertips surprised her. He was alive. The fact evoked no more emotion within her than had the speculation that he might be dead.

She started and whirled around, nearly falling at the rasp of

the key in the lock. He entered the room carrying a tray bur-
dened with a platter of sandwiches, a pot of coffee, and a box of
cookies.

"Chow time!" he announced in a voice that was macabre in
its gaiety. As normal as he had sounded the day before when he
called them into the bar for drinks. The last sane hour of their
lives before the cataclysm. She revised it with morbid realism.
The last sane hour of their lives!

"Wake up sleeping beauty," he ordered as he carried the tray
over to the card table they had been eating their meals on since
supper the night before. He laid out paper plates and coffee cups
at three places while the women took turns using the bathroom
that adjoined the bedroom. As a precautionary measure, he had
padlocked the shutter on the bathroom window and removed
all the bottles and implements from the medicine chest.

He rose from the chair, the fold-away kind, with exaggerated
gallantry as the women sat down at their places.

"I owe you an apology, ladies, for the simple fare," he said,
"but it has been a very, very busy day. Christmas Eve notwithstanding . . ."

The blonde woman sat trancelike with her hands in her lap,
staring at the flame of the single festive candle that burned in the
center of the table.

He lifted an eyebrow at her. "I felt the season deserved some
small recognition."

The dark woman watched him warily out of the sides of her
eyes as she cupped her icy fingers around the hot coffee cup. She
was uncertain how to interpret this change in his mood. Did his
light spirits signify a change in his homicidal plans as well? Or
was he the executioner, uplifted now that the moment was upon
him and the job would soon be done with? She listened, sifting
his every word, every nuance, every gesture, for some clue.

"I intend to improve on this tomorrow though. I mean, Christmas Day! I wouldn't be surprised if we have a turkey in the

freezer. Well, we'll see. Tomorrow." His good humor vanished abruptly. *"If*—if there is a tomorrow!"

The blonde began to cry again.

"Be still and eat your sandwich," he said. "It may be the last one you'll ever get."

"Stop torturing her," the dark woman said.

"Is that what you think?" He smiled. "You're wrong. I speak only the truth."

The candle flickered wildly as he exhaled across the table. The broken flame mottled his features, so that, in that instant, he appeared more bestial than human. A grinning, hooded cobra weaving from side to side, trying to decide, waiting, prolonging the moment, secure in his procrastination because his victims were helpless. But he would not wait much longer, of that she was convinced.

"How's our friend? Still out? Or do you think he's playing possum?" He glanced at the man on the lounge.

"He's not faking," the dark woman told him. "He's got a serious concussion. Maybe a fractured skull."

"I shouldn't have hit him so hard. I wouldn't want anything to happen to him—" he paused, baiting her—"before the time is right."

"And when will that be?"

"Well . . . that depends. Now, as far as he's concerned, I can take time. He won't give me any trouble. The same goes for weeping Wilhelmina here. She's a jellyfish. But now we come to you, dear. My instincts scream that *you* present a clear and present danger to me. That tricky mind of yours goes on ticking like a time bomb every minute I let you stay alive, and so—" He shoved back his chair and suddenly the rifle was in his hands aimed at her across the table.

She breathed quietly at first, then she stopped breathing altogether, as if the slightest vibration on her part would jar the taut finger bent around the rifle's trigger.

He stood up and let the muzzle come down off her. He grinned and winked. "So behave yourself while I clean up the dishes."

She shut her eyes and sagged limply in the chair.

He locked them in the room when he carried the supper dishes down to the kitchen. The clock above the dishwasher said six-twenty. He whistled as he stacked the dishes. "Jingle Bells." He was on the second chorus when he heard it. Someone was knocking on the front door! A coffee cup slipped out of his hand and smashed on the floor at his feet.

He was immobilized, physically and mentally. All of his reflexes were geared for dramatic confrontation. He was totally unprepared for this prosaic rapping at the door. His first impulse was to march down the hall and open the door!

He picked up the rifle and ran down the hall to the staircase. He bounded up two steps at a time. His lungs couldn't get enough air. The sound of the door knocker echoed through the vacant rooms below. A knell that quickened his frantic heart. There was an el jutting out at one end of the lodge. From the bedroom there it would be possible to look down at the front porch. He removed his shoes and moved in darkness along the hall. Through the doorway over to the east window. He flicked off the safety and tucked the rifle firmly under his right armpit, finger inside the trigger guard. With his left hand, he lifted the sash as far as it would go and undid the latch that fastened the shutters. Carefully, he eased open the heavy wooden shutter a few inches. Snow and cold air stung his face. Squinting against the blast, he peered out into the night. The overhang of the porch roof blocked his view of the front door. He waited. Soon a figure walked down the steps and stood with feet spread apart, hands on hips, looking up at the lodge. A vivid silhouette against the snow that glistened with an eerie phosphorescence in the darkness. A perfect target. Yet he made no move to bring up the rifle.

He wiped a hand across his eyes, expecting the apparition to vanish. It couldn't be real! A man walking boldly up to the house and announcing his presence. Pounding heavily on *his* door. It was too incredible! Who would do such a thing? Certainly not the law! One man. A lone unarmed man.

The sound of his own voice was unnerving. "What do you want?"

The man looked up at him, faceless in the blackness, not intimidated in the least.

"Ah, there you are! Mister—" The stranger laughed. "I'm sorry, I don't know your name, Mister—?"

He ignored the question. "Who are you, and what are you doing here?"

"I'm Fred Lewis of the A.P. Associated Press. I'd like to talk to you. No tricks. The fuzz don't know I'm up here. All I want is a story. I guarantee I'll tell it like it is. Any way you want me to tell it. Can I come inside? It's as cold as a witch's tit out here." He flapped his arms against his body to lend some urgency to the request.

A reporter! Straight out of *Front Page!* It was ludicrous. The poor fool actually believed in the legends!

Suddenly the solitude of the snowy night was broken. The voice of God, it sounded like, ringing across the mountain. He recoiled from it, ducking beneath the window ledge.

"You there, you damned fool! Get away from that place FAST! This is Captain Dorn of the Colorado State Police. You'll be killed. He's already killed six people. . . . Come back here immediately."

He recognized it then. A police bullhorn. There was no way to pinpoint its source. It seemed to be coming from all directions. He poked the muzzle of the rifle out the window and fired three quick shots into the air.

They put a fire under the reporter's butt. Whirling he ran. Slipping. Bellywhopping down the slope in front of the house. He went all the way down on hands and knees, feet pedaling to gain traction on the slippery boiler plate. He ran on clumsily through deepening drifts. He fell again and lay there spreadeagled in exhaustion.

The rifle poked between the shutters. The cross hairs of the scope swept in an arc until they split him in half. *Christ on the cross!* That was what he was reminded of. He withdrew the barrel, closed and locked the shutters. Room by room, he checked the terrain on all sides of the house. Nothing. Just the cold, desolate expanse of snow. The dark clumps of wood. The lights sparkling in the distance. And the wind crying in the loneliness on this Christmas Eve . . .

On his way back to the bedroom where his hostages were imprisoned, he kept thinking about the reporter. He didn't remember the name. A faceless man. Why had he spared him?

His brow creased and he shook his head. In his mind there was a dim answer. Something one of the women had said to him. He was angry with himself. And the pain was worse.

When they got back to the restaurant at Sam's Knob, Dorn took Fred Lewis into a back room and slammed him against the wall.

"What kind of a fool stunt was that?" he demanded. His eagle's beak almost touched the reporter's nose. "I ought to take you back to the airport and put you on the first plane!"

"If you cops had stayed out of it, I would have got through to him. He was talking to me, not shooting. You guys panicked him, that's what!"

Dorn let go of Lewis' coat collar and stepped back, his mind fastening onto a small hope. "You were talking or he was talking?"

"*He* was talking. Nothing much, there wasn't time. But I was standing right underneath the window where he was."

"Did you get a look at his face?"

"Not a chance. It was too dark, and the shutters were only open—yea much." He held up his hands a few inches apart."

The captain turned away in disgust. "What good are you anyway?" He paced, clomping the heels of his boots sharply against the floorboards, venting his frustration and helplessness.

A trooper opened the door and poked his head into the room. "A phone call just came through from that guy at the lodge. He said the next time anyone comes within a hundred yards of the place he's going to shoot them hostages on the spot. That was it. He wouldn't talk about anything else. He told it and hung up."

Dorn gave the reporter a long, contemptuous glare. "You hear that, Mr. Lewis? Now you go back down to the village and make sure that the rest of those reporters get the word. This is just another story to you. But to those three people he's holding up there it's life or death! You got it, buster?"

The reporter ran his tongue over dry lips. "Yeah . . . I got it, captain."

Dorn found Santini talking with the FBI agents and Sid Feldman in the bar. They were drinking whiskey and water, except for Feldman, who had his hands cupped around a mug of hot coffee. He was wearing a dark blue suit, white shirt, and tie underneath his open mackinaw.

"I'm taking my wife to a party later on tonight." He felt obliged to explain his formality to Dorn.

"Have a good time." The captain's face still mirrored the annoyance he felt toward Lewis.

Feldman flushed. "Of course if you'll be needing me . . ."

Dorn grinned. "No, you go ahead. I'm still burned about that crazy reporter."

"I heard." The accountant took off his glasses and slipped them, folded, into the breast pocket of his suit coat. His brown eyes looked naked and vulnerable without the glasses. "You know, I had sort of the same idea before. Just vaguely. You know, going up there with a white flag on a stick and trying to talk to him." He laughed in embarrassment. "Of course, I knew it was out of the question, really."

Dorn stared at him sternly. "You're damned right it's out of the question." The very idea of little Feldman entertaining such a dangerous thought shook him.

"If it is Jack, I could do it. I don't care what you say, he wouldn't hurt me." In frustration Santini slapped both hands hard on the table, rattling the glasses. "But, damn it! It can't be Jack. I've known him all my life. He couldn't do anything like this. So savage, so senseless. So insane!"

"Just because a man acts sane doesn't mean he is sane," Feldman objected. "There's a theory that the only difference between 'normal' and 'abnormal' is that so-called normal people are able to deceive us into believing they are sane."

"Come again, Mr. Feldman?" Dorn's forehead was puckered up like crepe paper.

Feldman was eager to elaborate on the theory. "We're all play-acting. A man invents a certain role for himself and tries to live up to it. If he's successful, then society considers him normal. But, if the role is beyond his capabilities and his performance is unconvincing, he fails and the illusion is exposed. Society regards him as abnormal. Insane."

"Hmmm . . ." Dorn scratched his stubbled chin with his knuckles. "Well, that could apply to anybody. Any one of us here in this room."

"That's right."

"Well, it's all very interesting, Mr. Feldman, but I think we better leave psychology to the psychologists."

"I couldn't agree more, captain. Which is why I thought you might want to talk to Dr. Alvin Kendall."

"Who's he?"

Feldman put his glasses back on, to Dorn's satisfaction. Without them it seemed as though part of him were missing.

"Dr. Kendall owns a lodge at Snowmass. He's up here now, as a matter of fact. He's one of the most eminent psychiatrists in the United States."

Dorn was interested. Dorn was desperate. He would try anything, short of spiritualism, to find some way out of this deadlock. And, if he knew of a good medium, he wasn't all that sure that he'd turn a deaf ear to the occult!

He could tell that the FBI were receptive to the idea too.

"Sure, let's have a talk with this Dr. Kendall. You know where to reach him?"

"I think so. Yes, I do." Feldman was ill at ease. "You see, I happened to stop by his place on my way up here, and he—Dr. Kendall, that is—said he'd be glad to lend whatever assistance he could to the police." He ran one finger around the inside of his starched collar. "That is, if you want his help. He's very politic, the doctor is."

Dorn stared at him stone-faced. He was aware that Santini and the FBI men were grinning at him. In a bland voice he said to the accountant.

"You just 'happened to stop by his place' . . . ? You know, Mr. Feldman, I have a feeling we ought to deputize you. Then you could work with the state police full time and you wouldn't have to take your wife to that party tonight."

Feldman shrank into his chair. "I should have spoken to you first, I suppose?"

He was grateful when Dorn laughed. "Hell! That's all right, Sid. Let's go talk to him right now."

They were at the lift before Feldman realized that Captain Dorn had called him "Sid." He looked up at the big state trooper and grinned. "Well . . . it's going to be a long, cold night—Les."

The name just loud enough so that only Dorn could hear it.

Chief Lanier met them at the lower lift station. His round face was sweaty despite the intense cold.

"Les, those newspaper people at the hotel," he burst out as soon as Dorn was out of the chair. "You've got to talk to them. They won't hold still much longer. They say the state police are stifling the press on this story."

Dorn's leathery face hardened. "Yeah, and if that ass Lewis had got himself killed, they would have been screaming about lack of police protection." He shrugged his wide shoulders. "All right, Max. We'll do it up big. A press conference just like they do it on television." He winked at the FBI men. "You fellows want to lend a hand? It'll help impress 'em."

Hardy and Anker were not so certain. "I don't know, captain. The FBI isn't on the case officially," Hardy reminded him.

"Just in an advisory capacity," Dorn said with a grin. He put a hand on Feldman's arm. "Maybe your doctor friend would sit in too. Pull out all the stops for the fourth estate."

They piled into two police cars and drove trough West Village to the Kendall lodge. Santini settled back in the seat, smoking a cigarette and watching the holiday pageantry of the winter resort unreel past the car windows on either side. The voice of pop singer Mel Torme blared out of loudspeakers all along the way. The yuletide classic:

"Chestnuts Roasting On The Open Fire."
Lyricizing of open fires.
Jack Frost.
Turkey and mistletoe.
Tiny tots all aglow.
The season to be jolly.
"Fa-la-la-la-la . . ." Dorn thought.

West Village, snuggled at the foot of Mt. Baldy, all covered with snow like a sugar-coated ice-cream cone, was a scene from a Christmas card.

Dr. Alvin Kendall was too much! A roly-poly jolly St. Nick with bushy white hair and white sidewhiskers. The carefully trimmed goatee spoiled the image a bit, but put him in a red suit and cap and he would do just fine, Santini decided, suppressing an urge to laugh when they were introduced.

Dr. Kendall was delighted that the police had consulted him and agreed to be present at the news conference. It was seven o'clock when they drove back to the hotel where the press was billeted. Kendall's elfin face became somber as he sat wedged between Dorn and Feldman in the lead police car. His eyes kept darting to one side, looking out the window up the mountain.

"If only there was some way I could communicate with that poor fellow . . ."

"We tried that. He won't listen." Dorn did not share Kendall's compassion. "I don't think of him that way, doctor. I keep thinking about all those people he shot."

"Of course, captain. But no amount of grief can bring them back to life. The objective now is to prevent any more loss of life. Including his. Yes, I do pity him. He's a sick, tormented man."

"I suppose he is." Dorn could understand Kendall's point of view even though his own was diametrically opposed to it. His objective, as a law-enforcement officer, was, first, to take the killer into custody. Alive if possible. And with a minimum peril to his fellow officers and to innocent civilians. Essentially, though, Dorn was going to take the gunman in. Dead or alive!

Very deliberately the sniper placed the butt plate of the rifle against his instep and pressed down until the pain of the metal plate grinding into his foot bone equalized the throbbing inside his skull. He had read somewhere that the human brain could not accommodate more than one extreme threshold of suffering simultaneously. It seemed to provide some small relief.

He continued to dwell on something the woman had said earlier:

". . . *Some of you have nothing in common at all. But the old tie has always been there. You've always kept in touch, even if it was only once or twice a year. Why?*"

The "why" of it nagged at him. Why indeed? Actually it wasn't accurate. Between 1950 and 1954, there had been little or no communication at all between various members of the old bunch. Tess and Kate had dropped out of sight altogether. He had no idea whether or not they had married or what had happened to them. And he had rarely seen Forrest Evans during that period either.

The first time all of them, the men, had met at a reunion had

been at the DiSalle hunting lodge in Maine. It had been a whim
on Forrest's part. One Saturday afternoon after he had gotten
tanked up watching a football game, Forrest had put in long-
distance phone calls to everyone he could locate. His sales talk
was hard to resist.

"*You* don't want to be the only wet blanket, old buddy. All the
guys are going to be there. It'll be great to get away from civili-
zation for a long weekend. And away from the broads, God
bless 'em! We'll hunt, fish, do any Goddamn thing we please.
Play cards around the clock if we feel like it, and the booze will
flow like—" he laughed—"like booze! What do you say?"

Jack Whittaker had been the only real holdout. But Forrest
played on the vague sense of guilt Jack always felt whenever
network business brought him to New York. Sometimes he had
drinks and supper with Wally Kaiser, but he avoided his other
old friends. His excuse was time. Producing a weekly television
show. Tied up in writing or production of a half-dozen other
TV projects. And his play in its final draft, with his agent
clamoring for it to show to some interested backers. Never
enough time to keep up with the frenetic present and the on-
rushing future let alone indulge himself in the past.

In the end, though, it was curiosity as much as Forrest's persuasion that made him accept the invitation. That, and the fact
that it was going to be a stag weekend.

The female disrupted the natural tribal camaraderie of the
male animal.

Once he got used to the idea of going to the reunion—it was
a reunion of sorts—he began to look forward to it with anticipation. He had imagined that his ties with the past were dead, but
he discovered that old friends and memories were not so readily
banished.

There was nothing memorable about the weekend. It rained
three of the four days. They sat around the lodge, playing cards
and talking about wives, children, love affairs past, politics, and
business. They drank too much. There was not one of them who

was not relieved when the last day was over and they were about
to go their separate ways.

"I feel like I've been on a retreat," Carl said.

"True in a way," Forrest agreed. "It's a healthy thing for a
man to escape from the crunch of everyday living from time to
time. We should do it again, say, in another six months."

"Count me in," Wally said promptly.

"I'm for it," said Carl.

To his surprise, Jack heard himself say, "Good idea. I'll try my
damnedest to make it." He meant it.

Charlie Roche went behind the bar and poured five stiff drinks.
"That calls for a toast! To the next time."

They lifted their glasses and drank to the promise. Next time.

In his own private thoughts, each of them must have asked
himself what enticement there could be to induce him to repeat
this unrewarding outing. Five men taking the time out from
contemporary interests and responsibilities, traveling hundreds of
miles (in Jack's case three thousand miles) to join this baffling
company. Five men who had outgrown whatever common interests they once had shared.

Why?

So he could measure his advancement on the scale of life
against the successes—and the failures—of each of his companions? A yardstick marked off in wrinkles, gray hairs, overweight,
alcoholic intake, the cut of a jacket, and company titles?

Perhaps.

Charlie Roche commented that the next time he was invited
to a "hunting weekend" he intended to hunt. They all laughed.

Actually, they had done some shooting on the one clear day.
Clinton DiSalle was a member of the National Rifle Association,
and there was a regulation rifle range on the property behind the
lodge. His den housed a small armory. Forrest, who had developed
into an excellent shot practicing with his father-in-law's gun
club, appropriated some rifles from the lodge's collection and
they all trooped out to the range.

Wally still had an aversion for lethal weapons but was finally persuaded to join them.

"After all, we're not out to kill anything. It's for sport," Forrest said. "Shooting at a paper target isn't any more blood-thirsty than chess."

Charles Roche, who had won medals for rifle marksmanship in national competitions, took the honors, although Forrest made it a contest. Jack, an ex-combat infantryman, had a respectable score. Carl and Wally, awkward and ineffectual at first, made re-markable improvement under Roche's instruction.

"You're doing fine," he encouraged them. "Both of you have natural ability. With a few more practice sessions, you'll be pressing Jack."

"What did you do?" a wife or a friend would ask after the weekend was over.

"Nothing much. Drank, smoked, played cards, talked."

"What did you talk about?"

"Nothing important enough to remember."

Only because he hadn't been listening.

The first night at the lodge, Carl Schneider brought up the subject of their last meeting, to Jack's discomfort.

"It was P.J.'s you remember? You and Wally." He took a quick, nervous gulp of his drink. "I behaved like a jerk. Broke a glass and cut myself."

"That's right, I'd forgotten." Jack laughed to cover the lie. "You had a few too many. It happens to the best of us."

"No, it wasn't that. I had a bad case of those old first-year blues. You know how it is that first year you're married? Ad-justing to each other, responsibilities and pressures you never had before."

"I know, Carl. It can be rough. Awfully rough."

"I guess you do, Jack," Carl said with real concern. "What a lousy break for you, what happened to Mae. How is she?"

"Just fine." He didn't care to dwell on it. "How's Wendy? And the kids? How many is it now?"

"How's Wendy?" Carl laughed. "Pregnant as usual. A boy three, a girl one, and one in the oven."

"That's great, Carl." Jack lifted his glass. "To the one in the oven."

"Thanks." When he finished drinking the toast, Carl looked grave. "Yes, sir, Jack, you wouldn't know that girl. She's really settled down. No more of those crazy notions about acting. She modeled for a while after we were married. Until the first kid began to show. But now she's perfectly content to be a hausfrau."

Charlie Roche had been eavesdropping on the fringe of two conversations. Now he approached Carl and Jack, grinning broadly. Of all of them, Charlie had changed the least both in physical appearance and temperment. His red hair was as bright and wild as ever; his eyes glowed with gleeful malice. In a room he circulated like a hurricane, buffeting everyone he touched with his turbulence.

He clapped Carl on the back. "I knew another guy who thought the way you do, old buddy. He married this wild chick, see, and he was bound to saddle-break her. So she's pregnant nine months out of every year for ten years. He figured it was the foolproof way to keep her tamed and out of trouble. What he didn't know was that only half those kids were his own!"

Carl laughed along with the other two men, but Jack could tell the joke had tapped a raw nerve. His high color. His silly grin. A boxer stung by a sneak punch. The way he kept putting the empty glass to his lips.

"I think we need a refill, Carl," Jack said. "Hey, Roche, get back where you belong, behind the bar."

Charlie held up his hands as if to ward off a blow. "Oh, no, you don't, Whittaker. Last time I tended bar at this dump, you clobbered me."

Jack winced. "That's one bash we'd all like to forget, I think."

"Not on your life!" Charlie touched Jack lightly on the chin

with his fist. The big stone in the ring on his finger flashed in
Jack's eye. It was the same ring he had taken from the Dead
German soldier in World War Two. "I still owe you one,
Whittaker," he said softly.

Wally Kaiser came up behind him. "And I owe you one,
Roche, or did you forget about that?"

Charlie looked around slowly, his wild eyes scorning Wally.
"Well, now, that's right. It sure took you long enough to make
up your mind, didn't it? But I always say: 'Better late than never.'
Be my guest!" Hands on hips, he thrust out his heavy jaw.

Charlie's voice had a nasal, hysterical quality that intruded on
all the other conversations in the room. The host, Forrest Evans,
was acutely aware of what the raucous and unpredictable Roche
was saying and doing. Now he came hurrying across the room.

"At ease, you guys!" he said anxiously. "What's with you guys
anyway?"

Charlie was delighted. He bent over and slapped his hands on
his thighs. "How about that! The man thinks we're serious." He
reached out and rumpled Forrest's hair. "For Christ's sake! What
happened to your sense of humor, old buddy? Loosen up, man!
That's what we're here for, isn't it? To horse around and have a
ball? Come on, don't look so grim." He put one arm around
Forrest and the other arm around Jack, leading them over to the
bar. "What we all need is another drink!"

Forrest shook his head and smoothed back his rumpled blond
hair. "This big ape!" He spoke around Charlie to Jack. "I don't
think he'll ever grow up, do you?"

"You're damned right I won't!" Charlie pounded the bar,
shouting at Forrest. "Set 'em up for my friends, innkeeper. The
best stuff in the house!"

Forrest shook his head again and sighed. Plainly relieved that
harmony had been restored.

Privately, so was Jack. For as long as he had known Charlie,
he had been walking a precarious ledge between good humor and
black rage.

Left to themselves on the other side of the room, Wally and Carl looked at each other.

"You know, he had me fooled," Carl said. "I thought he was serious."

"Roche?" Wally focused on the big, redheaded man slouching at the bar. "Why, of course he was serious. And so was I."

Carl was thoughtful for a moment, then he said gravely, "I guess there isn't a man in this room who doesn't have a score to even, is there?"

Wally smiled.

On the last night, Jack and Wally sat up playing gin in the den after the others had gone to bed. Wally had an unbelievable run of bad luck and the game ended at two o'clock with him owing Jack $150.

"Can I mail you a check, Jack? I underestimated this weekend and I'm short. Forgot my checkbook in the bargain, damn it!" He was pink with embarrassment.

The incident bothered Jack for a long time afterward. Not the money; he received Wally's check ten days later. It was *why* Wally had put off paying him.

They had shared the same room at the lodge, and, accidentally, he had seen Wally's checkbook lying in his open suitcase when they were unpacking.

Over a nightcap in the den Jack inquired casually, "How's the advertising business these days? Last I heard, you were setting Madison Avenue on fire. Somebody told me you were the brain behind the commercials on five of the ten top shows on the Nielsen charts."

Wally's unqualified appreciation of his own talent always amused Jack, and he sat back, waiting for a blow-by-blow account of how Wally had masterminded these prize accounts.

"They were good, as far as they went," Wally answered with uncharacteristic modesty. "But the trouble with the big agencies is, they'll only let out the leash so far. No matter how big the writer's reputation, he's still working under restrictions that strangle his creativity." He swirled the ice cubes around in his glass. "Diana kept telling me that from the start, but it took me a long time to get around to her point of view."

"Oh?" Jack remembered a tedious conversation the year Wally and his bride had visited them in California.

"Wally is too brilliant for the cliché mentalities who run the ad agencies. He should be heading his own agency."

"Well, I finally decided to kick over the traces." Wally's fingers beat a rhythmic tattoo on the bar. In spite of all he'd had to drink, he was tense. "I'm tired of squandering my creative talents on those jokers. If you're going to burn yourself out, do it for yourself at least—Di—I say. This sweet opportunity finally came along. Two other bright lads and me, we're going to start our own agency."

Jack was cautious in his praise. "It sounds great, Wally. But doesn't that kind of operation require a big hunk of front money?"

Wally's optimism was unconvincing. "Well, sure, man, it isn't going to be a picnic for the first year or so. We had to clean out our savings accounts, mortgage our homes, that sort of thing. Some of our relatives kicked in too. Long-term investments. But they'll clean up when our stock goes public."

He poured himself another drink. The whiskey and the lack of sleep were getting to him. He looked old and beat, with his haggard face and the spare tire around his middle inflating.

"I gave up forty thousand a year to swing this deal," He rubbed his red-rimmed eyes. "But it's going to pay off. I know it will."

"It will," Jack said. "You're the man to make it work."

"Damned right I am!" A muscle fluttered at the corner of his mouth. He lit a fresh cigar. "Now, what about you, Whittaker? I've been hearing some good things about you through the grapevine. You're pretty hot these days, old buddy. Big television writer-producer. A play on Broadway . . ."

"I'm not so sure about that." Jack laughed. "I *hope* it's going to be on Broadway. I don't have the backers yet."

"You'll find the backers, don't worry, Jack. Luck of the Irish." Some of the old swagger reasserted itself in the haughty tilt of one eyebrow. "Hell, you came out of the army and sat down in the hottest seat in the game. Television! The boob-tube empire! You never had to break your hump for anything, Jack. Success came looking for you. Not like the rest of us chumps. Know something, Jack? If I had gotten in on the ground floor the way you did, I'd be a network president today!"

Jack yawned. "Sure you would, Wally. What do you say we turn in? You don't really want that drink."

"Don't tell me what I want, Whittaker," Wally growled. "You sound like my wife!"

It was the only time Jack could remember that Wally had ever said anything critical about Diana. Up until now, he had been holding his own against the bellyful of Scotch he had consumed. The remark told Jack that Wally was on the verge of losing his poise. And face. The way he had come apart that unforgettable night after the Schneiders' wedding reception in the old apartment. The night Mae—he forced it out of his mind.

Jack wiped his sweaty palms on his shirt. God damn Wally, stirring up all those lousy memories. He pushed his drink aside. The alcohol was repeating on him, backing up sourly at the back of his throat.

"I'm going to bed." He tried to stand up and had to grab the edge of the bar to keep from falling. Both his legs were asleep. It was an unpleasant sensation. His nose and cheeks were tingling.

Familiar symptoms. Terrifying, as if the life were slowly draining out of him, but not serious, his doctor had assured him. Hyperventilation, induced by nerves. Breathing too deeply to relieve nervous tension, thereby drowning the brain in excessive oxygen.

He was a captive audience to Wally's drunken monologue.

"That's very appropriate when you stop and think abou' it." Wally giggled. "My busted hump. Tha's what I got, all right. A busted hump! You wanna hear somethin' funny, Whittaker?"

Jack held his breath to aid his body in restoring the balance of carbon dioxide to oxygen in its cells.

"Old Wally, you 'member what a swordsman I used to be?" He broke into song. *"Oh, if all the young girls were pink little rabbits, and I were a rabbit, they'd soon have the habit, oh-h-h-h."* He groaned and dribbled whiskey down over his chin and shirt. "All those grateful maidens I introduced to the delights of love . . . Well . . . now . . . you're not goin' to believe this, old buddy. I was old reliable, the long ball hitter in the grapefruit league where it didn't matter. But in the big leagues I am batting zero-zero-zero. What do you think about that?"

Jack was bewildered. His fuzzy mind couldn't make any sense out of Wally's ravings.

"Marriage!" Wally roared pounding the glass on the bar. "My wife is frigid! With me at least. I haven't been able to make her come *once* in all these years we've been married. Knock her up, oh, that's easy! She likes to be pregnant." His lip curled contemptuously. "That's a built-in excuse. She can relax and stop with that old routine 'Oh, dear not tonight. I have this splitting headache!' A lot you know about busted humps, my friend!"

Jack was feeling better. Oddly, Wally's confession of marital discord left him unmoved. There was a note of "rightness" about it that suited the ruthless and mindful forces which bent the destiny of all things in the universe. Wry, ironic, and altogether malevolent.

To have the man of God resist the seductress Sadie Thompson would warp the truth of natural law.

"Don't make so much of it," he told Wally. "There are worse disasters in life than having a frigid wife. You found sex easily enough before you were married. So find it again."

Wally would not be consoled. "You don't understand. Everything comes to you so damned easily, Whittaker. You always had the world by the handle."

Jack was struck by a wrenching sense of futility. He rummaged in his mind for the words of a poem:

And he was rich—yes, richer than a king—
And admirably schooled in every grace.
In fine, we thought that he was everything
To make us wish that we were in his place.

Dorn and his party were surrounded by reporters and photographers. There were television cameraman carrying small portable tape recorders. He kept nodding courteously to the garbled barrage of voices directed at him from all sides, and promised: "You'll all get a chance to ask your questions when we get inside."

A small banquet room had been quickly converted into a conference room. Camp chairs and a long table cluttered with microphones and cables. Captain Dorn took the center chair, flanked by Dr. Kendall and Sheriff Malone on his left and Chief Lanier on his right. (A courtesy Lanier had declined at first, but Dorn had insisted; it was the chief's bailiwick, after all.) Beside Lanier the conservatively dressed FBI agents looked relaxed but alert as Dorn opened the proceedings.

The captain introduced himself and the members of his panel to the press. He told them all that had happened since the sniper fired his opening salvo that morning, honestly and without minimizing his own impotency in dealing with the killer.

"Frankly, gentlemen, we don't know what's going to happen from minute to minute. There's nothing the police can do right now but wait him out." His gaze fell on Fred Lewis in the first row. "I guess Mr. Lewis has told you about his visit to the lodge and what came of it. Next time anybody gets too close to him, the gunman is going to kill his three hostages."

"Can't you use tear gas on him?" a reporter queried.

"Not a chance. The windows are all protected by heavy oak shutters. It would take a bazooka to blast through them."

Another question: "Why not cut off his power supply? Kill his light and heat."

"We thought of that," Dorn admitted, "but it would punish the hostages more than it would him. They're probably tied up and immobile. Besides that, it might force his hand, and that's what we want to avoid. If there's going to be any chance of getting those three people away from him alive, we must avoid pressuring him."

"Do you believe he'll get tired of the game in time and release them unharmed?"

Dorn deferred to Dr. Kendall.

"Oh, it's no game, sir," the psychiatrist replied. "This killer is a desperate and tortured man who is controlled and directed by hostile, destructive forces. That doesn't necessarily mean he is bound to kill them. Much would depend on the nature of his past relationship with the hostages. Love? Hate? Fear? Jealousy? Unfortunately, up until now, it has been impossible for the police to determine any of these significant connections. They don't even know the identities of any of the four people inside the lodge. . . . As for the possibility that he will release the hostages, I'd say there's less than an even chance of that happening. But . . . with every hour that he delays killing them, their chances keep improving. He claims that he has made up his mind to kill them, and himself. I'm sure he believes that, but he is wrong. There *is* doubt in his mind, and the longer he ponders, the more confused his thinking becomes, bolstering that doubt. . . ."

"Buy time, it's the best we can do right now," Dorn amended. "Dr. Kendall makes a good point. But, aside from the psychological reasons, there is a practical advantage that extra time gives the prisoners. There are three of them. And, unless he keeps them bound hand and foot around the clock, they may get a chance to overpower him."

"Why is the FBI so quiet?" a female reporter demanded, drawing the anticipated laughter from her colleagues.

Hardy rewarded her with a polite smile. "That's easy, ma'am. We just don't have anything very bright to say. Captain Dorn summed up the common viewpoint of the case very thoroughly. And, then, as he told you before, the Federal Bureau of Investigation is not officially involved here. Mr. Anker and myself are sitting here at the invitation of the state police. As advisers."

"Dr. Kendall . . ." a reporter who was taping the session asked, ". . . what kind of a man would you say this sniper is? Is there some recognizable pattern to these people?" He held the mike high to catch the doctor's answer, and turned up the recording volume.

Kendall began to comb his sidewhiskers with his fingers, but quickly put both hands in his lap when he became conscious of a television camera aimed at him. Laymen took enormous delight in picking apart the Freudian significance of his most innocuous idiosyncracies.

He spoke slowly and carefully. "If you mean would you recognize him on the street? That is, could you tell by looking at him that here is a man who is going to run amok and do mass murder? No—the answer would have to be no." He smiled. "I might be looking into the face of such a man or woman this moment. And *you* might be looking into the face of such a man *right* now!" He paused to let the appreciative response of the press run its course before continuing.

"But if a psychiatrist—or even a psychologically oriented internist—were to observe him over the course of a few general sessions, almost certainly a distinctive behavioral pattern would emerge. . . . As I said before, this kind of human being is controlled by hostile, destructive forces. He would display violent, if repressed, hostility toward authority. Authority representing, unquestionably, his father by whom he feels, rightly or wrongly, he was rejected when he was a child. Those who knew him as a child, family, friends, would probably tell us that he was an unusually good child. Well mannered, unobtrusive, quiet. Never demanding.

"As my eminent colleague Laing describes it, the kind of child who '. . . will leave no fingerprints or footprints in the world.'

"This child, and then this man, tends to withdraw more, and more from a world he regards as hostile and dangerous. Retreat from *them*. He defends himself against this outer world by shutting himself away within his own self. His inner world becomes a besieged castle—like the lodge he has barricaded himself away in. But the human psyche cannot exist this way. It starves and stifles within its own walls. There is no way for it to go—except mad!"

Dorn's mind turned off the rest of it as Dr. Kendall suffered through a long exchange with a couple of amateur psychologists in the audience relating sexual repression to violence and murder.

Dorn had told the press that all the police could do for the present was to wait. Buy time. Inaction was not his style. There *had* to be another way, he kept telling himself. Ever since the reporter's excursion up to the lodge, his mind had been manipulating one small discovery, attempting to apply it to the problem. The discovery was just how easy it had been for Lewis to get to the lodge, literally knocking on the front door, after the killer had held a troop of professional policemen at bay all day. The kernel of it was that Lewis was one man. A single infiltrator. That's what it was going to come down to in the end, if the stalemate continued. A one-man raid.

The conference broke up shortly afterward, with Dorn thanking the newsmen for their attention and civility and promising to keep them informed through his liaison officer, Chief Lanier, of new developments in the case, if and when there were any.

It was ten after eight when Feldman separated from the other men in the hotel lobby.

"My wife," he said to Dorn. Obviously he was sorry to be leaving. "She's waiting for me to take her to that party."

"Sure, Sid, you go ahead," the captain said, smiling. "I'll see you later."

Feldman pressed his lips into a thin line, thinking he would definitely see Dorn again before the night was over. He wanted to discuss an idea with him. And privately.

"I'll catch up to you after the party," he promised.

Within the next hour two vital communications were received at West Village police headquarters.

The FBI had located Charles Roche in Phoenix, Arizona, where he was due to address a meeting of the Rotary Club at breakfast on December 26.

More significant: United Airlines had reported that the passenger manifest of its 11:50 A.M. flight to Denver, Colorado, on the morning of December 23, contained the name C. Schneider.

Feldman walked through the swirling snow back to the three-room apartment where he and his wife, Alice, lived in one of the corporation-owned resorts. The streets were busy with celebrants getting an early start on the evening's festivities. The bars were doing a heavy trade. Song and laughter filled the night. He looked up at the mountain looming over the village, an immense, dark-hunched, dominating presence. It was outlandish that death and violence lay in waiting up there, just outside the halo of lights on this night of nights. Christmas Eve. Peace and good will toward all men. He shivered and pulled his mackinaw more tightly around his thin body. The white dress shirt and thin suit left him defenseless against the freezing wind.

Although Feldman was a Jew, he had not practiced his religion since leaving his parental home. He was married to a Christian girl who didn't practice *her* religion either. She merely took the pleasures it had to offer. Christmas, Easter, the excuses for fun and parties. Cynically, he thought, "I'm a better Christian than she ever was!"

Quote: *Christian:* Unquote.

Sidney Feldman had quit after his first year at the City College of New York to enlist in the Army the summer North Korean troops marched across the 38th parallel. In the eighteen years of his life he had never been out of New York State—not even to New Jersey!—and he jumped at his first opportunity to accomplish that feat. After two years in Korea as a company clerk in a field hospital on the outskirts of Seoul, the Army had deposited him back in New York City with his wanderlust unslaked. The GI Bill came to his rescue, providing a free college education at a school of his choice and a small subsistence allowance. Freed from parental dependence, Feldman headed for the wide-open spaces. On his way home from Korea, he had spent a night in Denver, Colorado, and knew immediately he had found his true spiritual home. Sid Feldman, who from his East New York bedroom window could see a plot of green grass as big as a sidewalk flag and a patch of blue not much bigger.

"Don't Fence Me In."

On the train ride from New York to Denver, Feldman kept humming that stirring ballad over and over.

At the end of his first year at Denver University he had gone back to New York for the summer. The following year, he had found a job as a camp counselor so he could spend the summer in Denver.

In his senior year, he met Alice Carew, also a senior, the daughter of a building contractor whose specialty was construction work at winter-resort sites, an endeavor destined to become the biggest Western bonanza since the Gold Rush of 1849. With the advent of the jet and helicopter age, the high mountains and deep snows of the world's most natural ski country would become accessible to anyone with the price of an airline ticket.

Alice was redheaded, cute, plump breasted, and round hipped. She was also round heeled, but he didn't find that out until it was too late. He had been largely ignored by Alice in his first two years at Denver. She was rich and spoiled and had her pick of the big wheels on campus.

Her whirlwind courtship *of*—not *by*—small, sedate Sidney Feldman, lately of New York, was the talk of Denver's social set, as well as of the student body, in the spring of 1957.

He lost his virginity to her on their fourth date in the cramped upper berth of a double-decker bunk in an unfinished dormitory at one of her father's construction sites. In retrospect, Feldman suspected that Papa Carew had provided her with the key.

Six months after the wedding, Alice gave birth to a stillborn male child. It was not premature. Alex Carew hadn't lost a daughter; he had gained himself an accountant. Figuratively speaking, Sidney Feldman had "balanced the books."

Not that any of them ever talked about it. Feldman had never once mentioned her extraordinary gestation to Alice. But she knew. That he knew. And that put him one up on her.

That one, and the satisfaction of rejecting all of the cush job offers A. W. Carew endeavored to ease him into. Sid was a good accountant, and he never had any trouble finding a job at the resorts where they wintered in their nomad existence.

Their marriage had been a succession of resorts in the winter— Sun Valley, Jackson Hole, Squaw Valley, Taos, and infrequently, Eastern resorts like Stowe, Vermont. Alice considered Eastern skiing inferior to Western, and that was fine with Feldman. He had exiled himself from the past totally. "You can't go home again," novelist Wolfe had preached.

Now it seemed that Alice had found a real home at Aspen. It was their second winter in Snowmass and Feldman was beginning to feel a sense of permanency.

He let himself into the apartment and went into the bedroom without taking off his mackinaw. His wife was sitting at her dressing table wearing only a strapless bra and a half slip.

"And I thought I was keeping you waiting," he said.

She spoke haltingly as she applied her lipstick with meticulous care. "I would have . . . but . . . Jim Ennis dropped in . . . for a drink . . . just . . . as I was getting . . . out of the bath. . . ."

He watched her pretty, vapid face in the mirror, her wide eyes mocking him with their bogus innocence. She had never tired of this game, even after he had learned to play it on equal terms with her.

"Old Jim was here, huh?" he returned casually. "How is he? Smashed yet?"

"No, he and Betty Rait are going to a party in Aspen."

"Oh, Betty was with him?" He could have bitten off his tongue. Score one for Alice.

"Yes, they were sorry they missed you. What kept you so long anyway?"

"That sniper who shot all the skiers this morning. I've been helping out the police."

She spun around on the stool, her voice mirthfully scornful: "*You've* been helping out the police? Oh come on now, sweetie. You sure you haven't been hitting the bottle?"

He blushed. It was humiliating, but he couldn't control it. He turned away from her and began to remove his muffler and coat.

"I told them as much as I knew about the people who own that lodge. They still don't have any idea who's up there, the killer or the hostages."

She snorted. "Just another case of the police having their hands tied by all the Commy liberals on the Supreme Court. Daddy phoned me this afternoon to find out what was going on first-hand." And with sarcasm. "Inasmuch as you're working with the police, you can tell him a lot more about it than I can. Why don't you phone him back?"

"Not now, Alice. Maybe later, after—" He stopped.

"After what?"

"When I have something concrete to tell him."

She leaned forward so that her round breasts, pink and powdered from the bath, almost spilled out of the half cups.

"You think this bra is too risqué, sweetie?"

"Is it a costume party?" he asked. "Then you could say you were coming as a topless waitress."

"Oh, *you!*" She laughed delightedly.

Her breasts never failed to excite him. She knew that too. Knew all of his vulnerabilities, and how she relished exploiting all of them.

Putting down Sid was Alice's third favorite kick in life. Right in back of sex and skiing. In that order.

If he had asked her to make love, this moment, late as they were for their party, she would not have denied him. *What the hell! She wouldn't have denied anybody!* His mouth formed a wretched little smile, the way a child smiles after getting his tooth pulled to show the world that it didn't hurt a bit! And to keep himself from crying.

He gazed down at her breasts, preening themselves like partridges in the nests of the half bra. And masochistically he savored the irony and absurdity of his life.

"You know what Daddy says," she prattled. "Daddy says the National Guard should run a tank against that lodge up there. Blast 'em to smithereens!"

That sounded like Daddy, all right!

It was after nine o'clock before Dorn was able to reach Charles Roche at his Phoenix hotel. Roche sounded drunk. And he was totally unconcerned about the shootings at Snowmass. If anything, he was jubilant.

"Yes, *sir*, captain. I heard all about it on the radio and TV. All the bars here are tuned in for the news bulletins from your neck of the woods."

"I'll bet," Dorn said evenly.

"But why call me about it, captain?" Roche asked. "I don't have anything to do with that crummy bunch any more. I should of cut them years ago. Half of 'em are radicals. And the other half are queer." He laughed nastily. "Not 'fairy queer,' I don't mean. Though I've sometimes had my doubts about that creep Kaiser. Then there's—"

"Mr. Roche," Dorn cut him off, "I don't mean to waste your time or mine. The reason I contacted you is on the long chance that you may have an idea where some people are who we can't locate."

"Me?" He laughed again. "I just told you I don't know them any more." Dorn could almost see the sneer. "Not since Labor Day."

"Uh-huh . . . Well . . . it was only a hope, as I said."

Curiosity got the better of Roche. "Who are these people you can't locate?"

The captain wasn't about to reveal the names, but then he decided that it didn't make any real difference.

"Jack Whittaker and his wife. And the Schneiders and Kaisers. But we're pretty sure the Kaisers are out of the country."

"That's where *he* belongs. Out of this country. For good. Wally Kaiser is one of the radicals I was telling you about."

"All right, Mr. Roche." Dorn was anxious to terminate this pointless conversation. "We're sorry to have bothered you—"

"Now, wait a minute, captain." Roche was the least bit antagonistic. "*You* called me."

"I said I was sorry to have bothered you."

"Hell! Listen, maybe I just can help you, captain."

"How's that?"

"Because I know all of that bunch. You don't. So, if it comes down to Whittaker, Schneider, and Kaiser, I can tell you—I'll lay a C note to your sawbuck—who's behind that rifle up at the lodge."

"Oh?"

"Sure. It's easy. Forget about Carl and Wally. Neither one of them has the guts. It's got to be Jack Whittaker."

"He's got the guts?"

"Sure, old Jack has the guts. He's also crazy enough to pull a stunt like that."

"That doesn't tie in with what other people who know him say about Whittaker." Dorn told him. "As I heard it, he's a cool customer."

"Sure, you know the type. The quiet, cool ones. You never know what they're really thinking or feeling because they're loners. Jack always had a flock of people around him. Oh, everyone thought Jack was the greatest. But no one really 'knew' Jack, because he was a loner."

He chuckled. "The only one who ever cracked that cement shell he lives inside of was yours truly. He swung at me a couple of times, did you hear about that?"

"Yes . . ." It was all Dorn offered, waiting for the other man to tell him.

Roche seemed to be savoring the memory. "I tell you something, captain. I just wish there hadn't been anyone around to interfere. Just old Jack and me. Now, that would have been one for the book. I think it would have proved I was right about Jack Whittaker all along."

"Right about what?"

He said it with genuine admiration. "That that pacifist front he always put on was a load of b.s. At heart I think old Jack is a killer. The old killer instinct, yes siree, captain. I'll be waiting to see who it is when you pull his carcass out of that lodge." He hiccuped. "Don't forget to send me that sawbuck you're gonna owe me."

The line went dead as Roche hung up the phone.

Dorn stared intently at the phone in his hand. The dial tone had a hypnotic effect on his fatigued brain. He started as Swenson poked his head through the doorway.

"Hey, captain. Your phone is off the hook. And your wife is on the other line."

Dr. Kendall had invited Lou Santini back to his lodge for a late supper after the news conference.

"My wife died two years ago, but I say without any modesty that I am an excellent chef," he joked. "Would my eggs benedict appeal to you, Mr. Santini?"

Santini smiled. "Sounds great."

Truthfully, he had no appetite for food. His hunger was a more ubiquitous craving. It began in the nerve endings, a tingling sensation just below the top layers of skin. A maddening itch

begging to be scratched. A dryness in the throat. The muscles
bunching thickly at the back of the neck. A gnawing in the belly.
The quickening tempo of restlessness. And fear.

After eight years off the stuff, the fear was still there. Fear
that one day it would exceed the limit of his endurance. There
was an inevitability about it. He was like a person with an arrested malignancy. Yes, his addiction was a malignancy. Arrested,
not cured. Every morning when he woke up he would ask himself: "Is this the day it's going to get me?"

He heard Kendall's voice only dimly. "I acknowledge my
eggs benedict are a masterpiece of beauty, Mr. Santini, but they
taste good too. Dig in."

Santini smiled and poked his fork into the rich mound. He
washed the first mouthful down with hot black coffee, but not
before the exquisite flavor of the egg, ham, and sauce stirred his
listless taste buds.

He chewed the second forkful, savoring everything. "It's delicious, doctor." He meant it, and ate with gusto now.

By the time the plate was clean, the tension inside him was sub-
siding. He slouched in the straight-backed kitchen chair and lit
a cigarette with his second cup of coffee.

"You said earlier that you've been off drugs for over eight
years." Kendall's eyes twinkled.

Santini was amused. "You're a mindreader as well as a head-
shrinker. How'd you know I was thinking about a fix a while
ago?"

"Elementary, my dear Santini—to cop a phrase from a master.
With the strain of all this on your shoulders, the terrible un-
certainty, it would be unnatural if you weren't thinking of a fix."
He put a cold pipe in his mouth. "That's not out of the Psychology One text either. It's personal experience. I had a bit of a
problem with alcohol when I was younger. And believe me it
wasn't easy to kick either. Do you know, to this day, when I
feel abnormally pressured, I still long for a tall glass with three
fingers of Old Grand-dad!"

Santini was interested. "Do you drink at all any more?"

"Oh, yes, I'll have a social drink. But, when I have a craving for it, then I won't touch it with a ten-foot pole."

"It's strange you should say that, doctor. There's a line in a new play Jack Whittaker is doing for a television special that says almost the same thing. Something to the effect: 'If you want a thing too obsessively, the safest thing to do is to walk away from it. Tomorrow it won't seem that important to you. . . .' There's more to it, but that's the gist."

"What's the name of your cousin's play?"

"It's an adaptation from Edwin Arlington Robinson's *The Children of the Night*. The one about Richard Cory."

"Richard Cory! One of the most fascinating themes in the collection." Kendall placed both hands on the table and pushed his rotund body out of the chair. "Come into the study. I want to refresh my memory."

The doctor's lodge was one of the smaller structures at Snowmass, but it was also one of the coziest. In addition to a large combination living-dining room and a roomy kitchen, there was a small den with a fieldstone fireplace. The walls of the den were lined with books from floor to ceiling.

"You been coming up here long, doctor?" Santini asked.

"Since it's been in business. Before that my wife and I spent several weeks every winter in Aspen. Oh, I guess for four years. Not that we were skiers." He laughed so hard his belly shook like his facsimile's in the Christmas poem, the younger man observed with good humor. "Can you imagine me on skis?" They both laughed heartily.

"No, the fact is we wanted to retire to someplace with lots of mountains and snow and sky. Never were the Florida kind." There was an almost inaudible catch in his voice. "After Margaret passed on, I was going to chuck the whole idea. Then . . . well, she wouldn't have liked that at all. Sometimes I actually forget she's gone, and think I can hear her puttering about in the kitchen."

Santini cast his eyes down in respectful silence.

"Now, where is that book? Ahh, here we are." Dr. Kendall sat down in a chair across from him in front of the fireplace and opened a thick leather-bound volume.

Adjusting a pair of steel-rimmed spectacles on his nose, he read:

> "Whenever Richard Cory went down town,
> We people on the pavement looked at him:
> He was a gentleman from sole to crown,
> Clean favored, and imperially slim.
>
> "And he was always quietly arrayed,
> And he was always human when he talked;
> But still he fluttered pulses when he said,
> 'Good-morning,' and he glittered when he walked.
>
> "And he was rich—yes, richer than a king—
> And admirably schooled in every grace:
> In fine, we thought that he was everything
> To make us wish that we were in his place.
>
> "So on we worked, and waited for the light,
> And went without the meat, and cursed the bread;
> And Richard Cory, one calm summer night,
> Went home and put a bullet through his head."

A full minute went by before Kendall looked up from the page. His face was grave. "Did Jack Whittaker ever discuss this play of his with you?"

"No, he just mentioned that he was doing it. And liked doing it." His concern went deep. The doctor could tell. "Jack said . . . there was more truth in that short work than there is to be found in most novels."

As it turned out, Feldman, who was "invisible" at most social occasions (as Alice liked to point out) and preferred to keep it that way, was singled out as a celebrity at the Christmas Eve party. The "Massacre on Mount Baldy," as the newspapers and television commentators referred to the shootings, dominated the conversation, and word had gotten around that Sid Feldman was working closely with the state police on the case. When he tried to discount his role, it whetted their appetites.

"Still waters run deep. . . ."

"Who'd of thought it, little Sid?"

"You're holding back something, Sid, that's for sure."

Feldman gritted his teeth, pulled in his head, and bucked the mob at the bar. He was drinking more than he customarily did at parties, but was feeling none of the salubrious effects the others seemed to derive from booze. Alice, peeved at his popularity, was engaging in one of her typical sado-masochistic games to humiliate him by cheapening herself. She danced by the group he was with, locking pelvises with a boy no older than eighteen. Feldman did his best to ignore her.

"This is the most exciting Christmas Eve I've ever spent!" a little brunette from Alabama said breathlessly. "Just imagine, at any minute that old killer might decide to come down the mountain and start shooting up on us!" Her bosom heaved, her cheeks were flushed. Her eyes were on fire.

A bitch in heat!

Feldman turned away from her in disgust, but there was no escape.

"What do you say we go up there caroling?" one half-wit suggested. "You know what they say? 'Music soothes the savage breast.'"

"You know that's not a bad idea. Something like that just might snap him out of it. The Christmas spirit and all. I bet if we could get through to him he'd let those hostages go. For the sake of their families."

Feldman found himself wishing the killer *would* come down and fire a few rounds into this bunch. In alphabetical order. Starting with Alice.

In any order.

They were all mad.

Mad as *he* was!

And what about Sid Feldman? He felt his sanity slipping away. He had to escape from this rat pack. There was no way to get his overcoat without attracting attention, so he sneaked out the back door and turned the collar of his light suit coat up around his throat. The cold slashed deep to his bones almost at once. He welcomed its bite. It was bracing, sobering. He breathed in the clean night air thirstily. Letting it wash away the taint of the whiskey, the smoke, and the foul breaths. He broke into a jog, heading for the sheriff's office.

"Now you'll be careful, Les? You won't take any unnecessary chances? Promise me you'll be careful, Les. . . ."

Dorn laughed softly into the mouthpiece of the phone. "Now you know I'm always careful, hon. Don't worry. Yes, I promise."

It was a replay of the same conversation that had been going on between Lester Dorn and his wife Janet for over twenty years whenever he was away from home at night working on a difficult case.

In the beginning her exaggerated concern for his welfare was irritating, even though he never would have let it show. She'd have been hurt at that. But, with repetition, somehow the old refrain assumed a special dimension in their ripening relationship. One of the countless reaffirmations of their love for each other. Like the touch of a hand in the dead of night. Or the affectionate slap he gave her on the fanny when he came down for breakfast in the morning.

"Now take care, love, and stop worrying. I'm glad the kids are with you. Tell 'em Merry Christmas for me, and I'll see them tomorrow."

He hung up the phone very gently, in the light way he moved

around the bedroom when Janet was asleep. He did not want her to wake up to the truth. Please, God, not yet!

Exhaustion overwhelmed him. He braced his elbows on the desk and covered his eyes with his palms like a child playing hide-and-seek. Dorn was "it." He let out a long, plaintive sigh, grateful for this rare time of privacy over the endless day. Sheriff Malone had driven back to Aspen with the FBI agents on a police matter unrelated to this case. Max Lanier was making the rounds of the bars to see that everyone was abiding by the law and the spirit of the night. Routine.

Routine.

His mind played with the word. His life, their lives together, had been routine. And even his work (Janet's chronic worrying notwithstanding) had been routine as police work went. Robbery, assault, rape, murder too, were as familiar to Dorn after twenty-five years as accounting statements and PR releases were to Sid Feldman. Yes, their life together had been as routine as eating, breathing, sleeping, making love. Nothing wrong with routine.

A good, generous life. Two kids. Steve, twenty-two, safely home from Vietnam, and in his junior year at Colorado U. Ellen, nineteen, married ten months and already expecting his first grandson.

Dorn had to smile at his smug vanity. Grandson! Indeed!

How routine could life be?

He supposed that there were men and women who would find his kind of life deadly dull. Maybe so. But Dorn liked his comfortable rut.

This coming summer, though, they were—he wasn't quite certain of the proper tense any more—going to break out, he and Janet. Their twenty-fifth wedding anniversary in June. And, ever since their first, he had promised her that in that historic year he would take her on a South Sea cruise. Hawaii, Samoa, Bali, all the picture-book paradises she had dreamed of seeing since her childhood. He had all the steamship folders in the bottom drawer of his desk at home.

And underneath them, locked in his fireproof strongbox where they kept their insurance policies and wills (how appropriate!), a piece of paper that could change all their plans.

Could change their lives! Nothing was ever going to be routine again for Lester and Janet Dorn.

When Dorn first noticed his civilian shirt collars were getting tight, he paid no attention. Starched collars had always made him uncomfortable. He was surprised when his softer uniform shirts began to bind his neck. On top of that he weighed himself and discovered that he had lost four pounds.

The state police doctor squeezed and prodded him about the throat and in the pits of his arms and groins. He looked concerned and took samples of his blood.

The next day the doctor called him at the office: "Les, I'm going to set up an appointment for you to see Dr. Smythe in Denver."

"It's bad, doc?"

"I don't know. That's why I want Smythe to look you over." He's the best."

"In what?"

There was a hesitation. "Thyroid and gland man."

"What's wrong with my thyroid and glands?"

"I think you have—a tumor."

"Cancer?"

"We can't tell, Les. See Smythe."

"Sure."

Dorn told Janet he was going to Denver on police work that day. Dr. Smythe confirmed the preliminary diagnosis. It was a tumor, with a "strong likelihood of malignancy indicated because of the involvement of the adjacent lymph nodes. . . ." That was what the report said.

Dr. Smythe wanted to operate the following week. The week of Thanksgiving.

"No, sir," he declined quietly. "Not until after the holidays. My son just came home from Vietnam. I can't spoil things for him and his mother. This is going to be a very special Thanksgiving. We've got a lot to be thankful for. The biggest Christmas ever too. I'm sorry, doctor, but it'll have to wait."

Dr. Smythe was blunt about it. "If it's malignant, waiting that long could be fatal."

Dorn grinned. "Cancer usually is, isn't it?"

"Damn it, captain! You're more intelligent than that! Thousands of cancer victims are being saved every year. And the ones that die, in most cases, are the people who waited until it was too late. Like you."

Dorn was apologetic. "I'm sorry. I know you're right, but it's a chance I'll have to take."

What he did not say to the doctor was that a man had natural instincts about his own physiology that superseded clinical knowledge. The swelling in his throat had been going on for six months before his first visit to the doctor. Whatever it was he had, his case was a slow process.

One month after he consulted Smythe, if there had been any change at all, it was negligible. By Christmas week, Dorn was contemplating an even more dangerous gamble. He could make it through the summer. They would make their cruise. He was convinced of it.

The knocking on the half-open office door jarred him out of his ruminations. He rubbed his eyes with the heels of his hands and looked up. Feldman was standing in the doorway, shivering and brushing snow off his suit and out of his hair.

"The desk clerk said it was all right." the accountant said. "Did I interrupt something?"

Dorn snorted. "Hell, no. I'm glad you did. In another minute I would have been asleep. And that would have finished me. If I don't keep up a head of steam, I'll just poop out. Say, what are you doing running around on a night like this without a coat and hat?"

Feldman laughed nervously as he came into the office. "I guess you could say I made a jail break."

Dorn grinned. "That party?"

"I've attended more uplifting wakes."

"You'll be in the doghouse with the wife?"

"She'll never miss me."

A statement that had a disturbing ring of sincerity. Feldman was on the defensive. And not, Dorn sensed, because he had run out on his wife to play cops and robbers. That would be the least of their troubles, he decided.

"I want to talk to you, captain." The accountant sat down in a chair alongside the desk and removed his glasses to wipe the melting snow off the lenses.

Dorn leaned back and lit a cigarette. "Shoot."

Feldman replaced his glasses and looked straight into Dorn's eyes. "I know how we can take the sniper. Maybe even alive if we're lucky."

Dorn resisted the urge to smile. He'd been right. Sid Feldman did want to play cops and robbers.

"*We can take*. . . !"

"I'm all ears, Sid."

Feldman leaned forward and said in a low voice that was intended to be conspiratorial: "The air-raid shelter!"

Dorn drew a blank. "What air-raid shelter?"

"The one at the lodge."

"You've got to be kidding. Why in the devil would anyone want an air-raid shelter up here?"

"It was Forrest Evans' idea. His engineering company began building them as a sideline when the Cold War started boiling right after Kennedy became President. The Cuban crisis. The Berlin Wall. You remember, there was a big war scare for a while. Some states even were trying to pass legislation to make it compulsory for every homeowner to build his own shelter."

Dorn remembered it vaguely. Ancient history. Like flying saucers. "So Evans built shelters?"

"They were constructing these big pre-cast jobs that could be installed the way a cesspool is. Quickly and cheap. Anyway, the craze died and Evans was stuck with all these shelters. He had three or four of them shipped up here when the lodge was being built and had his own crew put them in. Joined together they made one hell of a big shelter. . . . I remember one day when the three of them, the owners, were down at the main office, the others were needling Evans about it. He said they'd all be singing a different tune when the Russian ICBM's started to zero in on NORAD headquarters and all the missile silos around Aspen."

Dorn's fatigue had evaporated. He was charged with excited anticipation. He could not quite grasp the rationale behind it, but there was real purpose to what Feldman was telling him. Something big.

"You know the setup in these home shelters, don't you?" the accountant asked. "The good ones have an escape hatch. *Away out from the house itself!*"

Dorn contained an impulse to leap up and hug the little accountant. "You know that for a fact? That this shelter has another exit?"

"Positively, Les. They had to file a copy of the blueprints when they built the lodge. I remember, the shelter was an afterthought, and a separate sketch was stapled to the main plan."

"Can we get at those plans?"

"Sure, I have a key to the office."

"Great! What a break this is!" Dorn was only halfway out of his chair before the doubts crowded ito his mind in rapid-fire order. He sat down again.

"If you remember the shelter, Sid, so has he," he said. "He'd make sure no one could get to him that way. I mean, it would be obvious."

"Not necessarily," Feldman pointed out. "It only came to me after I left the news conference at the hotel. A chance thought. He's got so much on his mind as it is. All that concentrating on what he's doing right now. Moment to moment. My hunch is that he hasn't given the shelter a thought. Down in a corner of a dark storeroom. Half hidden by junk that's piled up over the years. I doubt any one of them has given it a look or a thought for years."

"Yeah, yeah. Could be you're right." Dorn rubbed at his chin before lighting up another cigarette. *If the thyroid didn't get him, then the lungs would, that was for sure!* "But the escape hatch at the outside exit, wouldn't it be locked from inside?"

"I don't know. It may be," Feldman conceded. "If it is, it could be opened. You people must have experts at that sort of thing."

"Depends. It won't be an ordinary lock."

"Acetylene torch?"

Dorn grunted. "And light up the night like the Star of Bethlehem?"

Feldman shrugged. "Let's not look for trouble."

"You're right." A frown deepened the haggard lines around Dorn's eyes and mouth. "It's not going to be simple even if we can open the hatch. The other exit can't be all that far away from the house. He keeps a sharp lookout. Can you imagine trying to sneak a squad of armed men up the mountain, crossing all that open ground and then going single file into that hole in the ground without him noticing it?"

Feldman leaned forward, his eyes suddenly very intense. "I thought of that too, captain. It can't be done that way. It's a one-man job!"

Dorn was silent a moment, as the idea filtered slowly through his objective policeman's mind. It distilled favorably.

"You're right, Sid," he agreed. "It's a job for one man. Two would be better. For cover. We'll only get one chance, because once he knows about the loophole, he'll find a way to plug it." And added solemnly, "If he hasn't done that already."

"You'll ask for volunteers, I suppose?" Feldman asked in a tight voice.

Like they do in the movies, Dorn thought. Feldman was a nice guy though.

"We'll work it out," he said. "The first thing is for you to get those blueprints of the lodge. I'll have one of the boys drive you over there. You can't go on running around town in those clothes."

Feldman stood up. "Thanks. I'd better stop home first and change. Anyway, I have to pick up the keys."

Sheriff Malone arrived back at police headquarters a few minutes after ten o'clock. He was puffed up like an excited toad, ready to burst.

"We got a positive identification from one of the stewardesses on that flight the Schneiders were booked on from New York to Denver yesterday," he announced. "It was the eleven-fifty A.M. flight leaving from Newark Airport. Arrived in Denver at one-forty P.M. This girl remembers Mrs. Schneider. The FBI got a photo of her from the television network where she works. She's an actress on some soap opera."

"The stewardess is positive?"

"Absolutely. But they're going to check it out again with the crew on the charter plane that flew them up to Aspen."

Dorn reached for the phone. As far as he was concerned, that pinned it down. Carl Schneider and his wife were one of the pairs at the lodge. And he was confident that the other pair was Jack Whittaker and his estranged wife.

"So what's the next move, Les?" Malone demanded.

"Just a minute, Paul." He spoke briefly to Corporal Swensen on the phone. "Listen, cancel that call to Mr. Wendell Gates in Connecticut. Thanks."

Malone's eyebrows arched like caterpillars. "I don't get it, Les. I figured that was your whole point. Find out who the four of them are up at the lodge so maybe we can get some help from their friends and kinfolks?"

"That was the original idea," Dorn acknowledged, "but something's come up that may give us a chance to wrap it up real quick."

Malone pulled off his fleece-lined hat, revealing a polished pate with a few strands of dark hair brushed sideways across the crown. He patted them with his fingers.

"What are you talking about, Les?"

Dorn recounted Feldman's plan.

The sheriff was impressed. "I remember hearing about some nut up at Snowmass who had built himself an air-raid shelter. It was a running joke for a time. But I never connected it with Whittaker and his bunch. Hell, Les! I'll bet my badge it's Whittaker behind that gun!"

"I don't know." Dorn's hand went automatically to the pack of butts in his chest pocket, but he willed it back to his side. "If Whittaker was planning something like this, why did he invite the others? The Evanses, the Kaisers, and Santini?"

"There doesn't have to be a reason. The man is insane. It probably hit him suddenly, just went berserk."

"No matter. We'd better get on up to Sam's Knob. Feldman is going to meet us there."

When they walked out of headquarters into the night air, Dorn was blinded by driving snow and the steam of his own breath. The cold quickly penetrated the multi-layers of leather and wool, raising goose bumps along the thin skin over his spine.

"It's getting worse," he grunted, pulling on gloves.

"That's good," Malone said, drawing down the flaps of his hat to cover his ears. "His visibility will be cut down if it keeps up."

Dorn didn't reply. He was concentrating on which of the troopers up at the restaurant command post he would ask to accompany him on the perilous mission.

He came back into the bedroom after completing a tour of the upper floor. Since the intrusion of the A.P. reporter, he had shortened the interval between his sentry rounds to a half hour, staggering the schedule so that, if the police were spying, as he was certain they must be, they could not fix the time when he would be at any given place.

The women were huddled on the bed, wrapped in blankets and quilts. The hot-water heating system was not functioning properly. The radiators were blocked by air bubbles occasioned by the long period of inactivity before their arrival. And he was not about to take the time to bleed them. From sundown, the little electric heater had been steadily losing ground against the incursion of the wintry night.

The brunette watched him with a growing sense of horror and fascination. He was never still. Pacing the room when he wasn't stalking the dark hall and the other rooms. His affliction was worsening. A transformation, physical as well as mental, that had been coming over him since the previous night. More and more he reminded her of an animal. The slope of his shoulders. The cruel cunning mirrored in his face. The coiled readiness of his body. There was a rhythm in his every motion that reached past the civilized consciousness, reanimated in quiescent memory cells passed on from far-removed generations of primitives. A Stone Age being waking at night to stare into the burning eyes of a saber tooth tiger.

His fingers were incessantly busy on parts of the rifle, the way a dog worries a beloved bone.

A sound carried faintly to them from a distant corner of the house. Not a sound to arouse suspicion. A branch blowing against a wall, she thought.

"What was that?" he hissed.

She had been praying for exactly this kind of opportunity. She took a deep breath and said: "I think it came from the back. Somebody may be trying to jimmy the lock on the back door."

Muttering to himself, he went out of the room into the hall. For an agonizing instant, he hesitated outside the half-open door, and she was afraid he was going to lock it. But then he moved down the hall.

He had stopped locking them in right after he had stepped up his inspection rounds. The first time she attributed it to an oversight. But when he neglected the ritual a second time, the idea had kindled.

"I think I can get away," she whispered to the blonde while he was outside the room. "Next time he leaves."

The other woman gasped. "You must be crazy!"

"Look, hon, you have got to get hold of yourself. Calm down. I'm going to need your help. . . ."

As soon as he was off to investigate the mysterious sound, she threw off the covers and leaped out of the bed. She went to her suitcase standing beside the dresser and opened it. Her fingers searched inside for the wig and the plastic facsimile of a human head that it was fitted around to hold its shape. Shuffling back to the bed, she pressed the plastic oval into the pillow and arranged the false hair over it and fanning out on the pillow case. Then she rolled up a heavy comforter and piled the other covers over it. She stepped back to the foot of the bed and surveyed her handiwork. In the dim light, her hasty improvisation bore a passable resemblance to a woman curled up asleep.

She reached over the bed and patted the blonde's hand. "Now just keep talking to my twin here, and keep your fingers crossed."

"He'll kill me when he finds out," the other woman sniffled.

"No, he won't. All he'll have on his mind is finding me. And if you can buy me enough time, "I'll be waiting for him—with a gun!"

In her stockinged feet she hobbled over to the door, and peered out into the dark hallway. He came out of a room at the far end of the hall and crossed into the opposite room.

She was light-headed, and her heart was running wild inside her chest, but her legs were steady and her resolve was strong. She slipped out of the bedroom and started the maddeningly slow journey to the stairs, with the shackles confining her to mincing little steps. She had to be careful, too, not to let the steel bands strike each other.

Each step was a conquest of sorts.

And then the stairs themselves. Breath held in against the one with a telltale creak!

Halfway!

Now only four more to go.

She smothered an irresistible urge to take the last two steps in a single leap.

She huddled against the wall at the side of the staircase in pitch darkness, waiting. Then his footsteps sounded in the hall over her head. She marked his progress. Passing the head of the stairs. On to the bedroom. The closing of the door. Silence.

She knew the layout of the ground floor well enough to find the den without bumping into anything.

She experienced a quaking panic as she reached the library and had to hold on to the door jamb to keep from collapsing. *Steady girl!*

She moved inside the room and closed the door softly behind her. Now it was safe to risk a light. She pushed the silent mercury switch on the nearest wall. The sudden glare was a physical shock. She recoiled, throwing an arm in front of her face.

It passed quickly and she opened her eyes, bringing the room into focus. There they were. The rifles and sidearms in their neat racks along one wall.

The surge of elation and relief within her was so powerful she pressed her hands to her mouth to stifle its vocal expression. *Damn female emotions! That was all she had to do, whoop it up!*

She rushed over to the gun racks as fast as her hobbled legs would allow, almost falling against it. She put her hand on an automatic pistol, a heavy-caliber weapon. She wanted a gun that was easy to handle and with the authority to stop a—there was only one way to describe it—wild beast!

She tried to remove the pistol from the rack. It wouldn't budge. The reason was simple. A heavy wooden bar secured the handguns firmly in their slips. And a formidable padlock of layered steel held that bar in place. The rifle rack was secured in similar fashion with a twin lock.

"Oh, no!" she cried out softly.

Despair, displaced quickly by a reprieve. She remembered the keys to the gun racks were hung on a hook out of sight behind the bar. Another torturous trip with the steel bands cutting at her bloody ankles. And at the end of it—catastrophe! The hook was bare. The keys were gone. Unquestionably in *his* pocket!

It was only common sense. He would never have been so foolish as to leave the keys to the gun racks out of his hands.

Overcome by weakness, she slumped down on one of the bar stools. Her eyes roamed idly over the faces of the bottles on the backbar. She would have liked to pour herself a drink, Chivas Regal, light on the water. Well, why not? The condemned were entitled to a measure of self-indulgence.

She tried to imagine how it would be when he came after her. There was no doubt in her mind about one thing. He would kill her on the spot. He could no longer risk letting her live. Not after this. The idea of death pumped adrenalin into her bloodstream. New strength flowed back onto her limbs. She was not about to sit there waiting to die like a sheep.

She switched off the light and opened the door. Held her breath, listening. The house was peaceful and silent. She started down the hall toward the kitchen with small, shuffling steps. Again she risked a small light. She opened a drawer and chose the largest, sharpest carving knife. The feel of the solid bone handle in her hand was comforting. Not that it gave her any real protection against a rifle. She was not naïve. The knife was strictly a defensive weapon, and, if it was to serve effectively in that capacity, the element of surprise had to be on her side. Along with good luck. He'd be stalking her. That was her sole advantage. Her next move would be to see if it was possible to improve on that advantage. She switched off the light in the kitchen. The cellar door was in a small el of the kitchen that led into the dining room.

She opened the door and made a slow, tedious descent of the steep stairs.

The lodge's cellar was enormous and partitioned into innumerable small, dark, dank dungeonlike rooms which served various purposes. Furnace room, laundry room, a room housing a large frozen-food locker, and storerooms for sporting equipment and other paraphernalia. In the well-equipped tool room and workshop, she found a flashlight and a box of fresh batteries. She fitted three of them into the flashlight and tested it. It gave a wide, bright beam.

She began an inspection of the cellar, looking for a place to hide. Ideally, it should be strategically situated so that, in order to get at her, he would have to leave himself vulnerable, if only for one moment, to her knife. It was a tall order, she knew, and her sense of desperation and hopelessness intensified as she went from room to room. The only possibilities that suggested themselves to her were the deep freezer (she could turn it off, but it was an airtight locker), an old steamer trunk in one of the storerooms, and a tool locker in the workshop. All three were obvious. And, once he discovered where she was hiding, he would have her completely at his mercy.

There was a room, smaller than any of the others, in one corner of the cellar in which an assortment of canned goods was stacked on shelves that went from floor to ceiling. From the thick layer of dust that coated everything, it appeared that nothing in the room had been disturbed for years. All those stores lying there untouched, forgotten, Why?

The lodge had always been, primarily, a male domain. Those times when the men were accompanied by women, the women went along as guests, and had very few domestic responsibilities, outside of clearing the table after meals and stacking the dishes in the washer. The men purchased all of the supplies and very rarely did they seek distaff advice in stocking the larder or in the preparation of meals, which were generally plain, hearty fare served in large quantities. "Rib stickers," as Jack Whittaker once described the portions.

She had been down in the cellar only one other time that

she could recall. She had already turned away from the room when it came back to her.

The shelter! Forrest Evans' brain child! Or, as the other men used to call it, "Forrest's Folly." That's why all those cans were stacked in the room. Emergency supplies. Forrest had been so proud of his idea in the beginning, like a child with a toy. He had once spent two whole days in it to simulate the "real thing."

He soon tired of the novelty and, in time, the joke became stale too. She hadn't heard anyone mention the shelter in years.

On one occasion Forrest Evans had showed it off to the women, but she had refused to take the tour. The idea of constructing a thing like that was monstrous. Accepting the inevitability of nuclear warfare and the ultimate suicide of the human race!

She went back into the room and shone the light on the wall. The steel-plate entryway to the shelter, painted the same white color as the concrete and dust-covered, was almost indistinguishable from the wall. It had a small wheel handle which operated like the rotating handle on a bank vault. The wheel was stiff from disuse and she had to put down her light and turn it with both hands. The seal gave way with a low *whooshing*. The steel door swung out smoothly on its hinges. Beyond the entrance there was a pipe tunnel, about twenty-five feet long, that reached to another door similar in design to the first one.

Her arms and legs were trembling. She felt as if she were smothering, confronting that grim passageway, so narrow in diameter that it had to be navigated on hands and knees.

Fighting claustrophobia, she climbed inside and pulled the door shut behind her. The handle on the back side of the door duplicated the outside handle, but there was no way to lock it. Knife in one hand, light in the other, she crawled to the far end as quickly as she could. The chains on her ankles made a deafening clatter against the steel pipe. It couldn't be helped. Hopefully, the din would be muffled by the earth around it.

The second door opened with less effort. Gratefully, she crawled out of the pipe into a chamber the size of a large telephone booth. She could stand erect. In this space a circular steel staircase led down to another slightly larger chamber. She aimed the flashlight beam down the stairwell, judging it to be about thirty feet deep. Down there she could see a doorway, twice as wide in diameter as the tunnel entry hatchways. That would be the shelter.

This was as far as she intended to go. When he came after her, when he reached the end of that narrow tunnel, that would be her chance. Her only chance. Quietly she closed the door and turned the handle.

She settled down on the floor to muster will and strength for what lay ahead of her. The cold of the steel plates penetrated her clothing, touching her flesh with icy fingers.

The chill of the grave.

She uttered a small animal cry of terror and pressed her knuckles against her mouth to keep it from welling up into a full-blown howl. She didn't think she could bear that, the sound of unbridled desolation reverberating off these subterranean steel walls.

"This . . . this . . . this . . . steel-lined coffin!" she whimpered.

Dorn conducted his council of war at one of the big tables in the main dining room. A large relief map of the mountain was spread out on the table. The troopers listened attentively as Sid Feldman drew a cross on the map with a black marking pencil.

"The shelter's emergency exit should be just about here. I'd say it's fifty feet from the back side of the ridge. Now that ridge runs from west to east, you remember? The lodge stands on the highest point, and just behind it the bluff falls off sharply. According to these plans—" he tapped the pencil on the architect's blueprints he had removed from the office files "—the exit is concealed under the little gazebo back there near the tall pine."

"What in hell is a gazebo?" Chief Lanier asked.

"It's a little outbuilding. In the summer it's screened in. Whittaker had it built so he could get away from the others and work at his writing. In the winter it's boarded up."

"And probably covered up with snow," Sheriff Malone observed.

"No, the gazebo isn't bad at all. I had a look at it this morning when poor Potts got killed," Dorn said. "It's set in between these clumps of trees on three sides, and the ridge acts as a windbreak on the west. I'd say there's no more than a foot or two of drifted snow around it."

Malone inspected a crude but precise sketch that Feldman had made of the lodge and the immediate terrain around it. "You still won't have an easy time of it in the pitch dark and snowing the way it is." The sheriff was pessimistic. "These landmarks won't mean a thing."

"True enough," Feldman admitted. "Remember it's essential, captain, for you to approach the gazebo from due east. Follow this gulley I've lined in. It curves right around behind these trees. You'll come up on the gazebo so that it's between you and the house. That way you'll have some cover if he spots you."

"Won't make all that difference," Dorn said. "That ridge is too high. The gazebo won't provide much cover if he catches on what we're up to. From that angle he'll still have a clean shot."

"Yes," Feldman agreed. "But not once you get in close to the gazebo. Then you'll be out of the line of fire." He tapped the sketch with a fingernail. "The best thing is for me to lead you up there. I know this mountain as well as I know the back of my hand."

Dorn couldn't find any objections to the arrangement, as long as Feldman didn't get in the way. And it would certainly make things easier for him and Corporal Dietzel with Feldman guiding them over unfamiliar terrain in snowy darkness.

"All right, Sid. That's a good idea, but only on the condition that, when we're there, you'll backtrack for the restaurant."

"Sure," Feldman stretched his arms over his head and yawned. "I'm bushed anyway. You can fill me in how it all worked out tomorrow morning."

Dorn was more than a little surprised. That was the last thing he expected to hear Sid Feldman say. Not Feldman, the self-appointed Sherlock Holmes of Snowmass.

Feldman answered the captain's inquisitive gaze. "I'm kidding, of course."

"Yeah." Dorn scratched his chin stubble and kept studying the little accountant. There was something perplexing about his behavior, something not quite right. Off key. He did not have time to meditate on it. He picked up his coffee mug and drained it. "Well, maybe we'll know all the answers pretty soon now. Come on, let's move out."

Captain Dorn and Corporal Werner Dietzel made up the "attack team." Each carried a .38-caliber pistol and a light, compact U.S. Army carbine. Dietzel, a husky young man with a blond crew cut and a stoic face, was the top pistol marksman in the troop. Backing them up were four expert riflemen armed with high-powered rifles equipped with the latest U.S. Army "snooper" scopes. These telescopic sights, operating on the principle of black light, made it possible to sight a target in pitch darkness as clearly as in daylight.

"If there's any shooting, you'll have a big advantage on him," Dorn told them, "with these scopes and four times the fire power."

Feldman led the way over the mountain in the direction of the lodge. All of the troopers wore white jump suits and white caps to make themselves inconspicuous against the background of snow. Underneath the suits they had on bullet-proof vests.

Feldman worked the party into a position east of the high ridge on which the lodge stood. They crouched in a clump of small pine trees bent almost double under the weight of a thick blanket of snow, no more than twenty yards southeast of the gazebo. Feldman had picked this spot because the tall pine tree growing at the base of the ridge would block the view of the sniper if he was stationed at one of the windows looking out in this direction.

"Just fine, Sid," Dorn complimented his tactical expertise.

"There's only about twenty feet of open space we'll have to cross where he'll get a clean shot." There was a hitch in his voice. "I guess this is as far as you come."

Feldman acted as if he hadn't heard. "I'm dying to get a look at that shelter."

Dorn laid a hand on his arm. "Now, wait a minute, lad. You know better than that. I can't risk you mixing in this, Sid. You're a civilian."

Feldman laughed. "So who wants to mix in it? Are you kidding? All I want is a look at where that exit is. You said yourself he doesn't have a clean shot. And, even if he did, I doubt he could hit anything in this." He held up his face to the dark sky. The fine snow, cutting down smartly, stung his cheeks like wind-whipped sand.

Dorn gave in. "I guess we owe you that at least. All right, Sid, but you stay close to me and behind me just in case."

"Anything you say, captain."

The lodge remained dark and silent as they dashed out of the trees, across the hard-packed snow behind the ridge, and ducked behind the gazebo.

"My guess is he's asleep," Feldman whispered. "After a hectic day like he's had, he must be exhausted. He's got to sleep sometime."

Dorn grunted his dissent. "Not now," he said. "This is the one time when he'll be twice as alert. He'll be expecting us to make our move, if we're going to make one, before it gets light."

Feldman did not reply.

The floor of the gazebo was raised about three feet above the ground in the old-fashioned tradition on cement blocks at the four corners. The crawl space beneath it was enclosed in a wooden skirt. The troopers removed a section of the skirt big enough for a man to squeeze through, and Dorn crawled under the structure to reconnoiter with a dim, hooded light. He found a steel door set into a slab of concrete. It swung open like the hatch cover of a submarine. Thrusting the light into the opening, he saw a steel ladder descending into a dark well. The light was too poor for him to make out the bottom.

When he crawled back outside, they all sensed the restrained excitement in his voice. "Well, it's there, all right. If he hasn't blocked up the other end, we're as good as in the house now."

"Let me get a quick look at it, and then I'll get out of here before the fur starts to fly," Feldman said. He unhooked a flashlight from his belt.

"You watch that light," Dorn warned him. "We don't want to give him anything to shoot at if he's up there watching."

Then he paid no further attention to Feldman as he gave his troopers a last briefing. "You riflemen fan out there to the right at intervals of five yards or so. That way you can cover the back windows and this side of the house. On your bellies and try and use those drifts for concealment. Now, remember, don't shoot unless he offers a fair target. You got that?"

He and Dietzel watched them crawl out to take up their positions in a sweeping semicircle off the north side of the ridge. When they were in place, he said to Dietzel. "You ready, Verne?"

"Yes, sir."

They turned back to the gazebo.

"Feldman's had his look by now. Let's rouse him out of there," Dorn said. He went to the opening and peered under the gazebo. "Sid . . . Time to git." No answer. "Sid?" He switched on his light and put his head and shoulders inside. The crawl space was empty. Feldman was gone. "God damn!" he said softly.

He backed out and looked back in the direction they had come from. The snow-laden pine trees swayed back and forth. They looked like figures kneeling in prayer marking the mournful dirge of the wind.

Dietzel laughed softly. "Say, he sure took off in a hurry, didn't he?"

"I dunno." He brushed snow off his eyebrows with the side of his glove. "Wait here, Verne." He dashed across to the pine grove and looked for some sign of Feldman in the ravine leading

back to Sam's Knob. He couldn't see more than ten yards
through the snow and darkness. Well, it was plain that the man
was on his way back. He rejoined Dietzel behind the gazebo.
The corporal was amused by Feldman's hasty departure.
"Didn't even wait to wish us luck."

Dorn glared at him, but said nothing. Motioning for the
corporal to follow him, he crawled under the gazebo and over
to the yawning hatch. He was motionless for a few moments,
staring down into the well pensively.

"No, no," he said to himself, shaking his head. He wouldn't
even let himself think such an outlandish thing! Then he swung
a leg over the side and felt for the ladder with his foot.

He tipped the bottle up vertically to his mouth and sucked
out the last few drops of bourbon. He cursed and glared at
the blonde woman balefully. She was sitting up in the bed with
her arms wrapped around her knees. For the last half hour she
had been prattling inanely.

"Why don't you shut up?" he shouted at her. "She's not even
listening to you. Your gibberish has put her asleep." He laughed
harshly. "Is she asleep? Let's find out." He drew back his arm and
hurled the empty bottle in the direction of the bed.

The blonde screamed and ducked away as it hit the mound on
the bed beside her with a dull thump.

"What the hell!" Slowly he walked toward the bed. At the
same time he unslung the rifle from his left shoulder. Something
was wrong. He'd hit her hard. Right in the back. Not a stir.
She just kept on lying there as if nothing had happened, with
her face buried in the pillow, pretending to be asleep. She was
a contrary bitch who'd been doing her best to deprive him of
the satisfaction that she was hurt and scared. But this was too
much even for her!

He stood over the bed now, staring down at her hair fanning
out on the pillow. His hand reached out. His fingers twisted in
her hair.

He recoiled in shock, with the wig coming away in his hand! Still clutching the wig, he ripped back the covers, exposing the rolled-up quilt.

"*You!* YOU!" he screamed at the quaking woman on the bed. "You tricked me!" He brought up the rifle and thumbed the safety. He had every intention of killing her.

"No, don't! Please!" She floundered across the bed toward him awkwardly on her hands and knees like some grotesque crab. She cringed before him, holding up her hands in supplication. "You can still catch her if you hurry. I told her she couldn't get away. But she wouldn't listen."

He was distracted from his purpose. *She.* Yes, it was the other one he had to be concerned about. This one could *wait*. *She* was loose. A long time loose. How long had it been since he had returned from his last tour? Fifteen minutes? She couldn't have gotten very far with those cuffs on her legs.

"I'll find her," he mumbled. The pain was numbing his brain.

"Yes, hurry!" she urged him.

He turned away from her and walked to the door. Halfway down the hall, he stopped. Oh, no, not this time! He came back and locked the bedroom door. Rifle held at the ready, he commenced the hunt.

The blonde woman fell back exhausted. Once again she let herself drift into that timeless state which lay somewhere between consciousness and unconsciousness, a world without end and where nothing existed that could harm her or frighten her or destroy her. She resented the distraction of the voice that kept trying to call her back from her safe dream world.

"No, leave me alone," she said petulantly.

"Please . . . water . . . I need water."

She was puzzled. It was a disturbing voice. A suffering voice. And she knew that was wrong. There was no suffering in her other world. Reluctantly, she let the voice pull her back to the real world. She sat up on the bed and stared at the trussed-up figure on the chaise longue. He was moving. He was talking.

"Water . . . I'm burning up. . . . Please, will somebody give me water?"

She got off the bed and walked toward him. Twice weakness and the chains on her ankles joined to make her fall. The last time she crawled the rest of the way on her hands and knees.

She bent over him, looking into his half-open eyes with disbelief. "You're alive. We thought—"

"Dead . . . Not far from it. What's happening?" He strained feebly against the wire binding his wrists, gave it up. "Can you get this stuff off me?"

Her fingers fumbled futilely at the tightly wound wire. She shook her head. "It's no use."

"Maybe you can cut them. Find some scissors."

She shook her head. "He took all that kind of thing away."

"Then get me some water."

She braced her hands on the side of the couch and pushed herself up. On her feet, at last, she set out at a weaving, snail's pace toward the bathroom. An interminable journey. He was lapsing into unconsciousness by the time she returned with a half-filled glass of water and a wet wash cloth. She fed him the water slowly. The drink and the cold cloth on his forehead gave him some relief.

"How long have I been out?" he asked her.

"Since yesterday."

"My God! What's going on?"

"He's going to kill us." Her voice was dull. She looked like a zombie. He's killed a lot of people. "It won't be long."

The shock was too much for him. He felt himself blacking out again, battled against it frantically. How could the whole world change so monstrously? How long had it been? Yesterday, she'd said. Twenty-four hours. It was too incredible.

Not long after their youngest child had turned ten, Wendy Gates Schneider had resumed her acting career, defying the

apoplectic threats and arguments of her irate husband, Carl.
"Besides, we can use the money," she told him maliciously.

It was the ultimate weapon that could always deflate Carl and
send him crashing down to defeat. Wendy used it with the skill
and versatility of a surgeon's scalpel to castrate him in all kinds
of battles that had no relevancy to their finances whatsoever.
The intimation that he had failed his wife and children. That he
had fallen behind his friends in the game of life in humiliating
fashion. That she could have done so much better in the marital
derby. Yet, of all the handsome, talented, successful men who
had wanted to marry her, she had chosen lowly Carl Schneider.

And he damned well better never forget it.

He never would.

Wendy was too realistic to believe she could make a comeback
on the stage at her advanced age of forty plus. She honestly
doubted she could have made it at ten. Otherwise, why would
she have married a chump like Carl? *Not just* to spite Jack
Whittaker. Spiteful she was. But not that spiteful. The truth was
—and Wendy suspected it was an eternal truth in every marriage, regardless of the maudlin and lofty rationalizations the
partners duped each other with—that a man like Carl satisfied a
very specific and urgent need within her. He was a whipping
boy, a doormat, a convenient scapegoat to blame her own failures on. And she could make him sit up and beg for sex the way
a dog panted for his Yummies. All in all, it was a satisfactory
arrangement, and, after she reinstated her career in television
drama, Wendy envisioned unlimited vistas in front of her.

She was still beautiful, and her figure was more lush than it
had been when she was a lanky twenty-year-old fashion model.
From a cool, ethereal blonde she had become a sultry, vibrant
brunette. She had acquired chic and maturity. That was the
vital ingredient.

And it was her maturity that made her realize that she and
Jack Whittaker had always been temperamentally unsuited to

each other. They'd have been at each other like cats and dogs if she'd married Jack instead of Carl. They would have broken up in one year, she projected.

Yet she was surprised at the thrill of satisfaction it gave her when Wally Kaiser told her that Jack and Mae were getting divorced. She probably would not have accepted that lunch date with Wally if she hadn't been so hungry to learn all the sordid details of their marital breakup. An irony that impressed itself on her later with indelible remorse.

The phone call from Wally on Monday morning had puzzled Wendy. Carl had spoken to Wally the previous Friday, and Wally had not mentioned that Jack and Mae were breaking up. Or had he? It would be like Carl to "forget" to tell her an intriguing item like that about Jack Whittaker. After all these years, he was still carrying the green-eyed monster around on his back where she and Jack were concerned.

Of course there was a possibility that Wally had withheld the news from Carl so that he would have an excuse to hold a tête-à-tête with her. It was a flattering thought, but she discounted it. Wally's ardor for her had cooled off a long time ago. In recent years when Wally made a pass at a woman, it was obvious that there was no serious intention behind it, but that he was motivated by some immature notion that it was expected of him. To prove that there was still fire in the aging philanderer.

There was nothing flirtatious in his manner. In fact he sounded very grim about Jack and Mae.

"It's a rotten thing to happen to Jack," he said. "Especially now."

"Oh, come on!" she said lightly. "So he broke up with his wife. It's the great American pastime."

"There's more to it than that, Wendy," he said with an air of mystery. "Look, can you have lunch with me today? I'll tell you all about it."

She hesitated, wondering whether Wally was going to start the old routine again after so many years of good behavior. Hand on the leg under the table. No! Her instinct told her it was not a line. He was too earnest.

"All right . . . if it isn't going to be a drinking luncheon, Wally. I have rehearsals later on this afternoon."

"That's fine. No boozing." There was an odd inflection to what he said next. "Thanks, Wendy. This could mean a lot to Jack."

"Our having lunch?" The suspicion was back. "Say, Wally, what are you up to anyway?"

"It isn't something I can discuss over the phone, Wendy. But it is important. To all of us. Not just Jack."

"All right," she agreed. "What time and where . . . ?"

By the time she left the studio at noon, her curiosity was overpowering. She took a cab to the restaurant he had named instead of walking the eight blocks.

Whatever doubts she had about Wally's purpose in arranging this meeting were resolved as soon as she saw him. He rose stiffly and took her hand when the waiter brought her to his table, ignoring the cheek she offered for the traditional friendship kiss. His face was grave and strained. He looked older and thinner than when she had seen him a few months earlier at the lodge.

"Thanks for coming," he said. "What are you drinking?"

"Something weak. Dubonnet, I guess."

"One Dubonnet on the rocks and another of these," he told the waiter, tapping his finger on the rim of his empty martini glass.

Wendy pulled off her gloves. "How are Diana and the children?" she asked, anxious to get over with the amenities.

"All fine. The kids will be spending Christmas with Di's folks. Carl said yours will be free-loading at your parents' too."

"Carl never said anything to me about Jack and Mae," she came straight to the point of this luncheon.

"Didn't he? Well, maybe I didn't tell him. I don't remember. All those last-minute details to work out. Did the old boy get off safely to that convention on Saturday morning?"

The subject of her husband's job was a stifling bore to Wendy. And those abominable sales conventions he was always rushing off to merrily! He had inveigled her into attending just *one*. That was it! Three days of scintillating dialogue about shoes and feet! She shuddered.

"Yes, he got off to his old bunion bash."

Wally chuckled. "Bunion bash. I don't imagine our boy would appreciate that."

"Carl told me you and Diana had a rugged week ahead of you too?"

He groaned. "Murderous. We're booked on a six-o'clock flight out of Kennedy tonight to Haiti. Reynolds, *Kaiser* and Price is bidding for an airline account plugging Caribbean package tours."

Wendy smiled furtively. He always managed to get the name of the firm into every conversation, with the emphasis on *Kaiser*.

"You plan to fly back on Thursday, don't you? Maybe I'll bump into you and Di in Denver. I've got a reservation on the noon flight out of Kennedy. It arrives at Denver a little after two. Carl won't be able to get out of Miami until late Thursday afternoon, so I don't have any idea what time he'll get to Snowmass."

"Well, that's what I wanted to talk to you about." He grabbed his martini off the tray before the waitress had a chance to serve Wendy's Dubonnet.

"Cheers." He gulped the drink.

Wendy frowned. "Hey, easy, boy. I thought this wasn't going to be a wet lunch."

"Sorry. You can coast on your one Dubonnet if you want to. I'm very up-tight and I don't mind admitting it. Ever since I saw Jack yesterday."

"You saw Jack Whittaker yesterday?"

"Yeah, At Kennedy Airport. He was on his way to Chicago and he asked me to have a drink with him. He looks God-awful. He's been on a binge ever since Mae left him."

"*She* left him?"

"Well, I don't know whose idea it was, but she walked out."

Wendy was skeptical. "I didn't think Jack was the kind to flip over something like that."

"It isn't just that. The breakup is just one of a long list of misfortunes that have hit him lately. His new play was supposed to open this coming summer, but the backers pulled out at the last minute. And he's been taking a beating on the market."

"I read not too long ago that he was writing a dramatic special for television."

"Yes, and he's having trouble with that too. You know how it is. He's in a dry spell. Nothing's going right for him. Incidentally, we were talking about you."

"Me? You and Jack were talking about me?"

"Yes, he's caught that soap you're in a few times. He says you're damned good." His eyes shifted down to the martini glass. "I know I shouldn't be the one to tell you this, Wendy. But Jack is seriously thinking of testing you for a part in his TV play. A big part."

"You're pulling my leg!" She didn't believe him for a minute.

"No, but it would be fun." He winked with a trace of the old wolfish gleam in his eye. "But, seriously, I mean it. He is considering you for the part. Don't let on I told you, please."

Wendy felt suddenly euphoric. "I think I will have that martini after all," she said in a dazed voice. "I—I don't know what to say. I didn't think Jack Whittaker knew I—" It almost slipped out: ". . . *knew I was alive.*" She dropped her hands into her lap to hide their trembling. ". . . that he took me seriously as an actress."

"Well, he does. But that's not why I asked you to lunch today, Wendy. The thing is, Jack's going up to the lodge on Wednesday."

She was perplexed. "So?"

"He'll be up there *alone.* The rest of us won't get to Snowmass until Thursday."

He sounded so sinister she had to laugh. "Well, now, Wally, Jack is a big boy."

He gazed at her with solemn reproach. "Wendy . . . I don't think you've been listening to me. This is a bad time of the year for lonely, despondent people like Jack. Lots of suicides around Christmas—"

"Oh, Wally!" She was shocked. "You aren't serious?"

"I'm damned serious! I don't think that, in his present frame of mind, he should be alone up there for even one night. Believe me, I know what I'm talking about!'

She was shaken. Being alone in that big dark lodge on a desolate mountainside at night with the wind whistling in the eaves was enough to drive anyone to suicide. Wendy didn't like the lodge, even in daylight. But at night! Alone! Just before Christmas! The idea of Jack Whittaker alone and full of despair wrenched at her heart. Fanned a tiny spark that was still alive in the ashes of her old love for him.

Her martini arrived and she picked it up gingerly with both hands, but it spilled over onto her napkin.

"What I had in mind," he went on, "is a change in our plans. If I put my mind to it, I can wind up my business in Haiti in one day instead of two. That way Di and I can fly back on Wednesday instead of Thursday."

"Oh, Wally, that's wonderful. Then Jack won't be alone." Impulsively she reached out and put her hand over his where it rested on the tablecloth. She felt warmer toward Wally than she could ever remember. She wondered why.

She was beginning to feel lightheaded from the two drinks on an empty stomach. All the tables around them with the spirits flowing freely and the laughing voices bubbly with the joyous season—it was infectious.

He was smiling at her benignly, patting her hand. "Well, what are friends for, dear? And I kind of thought you might like to come up to Snowmass a day ahead of schedule and be with us. The more the merrier. And Jack could use the cheering up." With studied casualness, he added. "I know you could do more to cheer him up than Di and I could."

"Wally!" She tried to pull her hand away, but he gripped it tightly.

"Wendy, you and Jack were very close at one time. I know that. And it wasn't all that one-sided as he may have led you to believe."

"Please, Wally! That was over and done with a long time ago."

"No treasured memories at all?"

"None."

His smile mocked the lie. "The point is, Wendy, at a time like this when one woman has just rejected him, it would give Jack a big lift to have a woman around who can relate to him in a positive way. Please—" he silenced the objection before she could make it— "I'm not suggesting anything like a romantic relationship. I'm talking about friendship. Platonic friendship. A man and a woman who have a respect and affection for each other that goes back over most of their lifetimes."

He was looking at her in that intimidating way he had always had of making a girl worry that her lipstick was on crooked or her deodorant wasn't holding up.

"We want to make sure Jack finishes that play you're going to get a role in, right?"

You son of a bitch!

The old Wally. So knowledgeable of human frailty and the art of abusing it.

She was genuinely distressed at the ugly prospect—not that she accepted it—that Jack Whittaker *could* kill himself. It was too preposterous! But there was the other covetous side of her nature, appalled that, if he did, her golden opportunity of getting a significant dramatic role in his play would die with him! Wendy was helplessly tangled up in her emotions.

"Oh, come on," he said jovially. "What difference is it going to make if you come up to Snowmass one day earlier? Your hubby is living it up in Miami. . . . Besides," he added slyly, "it will give you and Jack some time together to discuss your role in his play. Without old Carl to throw in the monkey wrench. Know what I mean?"

She did indeed! Carl's reaction to that gem was all too predictable. She smiled and Wally smiled with her. In one swig she downed the martini.

"I'll phone Carl tonight. . . ."

Carl was not in his room when she phoned him that night at the Desert Inn in Miami. She left a message for him to return her call as soon as he returned. But she still had not heard from him by noon of Tuesday. She tried again at three that afternoon, and the phone was picked up. A cacophony of deafening music, braying laughter, and raucous voices assailed her eardrum. Eventually, Carl got on the line. He was drunk.

"Sorry, hon. I kept meaning to call you, but something always got in the way."

She could hear the "something" in the background, a whiskey-tenor broad speaking to him *sotto voce:* "Let me get you a refill, honey."

"I'm going up to Snowmass tomorrow instead of Thursday, Carl," she said loudly.

"No kidding? How's that, dear?"

"Wally and Diana are going to get there a day early, and I thought—"

Her explanation was washed out by loud, hysterical screeching from his end.

" 'Scuse me a minute, hon." The bedlam was stilled as his hand covered the mouthpiece.

Wendy sighed indulgently and hummed a phrase of "Raindrops Falling on My Head," while she waited.

He came back on apologetically. "I'm really sorry, Wendy. What did you say?"

The background din was still deafening, and she could hear the woman nagging at him: "You got to tell me now, Carl, honey. Are you going with us to the Washburn party? I got to let Si know."

Wendy said it loud and clear: *"I am going up to the lodge tomorrow to have an affair with Jack Whittaker!"*

"Jack . . . old Jack . . ." he said vaguely and hiccuped. "You tell Jack we'll tie one on when I get there on Christmas Eve. . . . Wendy, you there?"

Smiling smugly, she replaced the phone gently in its cradle. In thirty seconds he wouldn't remember he had talked to her. He was that drunk. And occupied. She hoped that "something" would make it worth his while.

Wendy felt a lot better now about her decision to go along with Wally and Diana.

And Jack!

Who could tell? Maybe Wally was right.

"No treasured memories . . . ?"

She wasn't all that certain.

Nothing permanent, of course. Neither of them would want that. But—how to describe it delicately?

A brief interlude?

And the icing on the cake.

Jack's play!

Wendy felt elated and exhilarated.

Wally and Diana Kaiser were waiting for her at the gate when her DC-7 landed at Denver Airport at 2:15 P.M. on Wednesday afternoon.

Wendy and Diana touched cheeks warily like two boxers touching gloves before the start of a bout.

"You look absolutely fabulous, Wendy!"

"You too, Di. I adore your coat. Is it new?"

Diana laughed harshly. "I don't know. An ex-client gave it to my husband in payment for a bad debt. What do you think, dear? Maybe it's hot!"

Wally glowered at her. "That isn't funny, Di!"

"I don't think so either," she sneered.

Wally ignored her and put an arm around each of the women. "Come on. Jack is waiting for us at the terminal bar. He got in from Chicago about an hour ago."

He explained that Jack had been conferring with Hugh Hefner of *Playboy* magazine about writing an article on the modern film.

That was unexpected good news for Wendy in view of what Wally had told her of Jack's morbid depression on Monday.

"Oh, it doesn't mean a thing," Wally discounted her optimism. "You know Jack. He puts up a great professional front. I'm sure he impressed the hell out of Hef, and then folded up when he got back to his hotel room."

"I think it's all a lot of damned nonsense!" Diana snapped, pulling her autumn-haze mink more tightly around her well-girdled form. She was getting plump, Wendy noted with feline satisfaction.

Diana glared at her husband. "I'm convinced he planned this whole moronic outing to spoil my holiday. Can you imagine coming back to all this ice and snow when we could have spent the week in the Caribbean? At company expense, no less! You know, Wendy, it's been ten years since this man has taken me anywhere further than the local movie house?"

She never let up all during the long walk through the terminal.

They found Jack Whittaker in the terminal bar. He was sitting at a table staring into an old-fashioned glass that, from its dark color, was filled with straight whiskey. He didn't see them right away, so Wendy had an opportunity to study him with his guard down. He was drawn and red-eyed, as if he hadn't slept well. His gestures were belligerent, the way he slammed down his glass hard on the table, the way he pulverized his cigarette butt in the ashtray. The thrust-out jaw.

As soon as he became aware of them, the mask slipped into place. He greeted Wendy courteously, but there was no real welcome either in his smile or in his voice. "Well, hello, Wendy. I didn't expect to see you and Carl until tomorrow."

Wendy's mouth opened soundlessly, but Wally came to the rescue.

"What's sauce for the goose, you know, Jackson. Old Carl is living it up in Miami. Old Wendy decided she'd come up a day early and help us paint the town red tonight."

"West Village?" Jack snorted. "Now that is some comparison. How is Carl?"

"Oh, he's fine." Her throat was dry.

"And the brood?"

She laughed nervously. "They're not brooding, I can tell you that. Driving Grandpa and Grandma crazy."

Jack frowned disapprovingly.

"I can't get over the idea of you people deserting your kids on Christmas," he said, his gaze traveling from Wendy to Diana. "It's such an important family holiday. I remember once my father driving two days and two nights to make it home on time so he could see my sister and me open our presents on Christmas morning."

Diana's face was frozen. Wendy stared fixedly out the window at a 747 jet landing on a nearby runway. Wally smiled imperturbably.

"You and I were depression kids, Jack. It was an event to get a stack of gifts all at once. Today, Christmas comes two and three times a week at our house. Probably at Wendy's too. It's 'gimmee, gimmee, gimmee!' all the time. And we give."

Jack frowned. "I wasn't talking about the gifts, Wally."

Wally let out a groan. "Yeah, I know, old man, it's the 'spirit of Christmas' you're talking about. Good old-fashioned Jack. Jackson, we all love you." He laughed and rumpled Jack's hair.

Diana's face was ugly. "All right, kiddies, suppose you two save your *profound* discussions and your *not-so* profound drinking for later on. What about our charter plane?"

"I would have taken care of it," Jack told Wally, "but none

of us were very definite about our arrival times. The shuttle service is busy as hell today. We may have a long wait for a plane to Aspen."

Wally stood behind Jack and placed his hands on his shoulders. "You just sit and relax and finish your drink. I'll arrange everything." He chuckled confidently. "I have a couple of VIP cards in my wallet that guarantee preferred treatment. Don't you worry."

"Pompous ass!" Diana muttered as he strode away.

"Well, tell me about you and Carl," Jack said quickly to Wendy, pretending not to have heard Diana. "It's been a long time. What have you been up to?"

Wendy was disappointed. He knew what she was up to. Wendy Gates, queen of the television scene! Ready to knock 'em dead in Jack Whittaker's sensitive new dramatic work! She almost laughed aloud at her naïveté. What had she expected him to do? Sign her to a long-term contract right here at the airport bar?"

She smiled. "Oh, we're all just fine, Jack. How have you and—" She caught herself, but she might as well have finished it.

"Mae and I are separated," he said quietly. He shook a cigarette out of the pack on the table and turned it over in his fingers, inspecting it carefully before he lit it.

"That's right, I'd heard." She laughed to cover her embarrassment. "So many of our friends have been getting divorced or remarried it's hard to keep track of which ones are doing what."

He stood up with his empty glass. "The service stinks today. You save time going to the bar. What can I bring you gals?"

"Nothing for me!" Diana kept watching the doorway, her face surly. "And see if you can find out what's keeping that husband of mine while you're at it."

"I'll pass too, Jack." Wendy wanted a drink, but Diana's disapproval would have taken the pleasure out of it. She glanced at her hard profile, thinking:

"You always were a bitch, my girl."

"What time will Carl get in from Miami tomorrow?" Diana asked.

Wendy shrugged. "When he gets here. He couldn't be sure what flight he'd be on. Before midnight, I hope."

Diana shivered and pulled her coat around her again. "This damned climate! God, how I hate the cold!"

She complained about everything. The bumpy flight. The frigid weather. The food. The service. Wally's job. And mostly about Wally himself.

That was the curious thing. In the early years of their marriage, Diana had bored everyone to death boasting about her husband. Her "ideal" husband.

Now she was picking on all the petty, imperfect traits that made him human like everyone else. Wendy's ears began to ring from the incessant whine of her nagging voice.

She got up abruptly. "Excuse me, Di. I've got to find the powder room."

On her way out of the ladies' room she met Wally coming back from his mission. He was gay and exuberant, and from the high color in his cheeks she guessed he had managed to charm the hostesses out of a few extra drinks on the flight into Denver.

"Everything's set. We take off in forty minutes. Just in time for a quick libation . . . Oh, by the way, We're booked on this flight as 'Mr. and Mrs. Smith' and 'Mr. and Mrs. Jones.' "

She looked at him in amazement. "Why did you do a thing like that?"

He acted perplexed himself. "That's how Jack wanted it. From what I can gather some people, reporters maybe, have been on his trail. He doesn't want them to trace him up to Snowmass."

"How strange." A small thing, but it dismayed her.

"Yes . . ." he mused. "Classic symptom of paranoia, of course. Persecution complex."

"He *seems* so normal. A little tense, but so are we all these days."

"Jack's going to be all right now that he has his friends around

him," he said stoutly. He put an arm around her waist and
squeezed hard. "Everything's going to be just fine, doll. Big
Daddy says so."

Conversation on the flight to Aspen was curtailed by the
loudness of the Beechcraft's twin engines.

"Bad mufflers!" Wally shouted.

"No mufflers!" Jack shouted back.

Diana sat with her eyes closed and her mouth pressed into a
thin, suffering line, fingertips soothing her temples.

The taxi ride from the airport to the lodge was not any more
conducive to communication. The driver, who had resided in
Aspen for less than one month, felt obliged to entertain and
educate them with a monologue on the resort's attractions that
had obviously been memorized from a Chamber of Commerce
brochure.

The lodge had been made ready for them by a caretaker who
was gone when they arrived. The central heating was on, and
wood fires had been laid in the fireplaces in the den and in the
living room.

Wally and Jack carried the suitcases upstairs and left the
women to change their miniskirts and high heels for more suitable
garb. Diana called to Wally as he was going down the stairs.

"Give me the key to your suitcase, and I'll unpack for you!"

"Don't strain yourself, dear," he called back, winking at Jack.
"I'll do it later."

The two men and Wendy went into the den and mixed
martinis.

"First today," Wally said, upping his glass.

Jack studied his friend's bloodshot eyes. "I'll bet."

"Martinis, that is." Wally giggled. "Are we well stocked in
that department in case we're snowed in?"

Jack snorted. "There's enough booze in this joint to last out
a siege."

Their eyes met, and neither of them said anything else for a
long while.

. . . *to last out a siege* . . .

The nightmare was beginning.

As the afternoon wore on, and the men drank continuously, the relationship between them grew strained.

Predictably, when he reached a certain level of intoxication, Wally would talk of nothing else but his business. Reynolds, *Kaiser,* and Price.

"Ken keeps insisting that I put my name up front, but, hell! That would only disturb the rhythm of the title that all of our clients have grown accustomed to. Not that he's wrong. I'm the one who's carrying the weight of the organization on my shoulders, but you both know me. I prefer to stay in the background. . . . Say, there's a good boy, Jackson, fill 'er up again. . . .

"Listen, Jack, we're going to have a new issue coming out right after the first of the year. This is inside stuff, so please don't repeat it. Just a thing I want to let old pals like you in on. What am I talking about? None of the others are like you. My oldest and best pal." He put his arms around Jack and almost pulled both of them off their bar stools.

Jack disentangled himself. His face was wooden. His voice was flat. "Thanks, Wally, but I am not in the market for any stock at this time. Not until I get over the lumps I took last year."

"Oh, come on, lad, you know that ain't the smart way to play the market. Buy low, that's what the bible says." Wally reached for the bottle himself, knocking over Jack's glass.

"For God's sake! Watch what you're doing," Jack said irritably. "And I don't give a damn what the bible says. I don't *play* the market like some people." His expression was an accusation. "I *invest.* Wisely. So, even if the bottom falls out, I can ride it out. I don't overextend myself."

"Who overextends themselves?" Wally was offended by Jack's implication.

"Some . . . people."

"You go to hell, Whittaker! I know you mean me. Well, you're wrong. Bad luck . . . that's always been my trouble. . . ." He lowered his voice and stared morosely into his glass. "That's the key to the kingdom, Jack. Luck. You've always been lucky. Everything you touch turns to gold. Me . . . I just don't have the Midas touch." He turned on the stool and clutched Jack's arm. "Jack, you can't pass up this opportunity. Reynolds, Kaiser and Price shares are down to two and one half. Christ! That's rock bottom! You buy in now, with one hundred thou, you will be ass deep in a gold mine by the end of next year. I guarantee it, Jack. With your touch, we can't miss. Bounce back to twenty, you'll see!"

Wendy clutched her throat. She had an acute and frightening sensation that she was going to choke.

Smoke from a wet log in the fireplace hung in the air. The cold blue light of late afternoon filtered in through the frosted window panes, tinting the murky gloom so that objects in the room took on fuzzy outlines, as if she were looking at them through fine gauze. It was all unreal and grotesque. A reversed image on a television screen. Jack and Wally were turned about, faceless phantoms on a photo negative. The voices were wrong. Wally's voice saying desperate things she would have expected to hear from Jack.

"You can raise it, old buddy, I know you can. Your name alone. You've got the world by the tail."

"A hundred thousand! By God! Even if I had that kind of free capital, I wouldn't invest it in your company's stock."

"That deal I closed in Haiti. It's the turning point, you'll see. We've got it made now."

"What deal in Haiti?" Di's caustic voice came from the doorway. She had spent most of the afternoon upstairs lying down because of a headache. When she was young, Diana had possessed a rather fragile beauty. Now, in middle age, the skin was drawn tightly over the small, fine bones of her face (one indemnity from years of crash dieting), giving her a pointed, shrewish appearance.

She walked into the den, smoothing the tight stretch pants down her thighs with the flats of her hands. She smirked at her husband.

"The truth of the matter is, it's a wonder we weren't deported from Haiti! Lover boy got drunk, made a pass at a diplomat's wife, and insulted their president all in the space of a few hours."

Wally was livid. He got off the stool and faced her. His fingers were splayed tersely over his thighs. "You dirty, rotten bitch!"

"Don't lend him any money, Jack," Diana snapped. "Better donate it to your favorite charity. He's already up to his ears in debt. He's run the company on the rocks. His partners have demanded his resignation, and his creditors are screaming for his head." She put her hands on her hips and thrust her face into his. "I'd like to hand it to them personally!"

"You're . . . You're a . . ." His rage throttled him.

"Frigid." She laughed at him, mocking his inarticulateness. "Isn't that the word you're trying to say?"

"Arid!" He spit it out. "It isn't just the sex. You're a wasteland. Physically, emotionally, intellectually—"

"And what about you? The *big* man. Inside you're nothing. Just one big vacuum!"

"You did it, Di." The mask slipped away, baring his desperate anguish. An image seen in a shattered mirror "You never really wanted me to succeed. Just like my mother. Now there's another bitch for you!"

"That's a damned lie! You would have gone down the drain years ago if I hadn't been around to shore up that pathetic ego. I always treated you as if you were a little tin god!"

"Tin god! That's it, Di. Gold-plated tin. You brainwashed me!"

"Me?" she sneered. "You never could admit you were wrong. Every setback you had was always somebody else's fault."

"That was your line, Di, not mine. I got so used to having you bury my mistakes it got so I couldn't do anything right. This goddamned business of my own. Whose idea was that?"

"Don't blame me because you didn't have the guts or ability to make it succeed."

"But you knew all along! You wanted me to fall flat on my face. Right from the start you wanted me to fail."

Back and forth. A savage counterpoint of hatred between

husband and wife. Charge and countercharge. Treachery. Betrayal. Murder of the soul. A human being coming apart before their eyes. Jack and Wendy were repelled and horrified.

"Stop it, you two," Jack finally broke in. "I didn't come up here to listen to you two battling for the next three days. I've had enough family troubles of my own. I'm not interested in your hangups!"

Wally turned on him. "No, you never were interested in other people, Whittaker. Not really. Oh, you put on the good act. Sympathetic ear, pat on the back, reassuring smile. The perfect bedside manner. 'Go home and take two aspirins and go to bed and call me in the morning!' But just don't get too close to Dr. Whittaker in case it's contagious!"

Jack's face was crimson. "Look, Wally, if you're in financial trouble, maybe I can help you out. A couple of thousand . . ."

Wally began to laugh hysterically. "A couple of thousand! Thanks, buddy. That should be enough to buy me a one-way ticket to Timbuktu and get a jump on the loan sharks!"

Jack winced. "Jesus, Wally, I'm sorry. I wish I could do more. Honestly I do."

Wally didn't answer him immediately, and it seemed to Jack that he was making an effort to pull himself together.

But Wendy was not deceived. She had guessed the terrifying truth. The clumsy machinery of his lies about Jack laid bare: Jack was despondent over his personal and business troubles. Jack needed help. Jack needed *her* help. The bait: a role in his new play. All of it lies!

Classic symptom of paranoia . . . he had said.

An irrational mind. Yes, but not Jack Whittaker's mind. It was Wally Kaiser who was paranoid. The terrifying truth was he was quite mad!

"Yes, you're sorry, Jackson. You wish you could do more." Wally was speaking with quiet vindictiveness. "I'll tell you something, Jack. Everybody thinks you're such a great guy. You believe it yourself. A great humanitarian. A strong shoulder for the rest of us less fortunate peons to cry on. But I'll tell you the truth about yourself, Jack. The only thing you've got to give anybody is money and free advise. I know you, Jack. If a beggar collapsed on the sidewalk, you'd toss a buck in his hat and walk around him. You don't want to be involved in the lives of other people. Because that would mean you'd have to give of yourself. That precious self that you prize as if it's some kind of virginity."

"You're drunk." Jack got off the bar stool and started for the door. "I don't have to listen to this crap."

"Ask your wife, Jack," Wally shouted after him. "Mae knows. She's always known. About you and Carla March. All of it! The truth is you married Mae so you wouldn't have to marry a woman you did love. With Mae you were safe. You were afraid Carla would come between you and your brilliant career. Roche had your number, Jack, when he said you and your work were a beautiful incestuous affair!"

Jack whirled, his face the color of the snow heaped on the windowsill. "You crazy bastard!" He rushed Wally in a rage.

For a man who had had so much to drink, Wally's reflexes were remarkably alert. He met the attack with a vicious kick in Jack's groin, and in the same motion picked up a half-empty bottle of Scotch off the bar and smashed it against the side of his head as he went down to his knees. Jack rolled over on his side without a murmur and lay in an inert heap, with one elbow and one knee twisted up against the brass foot rail. Blood from a deep gash above his temple spread out in a bright stain on the pegged floorboards along the base of the bar.

The color of holly berries, Wendy thought idly. Her mind was numb.

Diana clutched her hands to her face and began to scream, until Wally sloshed a full tumbler of whiskey into her face. It went up her nose and down her throat, choking her. When she was able to get her breath again, Wally was facing them with the rifle.

Wally was perfectly composed now. He acted with the stolid determination and blind confidence of a robot. Calmly he ordered the women to go upstairs. He handed his wife a key.

"Open my bag," he told her.

When she saw the steel handcuffs on top of his shirts and linen, and the pistol, Wendy realized how desperately ill he was. All of the scheming that had preceded this moment. All of the interplay of personalities. All of the talk. The accusations and the recriminations. They were stage directions and dialogue in a script already completed in Wally's sick mind long before they had set foot on the plane. The ending was ordained.

It would have altered nothing if Jack had bought his stock or loaned him money. Nothing any of them could have said or done would have changed that sick mind. For Wally was bound to destroy them all.

"Why me, Wally?" she asked as he fitted the cuffs on her ankles.

He looked into her eyes. "Because you failed me too. Like Jack. Like her."

Diana began to sob.

"I failed you?" Wendy asked.

"Yes, I loved you once. Maybe I still love you, I don't know any more." He pressed the back of a hand against his forehead. "I'm confused about that. But I know I want to kill you. You don't deserve to live, Wendy. Not just because of what you did to me. You see, you rejected a man who loved you. You married a man you didn't love. And—you loved a man you couldn't have. Only because you knew you couldn't have him."

Wendy shuddered. Truth out of the mouths of babes; and don't forget madmen!

He remained in a squatting position in front of her after he had locked the cuffs on her ankles.

"You're worse than Di, Wendy. Because you've failed so many people. Including yourself. Though I suppose that's the tragic thing about all of us here, Wendy. Failing those who need us, or being failed by those we need. I used to think the world was held together by love." He laughed. "A cheap PR pitch by theologians. God is love. The truth is this lousy world is held together by hate. Hate! We spit in the face of love. We embrace hate. It's those we fear or envy who command our respect and devotion. Now, there's the original sin, my girl. We have failed as human beings. All of us. The judgment is in."

"What right do you have to judge me, Wally? Who gave you the right to judge anybody?"

He patted the rifle lying on the floor by his side and smiled. "The almighty power who gave us playthings like gunpowder, napalm and ICBM's. God is love."

"You're mad." Wendy shivered. She imagined that a hideous, invisible presence was invading the room. Cold tendrils touching her. Lightly on the backs of her hands. Inner thighs. Cheeks. There was no escape.

He stood up, sighing. "Now you ladies will have to entertain yourselves for a while. I'm going to fetch old Jack up to join the group."

All the way down the ladder, Sid Feldman kept up an animated dialogue with himself:

"You are out of your mind!"

"I couldn't agree with you more."

"Then why?"

"Like the man said about the mountain: 'Because it's there!' So he climbs up mountains. I climb down into holes."

There was something unflatteringly symbolic about that.

"What do you think you're going to do?"

"That's just the point. I'm not thinking. Alice is not altogether wrong about us, you know. We've always prided ourselves in being a thinking man. Think before we act. The trouble is we do so much thinking that the action passes us by, Sid boy. . . .

Now is the time for all good men to come to the aid of . . .
Action! That's our thing tonight, baby. 'Twas the night before
Christmas . . ."

"Glory be! Put in a call for Dr. Kendall. No, it's too late for
a psychiatrist. Sid, that isn't us talking. It's all that booze you
drank at the party!"

"The hell with *you*. And the hell with Alice!"

His foot came down hard on steel plate. He was at the bottom
of the ladder. Feldman switched on his flashlight. The yellow spot
framed a circular steel door imbedded in concrete. He twirled
the wheel handle and the door swung open, uncovering a steel
tunnel. A large pipe really. The beam of his flash picked out the
door at the opposite end of the tunnel.

"Here we go, Sid!" Feldman inhaled and crawled into the
black opening.

The shelter itself reminded him of the interior of a submarine.
A steel and concrete casing about eight feet in diameter with
fold-away bunk beds at one end. At the other end tiers of shelves
stacked with canned provisions. A small rectangular table with
four chairs placed around it. A bench along one wall holding a
sophisticated citizen's band radio receiver and transmitter. Above
it a control panel festooned with dials, bulbs, and switches. On a
small shelf above that a compact Sony television set.

"All the comforts of home," Feldman muttered.

It was a wonderful cozy setup. And the very least to be said
for it was that, in the event of a full-scale nuclear war, the
occupants would make their passage to the great beyond in
comfortable fashion sustained by all the familiar conveniences of
their earthly existence. There was even a liquor supply. Yes, it
was a tomb worthy of the Pharaohs.

He walked the length of the shelter to the other door. After a
moment of deliberation he bent and removed his shoes. Beyond
that door lay the unknown. Feldman decided it was a realm best
entered as quietly and unobtrusively as possible. He turned off

the flashlight and put it into the pocket of his mackinaw. Then slowly he rotated the door's wheel handle.

He took a single step outside the shelter and stopped. The darkness was total. He could not make out a hand held up only inches away from his eyes. The sensation of blindness was unsettling at first. For a few minutes, he stood motionless. There was no way to judge the design or dimension of the space he was occupying. Tentatively he lifted one arm straight out in front of him. Moved it in a cautious arc. The side of his hand hit metal. Another ladder? No, it was different. He explored it now with the fingers of both hands. The picture was beginning to develop in his mind. Testing with a foot. A step! The focus was clear now. He was at the bottom of a circular staircase. Grasping the rails on each side with his hands, he started to climb.

He had counted twelve steps and two full turns when the light burst against his face. Darts pierced his eyeballs. A banshee wail, summoning up all of the demons he had ever dreaded and dreamed about since his first consciousness of the supernatural. Lightning and thunder, crashing in on him from all sides. It literally drove him down on his knees. He clutched the railing desperately with both hands to keep from tumbling backward.

He looked up finally and forced his eyes open against the blinding light. Through the glare the hazy apparition materialized. A wild-eyed specter with tangled hair holding a wicked-looking knife in its upraised hand. In that instant, Feldman came as near to fainting as he ever had in his life.

"Don't!" he gasped.

They hung there suspended in time and motion like figures in a tableau. How long he didn't know. It seemed like eternity.

Then the light shifted and he could see more clearly. It was a woman.

"Oh!" Her voice had the pitch of a violin string stretched to the breaking point. "You're not—oh, my God!" The shuddering release of tension.

"It's all right. I'm here to help." His trembling knees were banging on the steel step.

"Who are you?"

"It doesn't matter. Are you—? Yes, you must be. But how did you get away?"

She lowered the knife and stood with her arms hanging loosely at her sides, swaying precariously from side to side.

"My God! Don't faint!" he implored her.

She shook her head. "I won't . . . How did you . . . ? Where did you . . ." She was going into shock, and speech was becoming difficult.

"From outside. There's another entrance to this shelter. Help's on the way. The police are right behind me." He looked back down the shaft hopefully, but there was, as yet, no sign of Dorn and Dietzel.

"Shhh!" She put a warning finger to her lips and looked at the doorway which led back through the tunnel to the lodge. Feldman heard something, indistinguishable sounds beyond the door, muffled by the thick steel and concrete.

"He's found me," she whispered. "He's coming!" She began to whimper like a frightened child.

Feldman reached up and took the light and the knife out of her hands. He put down the knife and grabbed her wrist.

"Come on! Hurry! Watch the stairs." He shone the light on the steps and started down. She sagged against him, and he almost fell.

"Hell!"

"My legs!"

"What's the matter with your legs?" He shone the light down on her feet and saw the steel shackles encasing her bloody ankles.

"Jesus!" he gasped, horrified. "All right, I'll carry you then!"

He put one arm around her waist and started down again. She was a large woman and her whole weight bore down on him. It was too much. He stopped and let her body slide down so that he was holding her under the arms. Half carrying her, half drag-

ging her, he made the descent. The chains on her ankles rang a
knell on each step. The twelve longest steps he had ever counted
in his life. They had reached the final step when he heard a
crash overhead. Instinctively, he aimed the light up the twisting
staircase and looked. Wasted motion and almost fatal. He had
an oblique glimpse of a man's face through a snarl of metal spokes
and steps.

The shot sounded like a cannon in the echo chamber of the
stairwell. The bullet struck the step directly over his head with a
clanging that made his ears ring. He doused the light fast and
dove for the open doorway that led back into the shelter. He
dragged the woman inside a second before the next shot went off.
He had the door half shut when the slug plowed into it. It
ricocheted off the heavy steel, buzzed past Feldman's nose, hit
the circular steel wall, and continued to carom from wall to wall
along the full length of the shelter, before it came to rest in a
pillow on one of the bunks.

Feldman slammed the door closed and turned the handle as
far as it would go. There was no way to lock it. So he grasped
it fast with both hands and braced his feet on the rough steel
plates.

"Run!" he shouted at the woman. "I'll hold him as long as
I can. The back way out."

She tried to get to her feet, and couldn't make it. She collapsed
and buried her face in her hands.

"It's no use. My legs won't move," she said in exhaustion.

"Then crawl! For God's sake, you can't stay here."

He was aware of increasing pressure on the wheel handle.
Gentle, testing pressure. He pressed back. Feldman couldn't ex-
plain the absence of fear. Tense, yes. Excited, yes. Apprehensive?
Well, he was no fool! But he was not afraid.

The hell with you, Alice!

As loudly as he could, he shouted: *"Dorn! Where the hell are
you, Dorn?"*

The contest with the door handle reminded Feldman of the

childhood games of arm wrestling that he had always been beaten at. And neither his strength nor his technique had improved with the years. Slowly, inexorably the wheel was being turned against him by the killer on the other side of the door. Finally, the ominous click of the locking mechanism disengaging.

"Dorn!" he called out frantically.

As the door was forced inward against his resisting body, a flashlight went on at the other end of the shelter. Feldman felt like a performer fixed in a theater spotlight.

"Down, Sid!" Dorn shouted. "Hit the deck!"

Feldman fell flat on his face the way they had taught him in Army basic and "ate dirt." His front teeth jarred on the steel plate.

Only, in this situation, the shots that buzzed over his head were real. Actually, as Dorn told him later, there were only three shots fired.

One fired by the killer, which imbedded itself in Dorn's bullet-proof vest.

One fired by Dorn, which went wild.

One fired by Corporal Dietzel, which hit the killer in the abdomen. He fell across Feldman's outstretched legs. Captain Dorn came down and rolled him off.

"You okay, Sid?"

"I—I think so." Feldman got up on his knees and looked down at the wounded man.

"You recognize him?" Dorn asked.

"Yeah . . . It's Mr. Kaiser."

Wally Kaiser was conscious, his eyes glassy in the beam of the torch shining into his face.

"Wally Kaiser?" Dorn asked. "Which one is he?"

Before Feldman could answer, Kaiser's lips moved. His words were barely audible: "Advertising . . ." The rest of it made no sense to the men: "Reynolds . . . *Kaiser* . . . and Price . . ."

Only Wendy Gates heard and understood. She cried quietly into her hands.

Jack Whittaker, Wendy Gates, Diana Kaiser, and her critically wounded husband were evacuated by helicopter to the nearest hospital. The women, listed in good condition, were treated for shock and lacerations of their legs and ankles. Jack Whittaker had a hairline fracture of the skull, but his condition was fair. Wally Kaiser was in the hospital's intensive care unit, and the doctors gave him a fifty-fifty chance to recover.

At five o'clock the next morning, Captain Dorn concluded his personal role in the case. A contingent of state police would remain on duty at the lodge at the request of the county district attorney's office to enforce security measures. To bar the curious public and to regulate the activities of authorized news-media personnel.

The FBI men had departed. Sheriff Malone was still up at the lodge. West Village Police Chief Max Lanier was playing host in his office to Dorn, Feldman, Lou Santini, and Dr. Kendall. He served hot coffee laced with Metaxa brandy.

Dorn, his face gray and pinched with fatigue, gulped the fortified brew gratefully: "Ahhh, that hits the spot, Max."

The rotund psychiatrist hefted his heavy mug and said. "I realize this is no occasion for levity, and my taste may be questionable in proposing a toast, but I intend to do so anyway. . . . A very merry Christmas to you all, gentlemen."

"Nothing wrong with good sentiments like that, doc," Lanier said. "For sure, this has got to be a happier day than yesterday."

Soberly they drank together.

It was the first opportunity that Dorn and Feldman had had to speak in relative privacy since the showdown with Kaiser in the shelter. All night long the two of them had been the chief targets of newsmen and photographers. They were both bone weary and letdown now that it was over. It was almost too much of an effort to speak.

Santini, Kendall, and Lanier were discussing Wally Kaiser. Feldman leaned forward in his chair and rubbed his palms together nervously.

"Captain, there's something I've been meaning to say," He kept his eyes fixed on Dorn's icy boots. "I had no right to pull what I did last night. No right at all . . ."

Dorn smiled thinly. "The way it worked out you were right, Sid. If it had come out wrong, you'd either be dead—or in jail."

"I don't know what came over me." Feldman laughed uncertainly. "What do they call it? Bottled courage. I suppose that was it. The liquor I had at the party made me reckless. I'm not a drinking man."

"Reckless" was the word all right. Dorn had been around too long to believe that a man could buy real courage from a bottle of booze. All that alcohol could accomplish was to dull the instinct for survival along with all of the other senses it deadened. Strangely, he wanted to protect the new image that Sid Feldman had earned for himself through his rash, irrational act in disobeying Dorn's orders and courting violent death.

"You saved that woman's life, Sid," he said. "Don't matter why you did it. You saved her life. And God only knows, maybe you saved the others too."

He didn't really believe that. If he and Dietzel hadn't got held up looking for Feldman, they would have been inside the shelter five minutes sooner. Time enough to save the woman and—no, there was no assurance that it would have worked out that way. Instead of them trapping Kaiser in the shelter, he might have trapped them in that narrow pipe leading back to the cellar. Now *that* would have been something. Kaiser would have had a field day, shooting fish down a rain barrel! And then he could have blocked up the entrance, and the police would now be as bad off as before. A standoff. Dorn was not a man for post mortems. Feldman had gambled, and he had won.

It was enough to win.

The specialist in Denver had accused him of pretty much the same thing he had been thinking about Feldman. His refusal to let them operate immediately was "irrational." It was "reckless." He was "courting death." He was gambling, too. If little Feldman could win on a long shot, maybe Les Dorn could win too?

"We live on hope," Dr. Kendall was saying to Santini. "And Wally Kaiser had lost that vital faculty. Coming up to this lodge was his ultimate retreat from a hostile world. The lodge becomes a significant symbol. I mean, if he wanted to kill these three people, he could have done it far more easily in New York. Just imagine the elaborate machinations he went through to arrange the rendezvous in Snowmass. Halfway across the country! The logistics would have been sufficient to discourage me. The key is that the lodge represented something unique and special to Kaiser. A projection of his own self, his own mind. The refuge of the mind. A refuge in which he could, at last, possess the three people in his life to whom he was committed in one form or another emotionally and psychologically. He had reached the stage in his illness where it became unbearable to be closed within the solitary confinement of his own self. He had to find another refuge against the hostile outer world. A refuge that was also accessible to these three."

"But he hated them, doc," Lanier objected. "He wanted to kill them."

Kendall's shaggy white eyebrows went up. "Ah! But would he have killed them, chief? He kept saying he would. Yet he had ample opportunity to do so, and still he did not kill them. No, I personally don't believe Kaiser ever would have gone through with it. In the end he would have released them. . . . You see, his murderous hostility was vented entirely on total strangers. He shot strangers."

Dorn was covertly observing Feldman all the while Kendall was talking. Unwittingly the good doctor was diminishing this moment of modest glory he was enjoying.

With good-natured sarcasm, Dorn told Kendall. "Trouble is, doctor, in order to prove your point we'd have had to shoot dice with the lives of three innocent people."

Doctor Kendall sighed and patted his protruding belly. "Yes, that's true, captain. There's altogether too much Monday-morning quarterbacking in our profession. But it can't be helped. You see, in medicine, the physician has an abundance of symptoms to work with, including a good deal of imaginery ones. The patient is eager to oblige. But in psychiatry the patient goes to fanatical lengths to hide his symptoms from his doctor. It can be frustrating, let me tell you. A man such as Kaiser. I could meet him at a cocktail party and judge him to be the most well-adjusted man in the world. That's a circuitous way of agreeing with you, captain. No, I would not under any circumstances have projected the viewpoint that Kaiser did not intend to harm the hostages before. That view is strictly hindsight, you're correct."

Santini stood up and stretched his long arms. "I don't know about you fellows, but if I don't hit the sack soon, I'll collapse."

"An excellent suggestion." Dr. Kendall bounced out of his chair in sprightly fashion for one so portly and considering the hour and his age. "You'll join me for Christmas dinner, my boy, won't you? You haven't eaten until you've supped on my orange glacé goose."

Santini grinned and draped an arm around the little doctor's shoulders. "It would be an honor."

Dorn laughed. "Hey, you two look like Mutt and Jeff."

Dr. Kendall was pleased by the simile. "We could do worse, eh, Louis? What a delightful species we'd be if we enjoyed the resiliency of those two indomitable characters. If we could shrug off our pratfalls and slights to our precious dignity with the outrageous aplomb of a Mutt and Jeff!"

Dorn and Feldman stood together on the steps of the police station after Dr. Kendall and Lou Santini had driven off in a car to the doctor's lodge.

The snow had stopped. And the halo of dawn spanning the mountain rims to the east held bright promise of a fine Christmas Day. Higher up, emerging from a cloud, was the brightest star that Dorn had ever seen. At least it struck him that way. Feldman stared at it too. A long time in silence.

They began to speak at the same time.

"The star—"

And then they burst into laughter.

"How corny can we get?" Feldman joked.

"Well, have a good day anyway, Sid. What will you be doing? Outside of sleeping, I mean."

Feldman shrugged and smiled. "Oh . . . My wife will think of something. . . . What about you?"

"Big family day coming up. The biggest." Dorn smiled. "My boy's back from Vietnam. First Christmas for my granddaughter too." He laughed at himself. "Hell, she's not born yet, but she's going to be there with us, just the same."

Feldman smiled. "You'll have a lot to celebrate. I'm glad you didn't have to sweat out that killer all day Christmas."

"Say, that's a personal note of thanks I owe you, Sid Feldman. You saved my Christmas." He cuffed Feldman's arm with gruff fondness. "We'll keep in touch."

They shook hands.

"You're sure I can't drive you home?" the trooper asked Feldman.

"Thanks, but it's a short walk. I like to walk."

Dorn thought about Wally Kaiser as he drove home. It would probably be better off all around if he died. The state wouldn't execute him. He was insane. If he did live, that meant he'd be shut up in an asylum for the rest of his days. A padded cell. That would be ironic. The final "refuge against the hostile outer world" that Dr. Kendall had been talking about.

His chances of pulling through were fifty-fifty, the hospital reported. Dorn touched the sensitive spot in his throat, wondering whether his chances were anywhere nearly as good as Kaiser's. This man who had murdered five people?

What the hell! Life and death were both a matter of chance.

From the instant the spark was kindled in a woman's womb until that same light was extinguished in some far-off battlefield, or in a speeding car, or on an operating table, or, more prosaically, in a bed at a ripe old age. Just chance.

Those five victims. One moment soaring across the snowy slopes of Mt. Baldy. Swapping jokes back and forth from their lift chairs. Planning their holiday entertainments. All young. Full of life, with not a care or fear among the lot of them. Certainly not the fear of death. And then the sudden, violent end of everything.

Like the fall of a card.

The throw of the dice.

The turn of the wheel.

"We live on hope . . ." Dr. Kendall had said. The little Santa Claus man with the big vocabulary had the right idea. When hope was gone, there was nothing. Nothing but the ruthless mathematics of the actuarial tables. Dorn had intense hope concerning the future. He was startled and a little self-conscious to find himself praying. Dorn was not a religious man. But then, he asked himself, why not? Wasn't prayer the natural extension of hope?

He looked out the side window at the star, bright and vigilant, keeping pace with the car.

Sid Feldman walked into the apartment while Alice and a man and woman he recognized vaguely from the party were on their third nightcap.

Alice was plastered. She gave a little shriek of pleasureable surprise and got up from the couch to greet him. She would have fallen over the cocktail table if the man, Harry, hadn't caught her.

"Sidney! You are a naughty boy," she simpered. She staggered the last few steps and held on to him for support. "Running out like that and leaving me all by my lonesome."

"You noticed?"

"Leave the man alone, doll," Harry said. He and his date, Cindy, gathered around Feldman. Harry extended his hand. "Say, what we've been hearing about you, Sid! Absolutely fantastic! You sure played it cool, man. But I knew you had something up your sleeve. Didn't I say that to you, Cindy?"

He realized suddenly that Feldman had ignored his outstretched hand, and brought it up self-consciously to pull at his long red nose.

Cindy giggled. "You know what they say? Still water runs deep."

"And dirty." Harry brayed like an ass.

Which he was, Feldman decided.

Alice threw her arms around his neck and rubbed her tummy against him. "Let's be dirty, sweetheart," she whispered in his ear and bit his lobe.

"Tell us all about it, Sid," Harry said, rubbing his hands together. "No sense going to bed now, anyway. Cindy, fix us all another round of drinks, will you, chick? Alice is too bombed."

Feldman reached back and unclasped Alice's hands from his neck. Firmly he pushed her away.

"Hey!" She cocked her head to one side petulantly.

To Harry he said: "I don't want a drink, and you can read all about it in the papers. Or buy my book."

Cindy squealed excitedly. "Ohhh! Are you really going to write a book, Sid?"

Feldman looked at her contemptuously. "I'm tired. I'm going to bed."

There was a chorus of indignant protest. Alice clutched his arm as he turned away from them.

"Oh, no you're not," she snarled. "This is my home and Harry and Cindy are my friends. You're not going to insult them by walking out. You did that once tonight." She took a noisy emotional breath. "Don't you dare walk out of here, Sid Feldman!"

He turned around. Without saying anything he looked her up

and down. Then he walked to one side and regarded her from another angle. He removed his glasses and walked around in back of her. With the curious detachment of a technician appraising a lab specimen.

"What the hell do you think you're doing?" She beat the air with clenched fists like a child in a tantrum.

"What you just said, Alice." As if by magic, new strength and vitality flowed into him. He felt as refreshed as if he had just awakened from a long, untroubled sleep, the kind of healthy sleep he hadn't rejoiced in for years.

"It made me realize something. I *do* dare walk out of here! Out of this room. Out of this apartment. Out of this town. Out! Out! Out! God only knows how far I'm going to go!" He threw up his hands high. Her expression was really something to see.

"You—you must be drunk or—or you wouldn't be talking like that!"

"Drunk with freedom!"

She shook her head. "I don't believe it."

"You can if you try." He headed for the bedroom. "Now, if you swell people will excuse me . . ."

"You get hit in the head or something when you helped capture that nut?" she called after him.

"Or something. Yes, I got something up there."

"You're crazy. What are you talking about? What did you get up there?"

He paused in the doorway and looked back, grinning. "A brave heart!"

"A brave heart?" Alice looked from Harry to Cindy helplessly. "Did you hear that? All this hero crap must have gone to his head. Well, I never!"

Just then Feldman's head popped into view from outside the doorway.

"That's from the *Wizard of Oz* in case you're wondering," he said brightly. "At least I think so."

He laughed all the way down the hall and into the bedroom. Then he took off his shoes, pulled a chair over to the window, sat down with his feet propped up on the sill, and watched the sun come up!

Wendy Gates was released from the hospital at 11:30 A.M. on Christmas Day. Before she left the hospital she visited Jack Whittaker's room. His condition had improved steadily since his arrival the night before.

"My, don't we look handsome with our head all swathed in bandages," she teased him. "Just like Richard Burton in that awful picture he wore the turban in."

Jack winced. "More like an Egyptian mummy, doll. I look as if they just dug me up." Gravely he inquired about Wally.

"No change. He continues to hold his own."

"I hope he doesn't make it," he told her candidly. "I'm for mercy killing. I don't think Wally could stand up to what's ahead of him if he does live."

She pulled the heavy wool sweater more tightly around her body. The deep chill of the lodge still lingered in her bones.

"It's terrible. I still can't believe what's happened to all of us. Wally Kaiser is the last person in the world I'd suspect of going—" She hesitated. "I was going to say 'going mad'. That's old fashioned, isn't it, but it describes what came over Wally as well as anything. Madness."

He shook his head as bewildered by the chaotic events as Wendy was. "We both heard what he said that day we got up here. But there had to be more to it than that. I mean men fail at business, marriage a lot of other things every day. But it doesn't drive them to violence and murder."

"They think there may be a small tumor pressing on his brain," she told him. "Diana says he's had migraine headaches as long as she's known him. They've been worse of late."

"Yes," he said in sudden recollection. "Wally was always

gulping aspirin the way I take antacids. Funny, you never attach much significance to things like that." Somehow he didn't accept the tumor theory. The poem kept throbbing in his mind:

> *"And Richard Cory one calm summer night,*
> *Went home and put a bullet through his head . . ."*

"How is Diana taking it?" he asked.

"Di's in shock, but she'll be all right."

"Di was born to martyrdom," he said cynically.

Wendy did not comment on the observation. She was standing beside the bed with her hands folded in front of her, shoulders back, feet close together. A pose she had been assuming since childhood, waiting to deliver her lines. In front of the class. In the theater wings. On the mark in the television studio.

"Mae is flying in this afternoon," he told her.

"That's wonderful, Jack. Maybe . . . ?"

"Maybe." He smiled. "After the past two days, I'm convinced that *anything* can happen."

"It's funny. It hits me that way too. You know something? I keep thinking this is New Year's Day, instead of Christmas."

"You're right. It feels new. . . . Listen, what about old Carl? Does he know what's been going on up here?"

"Carl knows. He got here about two, and by that time it was all over. He's up at the lodge with Forrest and Lou, looking things over. They'll be in to see you later on."

He was regarding her quizzically. "Wendy . . . Why did you let Wally talk you into coming up to Snowmass a day early?"

Her gray eyes were unwavering on his face. She reached out and took his hand. "What else, luv? I was going to seduce you so you'd give me a part in your new TV play, which I hear is brilliant." She rolled her eyes upward and uttered a long, histrionic sigh. "Ah, well . . ."

It was one of her best performances.

She tried to take her hand away, but he wouldn't let her go.

"So that could be a good idea. Listen. I've seen that show you're in. It's . . . it's . . ."

Wendy laughed. "It's just the right speed for me. Hey, you're forgetting I'm an old mama with four chicks. TV's fun and kicks. But I wouldn't want to live there. Listen, I've got to check out of here before noon or they'll charge me for an extra day. Good luck with the play, Jack. I'll be watching for it in *TV Guide*. Carl and I will." She tilted her head to one side. "You know, it wouldn't hurt you to call him once in a while. Carl. I think he adored you even more than I did."

He pulled his head to one side as if she had slapped him. "Don't, Wendy, please."

"Wally was right about a lot of things, Jack. . . ."

"I *know!*" He kept his eyes shut.

She glanced toward the door as a nurse wheeled a cart stacked with bedpans into the room. "Time for your enema, sweetie. . . . Now, how's that for an exit line?"

He lay there listening to the smart rapping of her high heels on the marble floor. Fading, fading, down the long corridor of time.

He cringed away from the contact of icy metal against his bare hip.

"Upsy daisy, Mr. Whittaker," the mannequin in starched white intoned tonelessly. "Here's your potty."